Praise for Joanna Chambers's
Unforgivable

"In *Unforgivable*, the familiar is given new life...a good story, well-told in fine prose, and characters that are imbued with some depth..."

~ *Dear Author*

"This was a very enjoyable historical romance and I will be looking for more by this author."

~ *Night Owl Reviews*

"*Unforgivable* was a fabulously written story..."

~ *Joyfully Reviewed*

"If you are looking for an emotionally charged and character driven historical romance I would definitely recommend taking a closer look at this book."

~ *Smexy Books*

Look for these titles by *Joanna Chambers*

Now Available:

Unforgivable

Enlightenment
Provoked
Beguiled

Unforgivable

Joanna Chambers

.

SAMHAIN
PUBLISHING

Samhain Publishing, Ltd.
11821 Mason Montgomery Road, 4B
Cincinnati, OH 45249
www.samhainpublishing.com

Unforgivable
Copyright © 2014 by Joanna Chambers
Print ISBN: 978-1-61921-647-1
Digital ISBN: 978-1-61921-373-9

Editing by Linda Ingmanson
Cover by Kim Killion

First Samhain Publishing, Ltd. electronic publication: January 2013
First Samhain Publishing, Ltd. print publication: January 2014

Dedication

For my mum who passed on to me her love of romance novels. And for my dad, who is a true romantic.

Part One: Spring

Rough winds do shake the darling buds of May...
William Shakespeare
Sonnet 18

Chapter One

May 1809

"I look awful," Rose said flatly.

The girl in the looking glass was gaunt, her cheeks hollow. She still carried the red, angry marks of her recent illness on her face and body. She was a stranger, and Rose hated looking at her.

"You look fine," Lottie said briskly, fastening the buttons at the back of Rose's gown. "And in a few months, you will look lovely. Your hair will grow, and my cook will fatten you up again, *cara.*"

Rose eyed her tragically shorn hair, all cut off in the midst of raging fever. Lottie's hairdresser had come yesterday afternoon and had done his best to style her short locks into something resembling a fashionable cap of curls, but she still looked like an early Christian martyr with her sad, shadowed eyes. Like Joan of Arc about to go to the stake.

When the buttons were all done up, Lottie looked up and smiled at Rose in the mirror. That smile roused an odd mixture of emotions in Rose. Fondness, resentment and an aching sort of envy. Carlotta Neroni—Rose's father's mistress—was very beautiful. In fact, she was Rose's polar opposite.

A few months ago, Rose had hated Lottie, even though they'd never met. She'd resented the beautiful soprano who reportedly sang like an angel and looked like one too. The woman who'd drawn her father away from her. And then Rose had fallen ill.

Chicken pox. A childhood ailment she should have recovered from within a week or two. By the time Papa realised how ill she was, she was delirious with blood poisoning and the physicians couldn't crack the fever. When Papa went to Lottie, it was probably for his own comfort; however, the result had been that Lottie had descended upon the household like a whirlwind. The physicians were told in no uncertain terms to stop bleeding Rose, her bedchamber was cleaned and aired, and the kitchens were commandeered by Lottie's Italian cook. Under Lottie's unsentimental ministrations, Rose had, against all the odds, recovered.

That had been weeks and weeks ago, and still Lottie was here, still fussing over Rose like a mother hen. She was looking at Rose now with that warm expression of hers that made her look as though she cared for Rose. Which was absurd, really, given that Rose had given Lottie no reason even to like her.

When she'd woken from her fever to find Lottie in residence, she'd been less than gracious to her. She'd been a querulous invalid too, but Lottie had borne her ill temper with cheerful amusement. Only in the last few weeks, as Rose had grown stronger and emerged from her selfish infirmity, had she realised how much Lottie had done for her. She'd tried, then, feebly, to make up for her poor behaviour, aware that her own father hadn't had the patience to care for her as this woman had.

"What time is this visit to take place, *cara*?" Lottie asked now.

"Two o'clock."

"And are you sure you wish to go?" Lottie's expressive dark eyes clouded with concern. "I am sure your father would understand if you told him it was too soon."

"I don't mind," Rose said. The truth was that Papa was bubbling over with enthusiasm to make this visit, and though he might agree to postpone it today, he'd only keep on and on about going until she agreed. It was easier to do it now. There was no point putting off the inevitable. It wasn't as though she was going to start looking beautiful any time soon.

Lottie smiled. "It's true what he says about you, you know."

"What does who say?"

"Your papa. He says you're an adventurous little thing when you're not laid low."

Rose smiled, even though Lottie was wrong. This was nothing to do with being adventurous. She couldn't remember what that felt like anymore. This was about getting something unavoidable over with.

When Rose descended the stairs half an hour later, her father was waiting at the bottom, watching her with an indulgent expression he occasionally wore when he looked at her. It was an expression that made her realise he did love her in his way, though most of the time he didn't much notice her. She pasted on a wavery smile for him.

Lottie had done her best. Rose knew she looked neat and presentable, though she felt like a child. She was just five feet tall and thin as a rake. Her height hadn't troubled her when she was plumper, but now that she was so thin, she knew she looked very, very young. It was even worse without her clothes. She hated her jutting hipbones and her nonexistent breasts; hated that she could see her ribs. She tried to eat the food that Lottie pressed on her: rich roast meats, creamy potatoes, toothsome puddings swimming in custard. But although her appetite had improved, it was still tiny.

Worse than that, though, worse than *anything*, was her face. Gaunt and drawn. And those marks. The worst one was the scab on her left eyelid that still hadn't gone and that made her eye look droopy. She'd tried to cover it with powder, but that had only made it look worse.

When she stared at herself in the mirror, she felt an awful, yawning hollowness in her stomach. She supposed the feeling was horror.

She wished she didn't have to meet Viscount Waite looking like this. He couldn't possibly find her the least bit attractive.

"Rosebud," Papa said as she descended the last step. "You look lovely, my dear."

His eyes shone with sincerity, and she realised he believed it. He must be blind, but then perhaps all papas were.

"Ready?" he asked. She smiled and nodded, not trusting herself to speak. The whole situation was so bizarre that she was having difficulty believing it was really happening. A week ago, she'd had no thoughts of anything but trying to get better. Now she was to meet, for the first time, the man who might turn out to be her husband.

She hadn't been out much since her illness, and it felt strange. She lifted the hem of her new gown carefully as she descended the steps from the front door to the street below. She leaned on her father in a way she never used to. He patted the hand that rested on his arm, and the small, thoughtless gesture made her happy and sad all at once. She'd grown up knowing she loved her father more than he loved her. Even today, his smiles and excitement were not really, not wholly, about her. Once married, she would be his responsibility no longer. He would be free.

The carriage was waiting at the bottom of the steps, and Papa handed her in, climbing in behind her and settling himself on the bench opposite. He thumped the ceiling with his cane, and the carriage lurched forward. He fiddled with his gloves, seeming uncharacteristically nervous. So unlike the father she knew. Miles Davenport was the most confident, debonair and charming man in England. But the most charming man in England had a serious look about him now. A serious look that he tried to temper with a smile.

This was another familiar expression. He usually wore it when he was about to leave her for a while. His mouth was smiling, but his eyes—the same grey eyes he had bequeathed to her—were a little anxious.

He leaned forward and took her small hands in his larger ones. "You needn't have him if you don't like him, Rosebud."

Rose looked at their linked hands. Papa ducked his head, looking up to intercept her downcast gaze. "I won't deny I want to see you settled. And this would be a brilliant match for you. But I won't force you to marry against your will."

"I know, Papa," she replied. But she knew too that her father had his heart set on this match. And besides that, she had to think practically. She was well aware that this wasn't the sort of chance that was going to come along very often—not for her. Papa's money came and went like the seasons. His profession, if you could call it that, was gaming. As the youngest son of a peer, he was a gentleman, but he had no income. As a young man, he'd been offered the chance to take orders but had rejected that opportunity, preferring to make his living at the tables. And although he was often successful, no one could win all the time.

He was currently enjoying the luckiest streak of his life—for the last two years, they had lived in relative splendour. Recently, he had sat Rose down and informed her he'd had a spectacular evening at the tables. One that had produced a veritable king's ransom in winnings. And he wanted to invest those winnings in her, in her future. To secure her a husband. A husband, Papa had said with a self-deprecating smile, who would be a steadier and more reliable protector than he.

The dowry he was offering must be substantial indeed if it was sizeable enough to attract Viscount Waite, the eldest son of the Earl of Stanhope.

"There will be no mention of marriage today," Papa continued in a soothing voice. "It will just be an opportunity for you to meet Waite and decide whether you wish to take the matter further."

"And for him?"

"I beg your pardon?" Papa looked bewildered.

"And an opportunity for the viscount to meet *me* and decide if *he* wishes to proceed," Rose asked patiently.

"Oh—oh yes, I see what you mean," Papa mumbled. But he didn't answer. Could her dowry really be so substantial that the viscount would agree to marry her sight unseen?

All too soon, they arrived at Berkeley Square. The coachman opened the carriage door, and Papa alighted, holding his hand out to help Rose descend. When she reached the ground, she straightened her skirts and set her shoulders back. Her calm appearance did not reflect her inner misery. In truth, she couldn't see how this meeting could be anything other than a disaster. The viscount was twenty-two and sounded like a typical young buck. He would be horrified when he saw her, so plain and young.

They walked up several steps to the very grand front door of Stanhope House, and Papa rapped on the glossy black door with his cane. It was opened by a butler of short stature and haughty mien who showed them into the drawing room. As he withdrew he advised them, in lofty accents, that the earl would be with them presently.

Scant minutes later, a man who had to be the earl entered the room. He was tall and broad-shouldered, but he had a slight stoop and walked with a limp, leaning heavily on a cane. His expression was grim, etched with pain and anger.

"Davenport," the man barked in Papa's general direction, but his eyes were on Rose, and he walked straight over to her. He came to a halt in front of her and stared, eyebrows bristling.

"Good afternoon, Lord Stanhope," Papa replied with an amiable smile. "May I present my daughter, Rose?"

The earl nodded, but his expression did not alter. He continued to stare, and while he did so, Rose curtsied. When she straightened, she offered him a small smile which died on her lips in the face of his frowning demeanour.

Papa looked much younger than this man. Of course, her father was only thirty-eight, while the earl looked to be somewhere in his fifties with iron-grey hair and deep grooves bracketing his mouth and creasing his brow. He did not look impressed with her, but she could not blame him for that. She knew she did not present a particularly impressive picture. He continued staring at her for long moments, and she had to fight the urge to look away.

To her relief, the earl's gaze finally lifted, his attention drawn by the doors of the drawing room opening again.

"Ah, there you are." He grunted at the two young men who entered the room. "Come in here and meet Mr. Davenport and his daughter." Rose wondered if he always spoke to his sons like that, in that dictatorial voice.

She turned her attention to the young men. Although they were brothers, they couldn't have been more different. The first man to enter was breath-stoppingly handsome, like one of those classical heroes in paintings. Or a warrior angel. He had hair the colour of sunlight and a face of compelling symmetry. And like an angel, he looked aloof. Indifferent.

"This is Lord James," the earl said shortly, adding brutally, "the spare."

The angel didn't so much as flinch, merely bowed over Rose's hand. "A pleasure to meet you, Miss Davenport," he murmured. His indifferent gaze absorbed the unpretty picture she presented. Rose wanted to curl up and die under that merciless blue gaze, but somehow she withstood his scrutiny and finally he moved aside.

If Lord James was the spare, that meant the second man was the heir. And he couldn't have been more different from his beautiful brother. Gilbert Truman, Viscount Waite, was large, half a head taller than his younger brother and considerably broader through the shoulders, though he had the leanness of youth. His thick, almost black hair was cut fashionably short. His face was arresting rather than handsome. Sharp cheekbones gave him a haughty look, and his nose was marred by a slight kink.

Like his brother, Waite looked her over as he murmured his pleasure at making her acquaintance. But unlike Lord James,

17

he did not appear bored and indifferent. In fact, she wondered if she detected something that might be kind in his hazel gaze before he turned away to greet her father.

She accepted Lord James's invitation to sit, perching on the edge of a delicate-looking chair. She was relieved she would not have to marry someone as perfectly beautiful as he. The contrast between them would be too cruel, a peacock and his dowdy little mate. But were she and Waite any more suited? He was so *big*, so masculine. He made Rose feel even younger, slighter and more insignificant than usual. Entirely lacking as a woman.

And yet, somewhat to her surprise, over the next half hour, Waite—and Waite alone—set about putting Rose at her ease. While Lord James and the earl sat, stiff and silent, Waite was all amiability. He talked in an easy, light-hearted fashion about this and that, drawing Rose out despite herself.

Although he looked forbidding, he had a pleasant manner and a surprisingly infectious smile. Like the rest of him, there was something not quite perfect about his smile. It was an off-centre thing, with a quirk to the left that made him appear to always be laughing at himself. It was...charming.

Rose found herself helplessly warming to him. After a while, she forgot about the marks on her face—even that scab on her eyelid—and stopped dipping her chin to hide beneath the brim of her bonnet. She wouldn't have believed it possible in the carriage on the way over, but she even found herself returning Waite's oddly charming smile with a shy half smile of her own. And it was impossible not to giggle at some of the sillier stories he told her.

How pleasant, he is, she thought. How thoughtful, to take such trouble to put me at ease.

"Have you seen the latest exhibition at the Royal Academy, Miss Davenport?" he asked after a while.

"I'm afraid not," Rose replied. "Although I will endeavour to visit it in the next few weeks."

"Do you enjoy painting? Many young ladies do, I believe."

She laughed at that, a derisive little snort that she'd been scolded for by half a dozen teachers and governesses. It merely made Waite lift his eyebrows in amusement; nevertheless, she blushed.

"I am not artistic, my lord," she explained. "I was the drawing master's very worst pupil at the ladies' seminary I attended. I am so very glad I don't have to attend any more of his lessons."

"You no longer attend this seminary?"

"No. I have been rather unwell, and Papa says that—" She paused. She had been about to say that Papa said she need not go back since she would likely be getting married soon. But it would be awkward, embarrassing, to refer to marriage at this first meeting. And after all, Papa had said marriage would not be mentioned today. "Papa says that now that I am better, I need not go back," she finished instead.

"And that pleases you?" the viscount prompted, smiling his quirking smile.

"Yes indeed," she agreed. "Now I can spend as much time as I wish doing the things I like, such as playing the pianoforte, and dispense entirely with the things I hate."

"Such as drawing?"

"Yes, and"—she wrinkled her nose—"*poetry.*"

"You are not fond of poetry? I thought all young ladies adored poetry. Poets are such romantic creatures, are they not?"

"I am afraid I must be a philistine," she replied. "As soon as I hear a rhyming couplet, my eyelids begin to droop."

Waite laughed. It was a warm laugh of genuine amusement, and at the sound of it, Rose felt her heart flip-flop in her chest. Such an odd feeling! She wanted to grin like an idiot. And stare. She wanted to stare and stare until she could remember every inch of him.

"Then we are both philistines, Miss Davenport," he replied.

We are both philistines.

It gave her a stupidly warm feeling, that comment.

"Well, all the most fashionable people are, you know," she said, adopting a serious expression.

As soon as the words were out of her mouth, she wanted to call them back. He wouldn't appreciate her odd sense of humour; wouldn't appreciate being bracketed with her in that way, as she laughed slyly at herself. Across from her, she saw Lord James frown, puzzled, and her heart sank. But then Waite laughed, a warm, rich chuckle, and suddenly everything was all right. Her own lips twitched, and when she braved a glance at him, she saw that his eyes gleamed with humour and warmth. Their gazes met in a moment of shared amusement. A moment that no one else in the room seemed to be in on.

A few minutes later, Papa rose from his chair to signal it was time to go. In defiance of all her expectations, Rose found she was reluctant to leave, but she obediently stood and walked to Papa's side. While Papa made their farewells, she glanced at Waite, and he smiled at her again, those bronze eyes of his dancing with good humour. She smiled back shyly, blushing slightly, her heart skittering with excitement and happiness.

Despite her fears, Viscount Waite had turned out to be everything she would have wished for in a husband. And amazingly, he seemed to like her too.

"Good-bye, Miss Davenport," he said when Papa had stopped talking. "It was very pleasant to meet you. I enjoyed our conversation."

"As did I, my lord," she replied, amazed at the steadiness of her voice. She curtsied, firstly to the earl, then to his sons, and then she placed her hand on Papa's arm and allowed him to lead her from the room. She felt like she was walking on air.

"Well, Rosebud," Papa said when the butler had closed the door of Stanhope House behind them. "What did you think? I thought Waite a very pleasant young man, I must say. And very attentive to you, my dear."

Rose realised she was smiling, widely, foolishly. Despite her apprehensions, everything was going to be all right. Better than all right, even.

Maybe even wonderful.

Chapter Two

After the Davenports left, James turned to Gil.

"You're too much the gentleman at times, old man," he complained. "An infant like that shouldn't be taken visiting. She couldn't have been more than fifteen. And what a little bag of bones she was! Now she'll be tediously in love with you because you were so nice to her. Which wouldn't be so awful if she was the least bit pretty but—"

"Don't be such a boor," Gil interrupted. "I thought she was an amusing little thing. Quite droll for a girl her age."

"She *snorted*!" James retorted. "Hardly ladylike."

"For God's sake, she's just a child!"

"And a damned ugly one," James retorted. "Did you notice all those marks on her face?

The earl interrupted then, his face flushed. "The chit's seventeen, and if she looks a bit peaky, it's because she's been very ill. She was at death's door a few weeks ago."

The brothers exchanged identical surprised looks. It wasn't like their father to notice a little nobody like Rose Davenport, much less defend her.

"Anyway, enough about that," the earl continued. "Need to talk to you, Waite. Come and see me in the library." He limped out of the room without another word.

James raised his brows at Gil. "What's all that about? It's usually me being called in for a dressing down."

Gil shrugged.

Despite his show of unconcern, Gil felt edgy as he walked to library. When he was younger, a visit to the library had always involved the meting out of paternal punishment. It had been a few years now since his father had beaten him, but he still felt like a boy as he made his way down the corridor.

Having been ordered to attend, he entered the library without knocking. It was an oppressive room, the walls lined with leather-bound books, the furniture dark and heavy. The earl sat at his huge mahogany desk, his face weary as he stared unseeingly at the polished surface, apparently unaware that Gil had arrived.

Gil felt an unexpected and unfamiliar stab of concern. He had never been close to his stern father, but today the old man looked every one of his fifty-six years. Older, in fact. He seemed to have aged a decade in the eighteen months since his countess had died. For all the earl's grim autocracy, it was the countess who had been the stronger partner in their marriage, and he had adored her. Since her death, he had floundered. Gil had heard reports from concerned friends and relatives about his father's uncharacteristic behaviour. It worried him, but he hadn't been able to bring himself to talk to his father. The earl was not a man to confide in his sons. He would be horrified if he knew just how much Gil had learned.

"You wanted to see me?"

The earl looked up, seeming almost surprised to see him for a moment. "Shut the door, Waite," he said. His voice was uncharacteristically quiet, quite different from his usual gruff bark.

As Gil shut the door, his father turned to the silver tray beside him and poured two glasses of brandy, handing one to Gil and swiftly draining his own. Gil held his untouched glass tightly, watching as the older man put his empty glass down and passed a shaking hand over his mouth.

There was a silence before the earl spoke, and when he did, he kept his eyes fixed on the desk. "I've made the most god-awful mess of everything, m'boy. And now I have to ask you to fix it. For all of us. For me, and for you as my heir. And for

23

James and Antonia." He looked up then, finally meeting Gil's concerned gaze, and his pale blue eyes were pleading. "Wish I didn't have to ask this of you, Gil."

It was that, that use of his Christian name, that made him realise something was truly wrong. His father never called him Gil. Always Waite.

Gil kept his voice calm. "Ask me what? What's happened?"

The older man set his shoulders back. He took a deep breath, then said, "I've lost all the unentailed property. Weartham and Kilburton, and Lofthouse too."

"What?" Gil said faintly. All he could feel was numb bewilderment. It was shocking. Impossible. "What?" he said again, more distinctly this time. His grip on the glass tightened, and he sloshed brandy on his hand. Absently, he noticed the coolness of drying alcohol on his skin. "How?" His voice was weak, disbelieving.

"At the tables. I've lost a fortune over the last few months. And then, two weeks ago, I found myself in a very deep game. I was so sure I was going to win! So I staked them all." The earl was sitting up very straight, his back like a ramrod, not even touching the back of the chair. "And I lost."

Gil felt like he'd been punched in the stomach. He knew what this meant. Stanhope Abbey was entailed; untouchable. But its existence depended upon the income from the unentailed estates. This meant ruin.

He'd been standing, but now he dropped into the chair on the other side of his father's desk, feeling as though his legs had been cut out from under him. For the last two years, he'd been learning about estate management, thinking about changes that could be made. He'd secretly planned to make Kilburton over to James when he became earl so James would have his own estate. Now these things would never happen.

He looked at his father again, at the broken old man who was staring back at him with watery, hopeless eyes, and suddenly, he was filled with anger.

"How *could* you?" he condemned, and his voice was ice. "Over a game of *cards*?"

In his whole life, he'd never spoken to his father other than respectfully—but this situation was beyond belief.

The earl said nothing, dropping his gaze to his desk.

After a minute's silence, Gil tried again. "So, who owns them now?"

"Davenport."

"*Davenport?*" Gilbert parroted, stunned. "The man who was just here?" He saw Miles Davenport again in his mind; his handsome, amiable face and his perfectly tailored clothes. He had felt a young man's admiration for Davenport's easy sophistication. Now he felt like a fool. "What was he doing here today? Why did you let him come here?" A new awful thought occurred to him. "Does he own *this* house as well?" He felt angry that he didn't know the answer to that already.

"No," the earl answered quickly. "The townhouse is part of the entailed estate."

Gil made no attempt to keep the bitterness out of his voice. "Well, thank God for small mercies."

"Davenport was bringing his daughter to meet you," the earl said.

"What? That little ghost of a girl? Why?" But even as Gil spoke, the truth was beginning to dawn.

"Davenport is prepared to make the properties back over to us—as a dowry—if you marry her."

Gil laughed, a harsh, incredulous sound. "That *child?*" he finally managed in scathing tones.

"She's seventeen. Old enough to marry."

Gil laughed again. "She doesn't look it."

The earl ignored that. "Davenport won the properties fair and square, m'boy. He could just sell them and put the money in trust for his daughter—she'd have a tidy fortune. It's generous of him to offer them as a dowry."

Gil stared at his father in astonishment. "*Generous?*" he exclaimed. "He took them from you on the turn of a card! And now he seeks to make his daughter a viscountess by tossing them back to you as carelessly as you turned them over to him?" He shook with anger. "And who is to pay for this? Me? Saddled with an ugly child for a wife? No! I won't do it!"

"If you won't do it, we're ruined. All of us." The earl's gaze was steady, but his pale blue eyes shimmered. And Christ, but Gil had never thought to see his father cry.

Gil had to swallow past a lump in his own throat before he could get his next words out. "What about Tilly?"

"What about her?"

I love her.

He couldn't say that, though. His father never spoke of feelings. He'd find it vulgar, incomprehensible, for Gil to do so. Instead, Gil resorted to the language of obligation.

"You know, Father. We're practically engaged."

"Practically? Are you or aren't you?"

"No, but—"

The earl sighed. "It wouldn't matter even if you were," he said. "Her father would never let an impoverished man have her."

And that was the hell of it. Not that Gil would even offer for Tilly if he couldn't afford to keep her in the style she deserved. Oh, she'd no doubt tell him she could be happy being a scullery maid so long as they were together—that was just the sort of thing she'd say—but he wouldn't want her to have to scrimp by on nothing. She was a carefree, blithe girl, and she had no idea how harsh the real world could be.

He pictured Tilly in his mind as he'd last seen her: dancing opposite him in a country dance, her pale gold hair swept up to reveal her swan-like neck. So very lovely. And then, quite unbidden, Rose Davenport, with her pinched, imperfect face, took Tilly's place, and he felt bleak and angry.

"Why didn't you tell me what was going on before Davenport came today?" he demanded.

His father paled. "He was insistent the marriage would only take place if the girl liked you. I thought that if you knew the full circumstances you might—well, find it difficult to be pleasant to her."

Gil laughed again, the same humourless bark. "As it was, I was positively charming to the little viper!"

"I don't think the girl knows anything about the dowry arrangements," the earl replied reproachfully.

"Thinks I'm going to marry her for her looks, does she?" Gil stood up, violently thrusting his chair aside, and strode to the window. The library was one floor up, looking down on Berkeley Square. It was the same lovely spring day outside that it had been this morning. Yet now the whole world looked different to him. Whatever happened now, he was facing a future he hadn't imagined this morning. One of two possible futures, each equally unappealing. The ruin of his family or a loveless marriage. And no place for Tilly in either of them.

Tilly. He'd been in love with her for a year already. When he'd confessed as much, she'd let him know, shyly, that she might be amenable to a proposal at the end of the season, and he'd been over the moon. Only a few months to wait and then they would be engaged, perhaps married this time next year.

It would never happen now.

Instead, he would have to choose between ruin and marriage to Rose Davenport. And really, there was no choice at all—it wasn't just himself he had to consider.

"I won't live with her," he said, still staring out of the window. He couldn't even look at his father." She can go and live at Weartham. I'll visit when I must."

"Once you've consummated the marriage, you can do as

you wish," the earl said. "She'll be your wife and your business. As for Weartham, I'll make that over to you now, if you wish."

Gil steeled himself before he turned back to face his father. "I'm afraid that won't do. You'll have to make over all the property to me, or put it into trust, until I inherit. If I'm to marry this girl, you'll have to resign yourself to a fixed quarterly allowance."

The earl flushed, a deep crimson wash that flooded up his neck and over his face. Not so many years ago, Gil would have been whipped for speaking to the old man in such a way. Even since he'd become an adult, he'd held back on any criticism of his father. But today changed everything. "I won't be forced into this marriage only for you to lose everything again on the tables next week," Gil continued implacably. "So, do you agree?"

The earl looked away. "I'll have Barton draw the papers up," he muttered.

Chapter Three

It rained on Rose's wedding day, a relentless downpour that didn't let up all day.

She stood at the window of her bedchamber in her chemise when she should have been getting dressed and watched the rain drive down, forming large puddles on the street below.

Four weeks had passed since her first meeting with Waite— *Gilbert*, though she still found it impossible to think of him by that name—and in all that time, Rose had seen him on only three occasions.

A week after their first meeting, the earl invited Rose and her father to a dinner party at Stanhope House, a grand affair at which their engagement was announced. She and Waite barely spoke a dozen words to one another. Ten days after that, Waite and his sister Antonia paid them a morning call. Waite had sat silent while his sister chattered about wedding gowns. And then, last week, the earl hosted an engagement party. Of the fifty guests present, Rose knew no one other than her father and Waite and his family. She felt young and dull and unsightly and had been relieved when it was over.

Waite was perfectly civil whenever they met, but the connection she'd thought she'd felt during their first meeting had been absent since then.

Papa told her that her dowry was substantial, but she still found it incredible that it was enough to secure this marriage. She and Papa lived modestly as compared to Waite's family. The earl's London residence, Stanhope House, was lavish and elegant, and the earl owned no fewer than four country estates. Antonia had told her the main country estate in Hampshire,

Stanhope Abbey, had one hundred and seventy-four rooms. Surely her dowry must be paltry compared to his wealth? He couldn't *need* it. If he needed money, there were dozens of wealthy merchants eager to marry their daughters off to peers of the realm who would doubtless be able to offer a hundred times as much.

Perhaps he had been cool with her because he felt nervous? She certainly did. They had never been alone, and whenever they met, she was horribly aware of everyone else watching them. Waite probably felt it too. If he did, it would doubtless make him as awkward as it did her.

In any event, it wasn't as though she could change her mind now. Ever since she had agreed to the marriage, her father had been beaming with happiness, vibrating with excitement. He had assumed Rose would be content to get married immediately, as had Waite, and Rose hadn't wanted to offend her future husband by asking for more time to get to know him better. Besides, it had all felt rather dreamlike till now. Until today. Until it was suddenly, and far too soon, the day of the wedding.

Despite her screeching nerves, there was no question of her not going through with it. She was *not* going to disappoint her father, or let Waite and his family down. She was seventeen. A grown woman. And she would not allow herself to act the scared rabbit. Her doubts were the natural reaction of a bride-to-be. In a few weeks, she and Waite—*Gilbert*—would laugh about them.

Besides, she had a new home to look forward to. When her father informed her that she and Waite would be living at one of the earl's estates on the Northumbrian coast, she had been touched. Her physicians had been saying for months that a period of recuperation in the country, and preferably near the sea, would be the best treatment for her. She had been surprised and gratified that Waite had chosen where they would live with so much care.

She was relieved too that she would be away from town. She hadn't relished the thought of attending *Ton* events, even as a newlywed viscountess. Not now, when her old school friends—young girls with apple-fresh cheeks and round bosoms and gleaming tresses—would be making their come-outs. She didn't want to be presented to the Queen. She didn't want to watch gorgeous, sumptuous fabrics being pinned around her skeletal form by fashionable dressmakers. She didn't want to be the inevitable wallflower at the events of the season; a wallflower with a thin, marked face and brutally short hair. Not even a married wallflower, thank you very much.

She was so grateful to be going to Weartham. It would be a welcome respite. A haven. Somewhere to get well again.

Papa had explained that Waite wouldn't be able to stay with her at Weartham all the time. He would need to spend time in London and at his other estates too, of course, notably at Stanhope Abbey. But perhaps that was a good thing? They would have time to get used to one another gradually rather than being thrown too much together at the beginning. And when she was better, they could travel together.

The thought of what married life would be like consumed her waking thoughts. Lottie had told her about the physical side of marriage. It sounded petrifying, though fascinating too. Lottie had tried to assure her that however frightening and embarrassing it sounded, it could be wonderful, but since that only made Rose think about Lottie and her father together, she had hurriedly cut the conversation short. It was easier, and more pleasant, to think about the other intimacies of marriage: learning each other's preferences, dining together every day, making plans for the future, bringing children into the world. She found herself reflecting too that, as time wore on, her hair would grow. Hopefully the marks would fade too. Perhaps one day she would be halfway pretty again.

She imagined what Waite would think of that, of the *real* her. She daydreamed about him coming home to Weartham, after an absence away, perhaps, and being stunned by her improved looks. She imagined his expression, how astonished he'd be, how thrilled. And how she would feel, to have her husband return to her, to their home. Not a stranger by then, but a *beloved*. Coming home to her.

The idea of that home, a house that had been in Waite's family for generations and that she need never say good-bye to, thrilled her in ways she could not give expression to. Her first permanent home. A home she would share with Waite. Together, they would be "we", "us". The Viscount and Viscountess Waite, man and wife, two parts of a larger whole.

A light tap at her bedchamber door interrupted her thoughts. She drew away from the window and the miserable sight of the driving rain. "Who is it?"

"Lottie. May I come in, *cara*?"

"Yes, of course." She went to the door and opened it herself, and Lottie slipped past her. Her long black hair was simply plaited, and she wore a loose crimson robe.

Lottie was not coming to the wedding, of course. Her presence would be scandalous. The bride's father's mistress. It felt strange, though, that she wouldn't be there. For the last few months, she and Lottie had seen each other every day. They had even become friends, Rose realised, half reluctantly. She saw more of Lottie, much more, than she saw of her father.

"Not long now, *cara*."

"I wish you were coming today," Rose said suddenly, surprising herself. Lottie blinked, then smiled more widely.

"Me too, *cara*," she said softly. "But we can't go shocking your poor husband's maiden aunts." Her gaze moved to the simple primrose gown and matching bonnet that lay on the bed. "Let me help you get dressed."

She helped Rose into the gown, fastening the long line of tiny buttons on the back with tender care. Then she turned Rose round and looked at her for a long time without saying anything. For some reason, that soft brown regard made Rose feel like crying, and she had to swallow against a lump in her throat.

"You look very pretty, *cara*," Lottie said gravely, ignoring Rose's snort of disbelief. "But a little pale." She pulled out a small, blue, glass jar from the pocket of her robe and opened the lid; inside was a thickish, oily red paste. Rouge. Rose had never worn rouge before. She let Lottie apply a tiny amount to each of her cheeks.

When Lottie was finished, Rose leaned forward and kissed her cheek. She felt stupidly like crying again. "Thank you," she said. "For everything. For taking care of me."

"You were very easy to look after, *cara*," Lottie said, and her eyes glistened.

"No, I wasn't," Rose said. "I was a little beast."

Lottie shook her head. "You are a fine, brave young woman, Rose. I hope you realise that one day."

Rose stared, taken aback. But before she could ask Lottie what she meant, the other woman added, "Are you sure about this wedding? No one else has asked you, I know. You are about to marry a young man you do not know at all. Are you quite sure you want to do it?"

"It's a little late to ask me that!" Rose teased, forcing herself to laugh. In truth, there was a part of her that wanted to whisper *yes*, she had changed her mind. But she had promised she would marry Gilbert Truman, Viscount Waite today, and it would be cowardly to run away just because—well, because the smile he'd given her that first day hadn't reappeared. That was a childish basis for any doubts she had. The fact was, Waite was probably just as nervous as she was. He was as new to the idea of marriage as she. But after today, he would be her husband and she would be his wife. They would face the future together, side by side.

"It's not *too* late though," Lottie said intently. "I know your papa wants this marriage very much—but if you tell him you cannot do it, while he may protest and try to persuade you otherwise, he will not force you. I won't let him, *cara*."

"Oh, Lottie," Rose mumbled, touched. "I am quite sure, truly. You needn't worry."

Lottie looked as though she would say more, but then there was another knock at the door, and this time it was Papa. She told him to enter, and he opened the door, smiling brightly.

"Time to go, Rosebud."

She pasted a matching smile on her own face and took his arm.

The wedding was to take place in an unfashionable church a good way away from Mayfair. There would only to be a few guests. It would be a private affair, Papa had explained. There was little point in having a great *Ton* wedding when Rose hadn't even been presented to the Queen and when she knew no one in society. Rose was relieved. She had found the engagement party a trial, even though fifty guests was paltry, according to Antonia. Fifty pairs of eyes judging her deficient looks had been more than enough for Rose.

The rain poured down all the way to the church. When they arrived and Papa opened the carriage door, she saw that the church was an unattractive square building with a squat-looking tower. It seemed to hunch over itself in the rain. It was not the sort of church she had imagined getting married in. In her girlish fantasies, she had walked into a lofty cathedral, and the sun had been streaming through a hundred stained-glass windows.

Thankfully, it was only a few steps from the carriage to the portico where the vicar waited for them. While Papa spoke with the vicar, Rose peeped down the church. Waite stood at the altar with his brother beside him as his groomsman. They looked magnificent in matching dark blue coats.

Rose felt a queer ache looking at Waite. He was everything a woman should want in her husband, yet Rose could take no pleasure in the moment, and she realised, with some horror, that she felt unworthy of him.

Hastily, she looked away from him to the guests sitting in the pews behind. The earl was sitting with Antonia and an older lady who had been introduced to Rose at the engagement party as Cousin Harriet. Behind them sat a middle-aged couple— Waite's uncle and aunt. On the other side of the church were Papa's brother, Sir Philip Davenport, and his wife Celia with their son John.

All at once, it was time to get married. She laid her hand on her father's arm and smiled at him. He beamed back at her, looking handsome and happy.

Rose walked down the aisle with considerably more composure than she felt. Her fingers did not tremble when her father placed them in Waite's large hand. Her voice emerged clearly and promptly as she spoke her vows. Not by one gesture or a single word did she reveal that she had ever entertained the slightest doubt about this marriage. All in all, she was rather proud of her performance.

As for Waite, he was impeccable. He bowed over her hand when it was placed in his own. He spoke his vows in his deep voice without hesitation. But still, there was no warmth in his eyes for her, not even when he lightly brushed his lips against her own after the pronouncement that they were now man and wife. And as they walked back down the aisle, past their smiling wedding guests, Rose wondered for the first time whether she had actually imagined the kindness in his eyes at that first meeting.

Gil was on his fourth glass of brandy.

"Are you ever going up?" James asked, cradling his own glass in his hand and staring into the amber depths. "It's after midnight."

Rose had retired several hours ago, not long after the seemingly interminable wedding breakfast had finally ended.

"Is it? I'd better go, then," Gil replied, trying to sound nonchalant. He stood and drained his glass, casting a glance at James, who was lolling in a fireside armchair. James looked amused, damn him. His light chuckle followed Gil out of the library.

Gil slowly climbed the stairs, a single candle in his hand. He thought of Tilly in all her pink-and-gold beauty. It should be her he was going to tonight. Not the plain, oddly collected girl he had married today.

He'd been aghast when he'd learned that Rose had been put in his mother's old bedchamber. No one had slept there since his mother had died two years ago. He hated that Rose would be there. Hated that he was being forced to spend his wedding night in that room.

It was unavoidable, though. The gesture—his father's—was a mark of respect to the bride. Gil could hardly gainsay it. However unwillingly, he was married now. Stuck with Rose Davenport forever. *Till death us do part.*

When he arrived at the door of Rose's bedchamber, he paused to steel himself. It really shouldn't be this hard, he thought. She was just a girl, and he had done this before. Although not with a virgin. Mortifyingly, his father had taken him aside last night and told him to *"break the girl in gently"*, reminding Gil that she'd been ill. As though it wasn't patently obvious from looking at her. Gil just wanted it over with. And in truth, it was probably best to be as quick as possible. He took a deep breath and entered the bedchamber without knocking.

The room was dark. Apart from the candle he had brought with him, the only light in the room came from the shivering glow of the fire as it slowly died in the grate. Rose lay in bed,

36

the blankets pushed down to her waist. She was asleep, innocently unaware of his arrival.

He stood at the foot of the bed and looked at her: a young girl clad in an overly fussy nightgown that drowned her slender form. Her hair was very short, a boyish cap of soft, dark curls. His father had told him during last night's dreadful interview that it had been cut off during her illness—again, as though it wasn't obvious. It looked as though it was only just beginning to grow in again.

Her profile was fine, he noticed, although her face was pale and very thin. But the dim light from the fire was kinder to her than the harsh light of day. Those red marks seemed less obvious in this light. He wondered if she would always be disfigured. His father had said he was sure the marks would fade, but what did he know?

She let out a little shuddering sigh, and his eyes were drawn to her mouth. It was a soft, childish mouth, slightly sad looking. He remembered that just before the vicar had begun the ceremony, her mouth had trembled, and he had thought she was about to cry. An illusion, actually. When he had looked into her eyes, he had seen she was perfectly composed, placid even.

It was difficult to see the shape of her body beneath the blankets, but he could just make out the line of slender, coltish legs and, beneath the voluminous nightgown, the hint of a bosom. *Thank God. Not entirely childlike, then.* Still, it wasn't going to be easy. She was so very different from Tilly, so unappealing. And the fact she was a virgin worried him.

"Rose," he said softly. "Wake up."

She stirred from her sleep, slowly blinking her eyes open and focusing upon him. When she realised where she was, she flushed and sat bolt upright.

"I'm sorry. I fell asleep!"

Gil didn't answer. He merely blew out his candle and set it

aside. Then he silently got to work removing his clothes. His boots, his waistcoat, breeches, shirt, drawers and stockings—all were discarded with calm efficiency. When he was naked, he advanced toward Rose. His eyes had grown used to the almost-darkness now, and he could just make out her apprehensive expression by the fire's glow. Despite everything, he felt for her. She was very young.

"I'll try to be as gentle as I can," he said stiffly, "but this might hurt a bit, I'm afraid. I'm told it can be painful for ladies, the first time."

He pulled the blankets down. Rose scooted over to the other side of the bed as he got in beside her. She looked rather as though she would like to jump out of her side and run out the door. Instead, she carefully lay down beside him, her arms rigid by her sides, regarding his large, naked body with a kind of horrified fascination. Get it over with, he thought bleakly.

"Take your nightgown off, Rose," Gil said in the same soft, neutral voice. She looked pained and reluctant, but when he kept staring at her silently, she raised her shaking fingers to the buttons and fumbled a few open. She looked up at him then, her eyes beseeching.

"Take it off," he said again, somehow finding it impossible to be kind.

She closed her eyes, looking miserable, and sat up. In one swift movement, she pulled the nightgown over her head. He took it from her and dropped it on the floor.

"Lie down," he said. Her fingers searched for the bedcovers, but he shook his head, and eventually she lay down as he wanted, uncovered and naked before him. He cast his eyes over her assessingly. Her body was thin but surprisingly enticing. Unmistakably a woman's body. She had beautiful legs, and her small breasts were nicely shaped with dusky nipples. His cock stiffened obligingly, and he felt a bolt of intense relief. He would be able to do this.

Without looking at her face, Gil placed his hand on her

right breast. It fit his palm snugly, and he played with it idly, watching as the nipple hardened beneath his fingers, ignoring Rose's sharp gasp. He kept playing with her right breast as he dipped his head to the other one, rolling his tongue around the hard nubbin and sucking wetly, registering her faint moan with detached interest. If she got wet for him, it would make it easier, so he spent several minutes tonguing and teasing her breasts, his own excitement building as he did so.

After a while, Gil lowered one of his hands to Rose's slightly parted thighs, insinuating his fingers between her legs and pushing them farther apart. She stiffened briefly but did nothing to impede him. Without ceremony, he slid his longest finger deep into her already wet quim, using his thumb to circle the fleshy pip at the entrance. Rose bridled, then calmed. A moment later, she moaned softly and whispered his name, a question in her voice. She was ready enough for him now, her slickness all over his fingers.

Gil took his hand away and covered Rose's body with his own, settling himself between her parted thighs. He saw that she wore an expression of mingled shock and desire, and quickly closed his eyes. He didn't want to look at her as he ploughed her. Instead, he distracted himself by kissing her, closing his eyes. It occurred to him, as his mouth moved over hers and he coaxed her lips apart, that this was their first proper kiss.

He didn't want any illusion of romance arising in her mind, so he made the kiss a deep, sexual one, thrusting into her mouth with his tongue. His cock bumped against the entrance of her quim. He was becoming ever harder as he anticipated the pleasure of penetrating her. Rose had wrapped her arms around his neck, and some instinct was driving her to grind her pelvis against his cock. It excited him wildly. He *wanted* her. He felt appalled and relieved all at once.

Gil broke the kiss, sliding his hand between them to part her folds and guide his cock inside her. Christ, but she was tight! So tight that he wondered for a moment whether this was going to be physically possible. He had to push, and push *hard*.

Rose didn't cry out as he breached her flesh, but a soft whoosh escaped her lips. She pushed against his shoulder, and when he lifted his head, she searched his face with panicky eyes, but he couldn't look at her. Instead, he turned his face into her throat and thrust even harder, forging a passage for himself in her untried depths. He kissed the flesh of her throat passionately with his open mouth, trying to ignore the fact that Rose's body had gone stiff and still; that her enjoyment had apparently evaporated; that she was just tolerating this now.

Through a supreme effort of will, he managed to ignore her discomfort, focusing on finishing as soon as he could. But even excited as he was, he winced when he heard a noise at the back of her throat that was plainly a suppressed cry of pain. Get it over with, he thought again. And he thrust again and again, driving into her, concentrating hard on his own pleasure, trying to bring himself to a swift completion.

After a few moments, he came fiercely, gasping. Despite everything, her discomfort, his resentment, her lack of allure, his orgasm was intensely pleasurable, and he felt ashamed when it was over.

Rose held herself very still beneath him as he regained his breath. As he levered himself off her, he saw disappointment and bewilderment in her eyes. But he quashed the incipient swell of regret ruthlessly.

He got out of bed straightaway and pulled on his drawers and shirt. For a moment, he hesitated, feeling he should say something. But what was there to say? Without a word, he gathered up the rest of his clothes and walked to the bedchamber door.

"My lor—Gilbert?" Rose called out. Her voice sounded tentative and very young. He turned around, an expression of polite enquiry on his face. She was sitting up, the bedcovers pulled up to her chin. "Where are you going?"

"To my bedchamber. To sleep." He made his voice sound faintly surprised and felt like a brute when her shoulders slumped.

"Oh, I see," she replied in a wavery voice. "Well, good night, then."

"Good night." He nodded at her with ludicrous formality and left through the door connecting their chambers.

Inside his own bedchamber, he tossed his clothes onto the floor and stripped off his shirt and drawers again, crossing to the ewer and basin to wash away the traces of her blood.

When he was clean, he threw himself onto his bed and lay for a long time, looking at the ceiling. They were leaving for Weartham tomorrow. He wondered how long it would be decent to stay before he could come back to London. Would a week be too short? The thought of a week, or worse, two, in Rose's company depressed him. He had nothing to say to her, no wish to spend time with her. No wish to repeat what had just happened, no matter how good his climax had felt.

Was this how life would be from now on? Dreading and resenting the duty visits he would have to pay his wife? It was not the life he had hoped for. Just a month ago, he had been dreaming of a very different marriage to Tilly. One in which he would not dread the marriage bed or feel like the worst sort of boor afterwards for tupping his own wife.

It was almost dawn before sleep finally took him.

Chapter Four

The next day, the newlywed Viscount and Viscountess Waite left for Northumberland, with Cousin Harriet in tow.

Miss Harriet Browne was a lady of around fifty years. Her role in life was that of poor relation to the Earl of Stanhope. For many years, she had been companion to the earl's mother and, more recently, his sister. Now she had been asked to go to Weartham to live. A companion for Rose for when her new husband was away.

Rose had been informed of this by her new father-in-law on her wedding day. Since she was entirely in awe of the earl and since Cousin Harriet was standing beside him and beaming when he imparted the news, Rose had not felt able to protest. Besides, she had been too busy wondering just how much time Gil intended to spend away from Weartham, if he felt she needed a companion to fill his absences.

The first day's travelling was brutal. Despite the luxurious upholstery of the earl's carriage, Rose was jolted and jarred till her bones ached. Harriet pointed out, sympathetically, that it was harder on Rose because she was slender and her bones were nearer the surface, whereas Harriet was more "padded". Rose tried to smile at this gentle self-deprecation, but her stomach was upset by the constant motion, and it made her peevish.

She liked Harriet, though. Harriet was chatty when Rose felt like talking and silent when she needed to think. Rose felt like she could be herself with Harriet.

She couldn't be herself with Waite. *Gilbert.* With him, she felt like a tongue-tied schoolgirl. Not that she had much opportunity to speak to him as they travelled.

After the first few hours, they stopped at a small hostelry. Even by then, Rose felt sick from the lurching of the carriage and the smell of the warm leather upholstery. It was a relief to climb out and walk in the open air. She followed Waite and Harriet into the taproom of the inn, which was far from plush. In fact it was dingy and dark, the chairs and table rough-hewn and uncomfortable.

"My apologies, ladies," Waite said as he seated them, wiping a rough wooden chair with his fine silk handkerchief before Rose sat down. "But there is no other hostelry for many miles. I thought you would prefer to stop now rather than wait."

Rose smiled up at him shyly. "Thank you," she murmured. She felt a little hurt when he nodded stiffly and looked away.

She didn't feel hungry and merely picked at the food the landlady brought them, unenthusiastically sipping a little ale. She wondered whether, after their meal, Waite might join Harriet and herself in the carriage. But when they left the taproom half an hour later, Waite signalled to a groom for his horse. Apparently, he hadn't yet tired of his long hours in the saddle.

While she waited for Harriet to climb into the carriage before her, Rose glanced at her husband again. He was talking to an older gentleman who also seemed to be waiting for his horse. Next to the older man, Waite stood a full head taller. He was young and strong and perfectly groomed, from the top of his dark head to the toes of his well-shined boots. When he laughed at something the man said, he flashed white, even teeth and—amazingly—a dimple in his left cheek. Bright-eyed and laughing, he looked almost as youthful as herself, she thought. Perhaps two and twenty wasn't so very much older than seventeen after all.

Waite turned to his horse which a stable hand was holding for him. He disdained the mounting block, casually wedging his foot into the stirrup and mounting the beast with athletic grace.

Rose's mouth went dry at the sight, and she was overcome with an almost childish admiration for this casual display of physical prowess. She stared at him, eyes wide, like a little girl watching her older brother doing something dangerous and forbidden. And then his eyes met hers, catching her gawping at him. For a moment, their eyes met, and she saw that his smile was gone, his expression very cool now. She couldn't imagine what he made of her, of her gaucheness, and she looked quickly away, flushing hotly, scrambling into the carriage after Harriet.

It was seven o'clock in the evening before they finally stopped for the night at a bustling inn. Their rooms had been reserved, and Rose was shown into a bedchamber several doors away from Waite's. She wasn't sure how she felt about that. Relieved, she supposed, though oddly disappointed too.

Her new maid, Sarah, asked her what she wanted to wear for dinner. Rose shrugged. "You choose," she muttered. She couldn't work up any enthusiasm for the pretty gowns her father had bought for her in the weeks before her wedding.

Sarah pulled out the pink silk. It was high-necked and a little fussy. Rose let Sarah button her into the gown and then—against her better judgement—allowed her to thread a pink silk ribbon through her short hair, fastening it with a little pearl hair ornament. Rose stared doubtfully at her reflection in the looking glass.

"You look ever so nice, your ladyship," Sarah said. She'd been "your ladyshipping" Rose to death since yesterday.

She didn't look nice, though. And it wasn't the dress or the ribbon. Nothing could look nice on her. On that girl in the mirror. For a moment, Rose let herself remember how she used to look, with shiny, luxuriant hair and unmarked skin.

She turned from the mirror. "I'd better go down."

A private dining room had been reserved for them for dinner. It was small but like a palace compared to the hostelry they had eaten at earlier that day. A good linen tablecloth covered the table, and it was set with silverware and wineglasses. The food was plain but good.

As they ate, Harriet and Waite conversed with ease, but Rose couldn't seem to get a word out. She sat silently, trying to eat, all the while feeling terribly self-conscious.

The meal was served by a pretty maidservant. She had a peaches-and-cream complexion and bouncing golden curls under her cap. As Rose watched her enter the dining room bearing a tureen of soup, she found herself wishing she hadn't let Sarah put the pink ribbon through her hair. She felt foolish. Pathetic. An ugly little monkey dressed up in silken finery.

Later, she caught the girl staring at her. When their eyes locked, the girl hurriedly looked away and bustled out of the room. Rose had to swallow against the lump that rose in her throat, a clod of hot tears that choked her. Fighting for control, she pretended to be absorbed in her dinner, grateful for Harriet's bright chatter.

At last the meal was over, and Harriet and Rose stood to retire, leaving Waite to his Port. As they left the dining room, the pretty maidservant was walking along the corridor toward them, carrying a decanter of dark ruby wine for Waite. She bobbed a small curtsey at them as she passed.

Rose slowly walked up the stairs, imagining how Waite's face would look when he saw the maidservant enter. She really was very pretty. Rose was sure he would smile at her, take pleasure in the sight of her. What man would not?

Harriet chattered all the way upstairs and for several minutes outside Rose's bedchamber door before she finally said good night. It was a relief to go into her bedchamber alone. Well, alone except for Sarah, who helped her undress and packed away the now-hated pink silk before she herself retired.

It was only when Rose slipped between the cool sheets of her bed that she realised how very tired she was. She would never have thought that merely sitting in a carriage could be so exhausting. And she had many days of travelling ahead of her.

As she drifted off to sleep, it occurred to her that Waite might come to her tonight. But when she woke in the morning, she was alone.

The next few days unfolded in much the same way. The pace of their travel was relentless. Every day was an early start with only the briefest of stops for refreshment and comfort and Waite riding all the way. It would have been terribly boring if it were not for Harriet.

Each night they arrived at an inn, always the same sort, respectable and comfortable. They dined together, as they had the first evening, Rose usually staying silent while Harriet and Waite talked. And then they retired, each to their own bedchambers. It seemed that Waite—Gilbert—did not intend to visit her bedchamber at all during the journey. She wondered why. Perhaps he thought she would be too tired? Perhaps *he* was too tired? He was riding all day, every day, after all. Surely he would visit her again when they got to Weartham?

She wondered what he'd made of their wedding night. So far as she was concerned, it had been very far from wonderful. But then Lottie had warned her that it wouldn't be very good the first time and possibly not for a while after that.

She had thought that Waite had enjoyed it, though. He had finished, after all. And he had *seemed* enthusiastic, at least toward the end. Each night, she relived the feel of his heavy body covering her, his hard flesh driving into her as his mouth moved over her throat. She remembered his helpless groans, signalling, she'd thought, his pleasure. Although the experience had been painful for her, the memory of it, strangely, was not entirely unpleasant. There had been a few magical minutes at the beginning when he had kissed her and touched her intimately, and she had felt a tense, temporary pleasure in his arms.

Those initial minutes had been exciting. Despite how it had

ended, she was curious to discover more. But she was a woman—she would have to wait for her husband to visit her.

As soon as that thought crossed her mind, she frowned. *Did* she have to wait for him to visit her? Perhaps he thought she had hated their wedding night and was holding back until she signalled that she would welcome him in her bed again? Perhaps he was being considerate? It was a novel thought, and one that made her bite her lip with uncertainty. She stared out the carriage window, not seeing the countryside they travelled through, thinking instead of what she should do tonight, after dinner.

Tonight was their last inn stop. They would arrive at Weartham tomorrow afternoon. It would be very easy to let tonight follow the same pattern as all the other nights of this uncomfortable journey. It would be very easy to simply wait to see what tomorrow night would bring at Weartham. Yet Rose was seized all at once by a need to *act*. Perhaps her adventurous streak, which had seemed to entirely vanish when she had been ill, was beginning to reassert itself?

She rested her forehead against the glass of the carriage window and imagined going to Gilbert tonight, pulling the bedcovers aside and sliding into bed beside him. He would put his hands on her, and this time, she would put hers on him. She would *explore* him.

She smiled at herself in the carriage window. She was being ridiculous.

Or was she? Why should she not go to him tonight? After all, what was the worst that could happen? Surely he wouldn't reject her? He was her husband, after all.

After dinner that evening, Rose retired to her bedchamber as usual. Thankfully, there was a connecting door between her bedchamber and Waite's so she wouldn't have to venture into the inn corridor in her nightgown.

Sarah helped her undress and slipped her nightgown over her head. She felt like a child, having a servant dress and undress her. Her nurse had stopped doing all her buttons for her years ago. But she needed a maid now that she wasn't wearing her old gowns with their practical fastenings. Her new gowns were all frivolous impracticality.

After Sarah had brushed Rose's hair—a task that took all of half a minute—Rose dismissed her, then sat at the dressing table for a long time, paralysed with uncertainty. The thought of Waite in bed next door was both exciting and alarming. She wondered whether he would be pleased or disapproving of her taking the initiative.

She wandered over to the connecting door and stood in front of it for a long time, her pale hand resting lightly on the wooden panel. Twice she lifted her hand, and twice stopped just before she made contact, feeling uncertain and ridiculous. Eventually, she steeled herself, made a fist and firmly knocked. Her stomach was in knots as she waited. She had to clasp her trembling hands together to still them.

After a moment, the door swung open. Waite stood on the other side looking surprised. His broad chest was bare, although he still wore his breeches. She must have caught him in the act of getting undressed.

He looked very male. Alien to her in every possible way. His chest was lightly covered with dark, crisp-looking hair, and his body was large and hard and muscled. There was no softness to him at all. Rose flushed scarlet.

"Yes?" he said, appearing surprised. "Is something wrong?"

Rose swallowed. "No," she squeaked. "I just thought, that is—" She swallowed again. "I thought I would—come to your bedchamber tonight."

Waite frowned and looked away. Immediately, she wanted to sink through the floor. It was quite obvious that her approach was not welcome.

"All right," he said eventually, his voice unhappy. "But go to your own bed. I'll come to you in a few minutes." He closed the door then, and she stood staring at it miserably for a moment before she turned around and walked back to her own bed.

She wished, desperately, that she hadn't knocked on that door. But there was no undoing it now. So she removed her nightgown and slid under the bedcovers, hoping that it would be possible to stay under them, shielded from Waite's gaze. As soon as she closed her eyes, she saw his frowning, averted face again.

The minutes that followed felt like an hour to Rose as she lay waiting, staring at the ancient beams in the ceiling, trying to hold back the hot tears that were lodged in her throat. The weeks of doubt had finally coalesced into a firm certainty.

He doesn't want to be married to me.

She had assumed he felt as she did: hopeful, determined to make something of this arranged marriage. Plainly, he did not. He must have only wanted her dowry. Or perhaps his father did. He certainly did not wish to share her bed. He was probably counting the minutes until he could rush back to London.

By some miracle, Rose managed not to cry.

When he came through the door, he was wearing a dressing gown. Rose hurriedly blew out the candle beside the bed while he undressed. In the dark, mercifully, she could not see him. And he could not see her.

Over the next few minutes, Waite told her what to do, and she obeyed numbly. She felt his hands on her, on her breasts and her hips, but it wasn't like last time. She couldn't take pleasure in his ministrations tonight.

After a while, he managed to coax a slight, mechanical response from her with his searching fingers, enough at least to lubricate her against pain. This time though, she was embarrassed by her wetness, mortified that he could cause even that weak physical response in her when she hated him so. She concentrated hard on the hate, managing to drive the hint of incipient pleasure away.

There was little pain when he entered her, although she felt uncomfortably full. She lay perfectly still beneath him while he moved on top of her. His physical invasion of her body felt horribly, hatefully intimate, and she wished with every fibre of her being she had not invited it. She never would again.

Her eyes had become accustomed to the dark now. She risked a glance and saw that Waite's eyes were closed, his face taut with concentration. She wondered if he was thinking of another woman as he did this to her. That pretty serving maid, perhaps. Well, who could blame him? she thought bleakly. She was ugly. It probably sickened him to look at her.

In a matter of moments, he was finished. She felt the hot flood of his seed into her core and realised that this night might result in her conceiving a child. She hoped it did. Perhaps if she presented him with an heir, they need never do this again.

He rose from her without a word and put his dressing gown on. He walked to the door between their chambers. "Good night, Rose," he murmured softly. He didn't open the door, though, and she sensed him looking at her in the silence. She ignored him, merely turning to the wall.

After a moment, she heard the soft click of the door as it opened and closed behind him.

Even then, Rose did not give in to tears. Instead, she turned her misery to hate. She fantasised about how she could punish him. There were physical punishments, of course; throwing something at him would be satisfying, something large and hard. But physical pain wasn't good enough; she wanted to pay him back in kind. She wanted him to experience the same feeling of cruel rejection that she had just experienced. She wanted to be beautiful and for him to desire her desperately. She wanted him to beg her for a crumb of her precious attention.

She knew she might as well wish for the moon.

Never again, Gil thought as he discarded his dressing gown and got into bed. He didn't know quite how he had got through that experience. He felt hollow and horror-stricken, as though he'd just been through a battle. The wedding night hadn't been easy, but at least she had been willing and receptive to his touch. This time—Lord, he felt like a rapist. She had asked him to come to her, then lain beneath him like a martyr, regret and misery pouring off her in waves.

Gil stared at the ceiling, trying to nourish his anger. It was hopeless, though. Instead, he found himself remembering something his mother had said to him at the first ball he had ever attended. She had persuaded him to ask a plump, painfully shy young girl to dance with him. *"Don't make her feel as though you are asking her out of politeness,"* his mother had said. *"Be kind. Make her feel as though you really want to dance with her."*

Kindness had mattered to his mother.

He had not been kind to Rose tonight. All his anger and resentment about this forced marriage withered in the face of that simple truth. He had been beastly. Cruel. He'd let her know he hadn't wanted her. And the astonishing fact that he'd easily become hard, easily climaxed didn't help in the least. In fact, it made it worse somehow.

There was no undoing it, though. And having behaved like such a boor, he couldn't think what the next day might bring. He wanted to jump on his horse and race back to London.

The rest of his marriage stretched before him, decades of it. An inescapable prison. A life sentence.

He felt wronged by it. By Rose. And now he had wronged her too.

If only he could undo it.

All of it.

Chapter Five

They arrived at Weartham late the following afternoon. The carriages rumbled up the long drive, coming to a dusty halt in front of the house. It was a substantial house built of mellow sandstone, and in the bright afternoon sunshine, it looked warmly welcoming.

During the journey, Harriet had told Rose that, although Weartham was the smallest of the Earl's estates, it had been Waite's mother's favourite. The earl used to take the whole family to Weartham for a month or two every summer. Harriet too. She had spoken fondly of those summers. And perhaps her memories of blackberry picking, village fetes and long walks by the sea had infected Rose. For as soon as she saw the house, it felt oddly familiar. And then she noticed the line of servants waiting outside.

Were they standing there to welcome her? Or to be inspected by her? Rose was going to be mistress of this house, and she had absolutely no idea what was expected of her.

Stiff with shyness, she watched from the carriage window as Waite gracefully dismounted his horse. He waved the hovering footmen away and opened Rose's carriage door himself, offering his hand to her to help her descend. She grasped it with numb fingers and stepped down.

He led her to the steps of the house where the servants waited and introduced her to the housekeeper, Mrs. Hart. She was a slim, neat woman in her middle years, and when she curtseyed to Rose, her expression was very composed and quite devoid of curiosity. As Rose made halting conversation with Mrs. Hart, Waite drew away from her, stepping back. She felt her sudden isolation keenly, though she said nothing to give any hint of her feelings. Instead, she followed Mrs. Hart down the line of neatly turned-out, expressionless servants, taking note of each name in turn. The maids bobbed their curtseys and the men bowed. They kept their eyes lowered for the most part as Rose repeated their names, but she felt their gazes upon her when she moved down the line, felt them looking at her surreptitiously.

They must be wondering why their master had married such a plain, drab thing.

At length, they entered the house, Rose and Harriet walking beside Mrs. Hart and Waite bringing up the rear with Mr. Thomson, the steward. The rest of the servants melted away.

"I will take tea in the library with Mr. Thomson," Waite told Mrs. Hart once they were inside. "The ladies might wish to take refreshments in the drawing room."

Rose realised that everyone was looking at her expectantly.

"Ah—yes. Yes, that would be nice," she stammered. "Harriet? Tea?"

She hated the uncertainty and nervousness in her voice. Harriet smiled at her. "Tea would do very well," she agreed calmly.

Mrs. Hart inclined her head and glided smoothly away. Waite strolled off with Mr. Thomson, already engrossed in conversation. For a moment, Harriet watched the two men walk away; then she turned to Rose and smiled. "Let me show you the drawing room."

She led Rose down the corridor and into a restful, sun-bathed room furnished in pale cream and gold. Rose spotted a collection of miniatures arranged on the wall and wandered over to take a closer look. One miniature, of two small boys—one dark and one fair—caught her attention.

"Gilbert and James," Harriet confirmed behind her. Rose

stared at the two children. The fair boy—James—was innocently beautiful. The darker—Gilbert—looked like a scamp. Rose stared at the charming little painting, wondering how such a warm, mischievous-looking boy had turned into her cold, stern husband.

It was only when Mrs. Hart brought the tea tray that Rose wondered if she should invite the housekeeper to join them. Housekeepers sometimes took tea with the lady of the house, didn't they? Was it expected that she would ask Mrs. Hart to do so now, on the first day? Or would that be a *faux pas*?

She glanced at Harriet, hoping for a hint, but Harriet merely smiled at her and wandered over to the window. Was it that Harriet didn't want to take charge in front of Mrs. Hart? Or was there nothing to worry about at all? Was she being ridiculous?

She felt paralysed by uncertainty. In the end, biting her lip, she said nothing, and Mrs. Hart quietly withdrew.

"Do you think I should have asked her to join us?" Rose asked anxiously when Harriet turned back from the window and walked over to the tea table.

"Oh no," Harriet answered easily. "Tomorrow will be fine." She sat herself down on a small sofa and leaned over to take possession of the teapot. "Shall I pour?"

After tea, Mrs. Hart reappeared and asked if Rose would like to take a tour of the house. Rose accepted and was grateful when Harriet agreed to join them. She felt sure that Mrs. Hart was surprised by her extreme youth, and she winced every time the older woman said "ma'am" or "my lady".

Weartham Hall had been built in an E shape, Mrs. Hart informed her as they walked down the corridor—in honour of Queen Elizabeth, when that formidable woman had graced the throne of England. Perhaps it was fitting, Rose thought, that this house, beloved as it had been of Waite's mother, and now to be his bride's home, had been built in honour of a woman.

The fact that this was a woman's home was underlined by the light, feminine style of the decor. It had been renovated by Waite's mother a number of years previously, but nothing looked worn or in need of replacement. The windows sparkled; the wooden floors shone. Everything was immaculate. Mrs. Hart clearly ran a tight ship.

She showed them the ground-floor rooms first: the drawing room, dining rooms, library and music room. Rose couldn't resist fingering the pianoforte keys.

"Do you play?" Harriet asked.

"Yes, I love playing," Rose answered, smiling shyly. Beneath her fingers, the keys were smooth and responsive. She would love to sit down for a while and lose herself in music. Instead, she followed the others back out to the corridor.

The first and second floors contained numerous bedchambers and dressing rooms. Her own suite of rooms included an east-facing sitting room, which would get the morning sun.

Mrs. Hart completed the tour of the house with a visit to the kitchens and laundry. Rose smiled and nodded at the servants as she followed Mrs. Hart around, trying to conceal her nervousness. It was difficult to believe that she was mistress of this house now, and that she would be expected to give the efficient Mrs. Hart her instructions each day. She knew she would feel foolish doing so, at least at first. She was glad Harriet would be here to guide her.

After the tour of the house, Harriet suggested they walk around the grounds. The late countess had been a keen gardener, and Weartham boasted a series of separate gardens, connected by a long, winding walkway. There was a formal garden, a rose garden, a kitchen garden with carrots, peas, asparagus, lettuces and herbs. There was an orchard with apple and pear and plum trees. And beyond all those carefully tended domestic gardens, there was a wild garden.

By the time they reached the orchard, they were both tired.

55

"Let's have a rest," Harriet suggested. She headed toward a bench in the shade of a pear tree and sat down, sighing contentedly.

Rose stayed where she was. "I think I'll just go and look at the wild garden," she said. She was bone-weary, but she wanted to see it before they went back. It felt like forever since she'd been in the country.

"All right," Harriet said placidly, fanning herself. "I'll wait here."

The entrance to the wild garden was through a doorway in the wall that surrounded the orchard. As Rose passed through, she left the careful ornamentation of the formal gardens and the useful practicality of the kitchen gardens behind her, and took her first steps into a meadow of wildflowers.

The scent was heavenly. Not the heavy glamour of the hothouse blooms that had filled Papa's house in London, but a sweet, fresh, grassy scent that reminded her of childhood summers in the country at Uncle Philip's house or at friends of Papa's.

A path of sorts led her to a little bridge beneath which babbled a perfectly English brook. A few feet away from the bridge, there was a fairy-sized waterfall that gushed into a clear, cold-looking pool. On the other side of the bridge stood a small, artfully ruined folly, a temple in the classical style, its white stone mouldered with green.

Rose went up the steps of the temple, trailing her fingertips across the cold marble of the pillars as she moved into the centre of it. It was shady and cool, refreshing out of the warmth of the summer day. She turned slowly. One half of the inner wall was blank but there was a fresco on the other half. It depicted Persephone, contemplating a pomegranate. Rose thought she looked rather desperately hungry.

Rose stood there for a few minutes, looking around. She realised, suddenly, that she was smiling. These were the first moments of contentment she had felt in many weeks. This was to be her home, this quiet, welcoming house with its beautiful grounds and its small army of efficient servants. It would be the perfect home, were it not for the man who came with it. But then Waite would probably depart for London soon. And once he was gone, she suspected it might be some time before she saw him again. It was awful, but the thought brought her nothing but relief. Relief tempered with sadness. She wondered if this was how their marriage would be—if she would come to dread her husband's visits and find all her happiness away from him.

It was a depressing thought, and it shattered her brief moment of happiness. But she could not shake it off as she wandered back over the little tumbledown bridge and through the meadow to Harriet.

If Gil could have justified leaving Weartham within two hours of arriving, he would have done so. As it was, he convinced himself that a week would be a long enough stay. He was foolish enough to mention his plans to Cousin Harriet when she asked about them later that day.

"Surely you should stay a little longer," she said, plainly shocked. "This is your honeymoon! What can possibly be so urgent in town to require you to leave?"

"I'm afraid," he lied smoothly, "that I have pressing business that cannot wait longer. I'm quite sure Rose will understand."

Harriet pressed her lips together in a way that told him she was not pleased, but she said no more on the subject.

Dinner that evening followed the same pattern as all the previous evenings since they'd left London. He and Harriet carried the conversation while Rose stayed largely silent. Rose dutifully responded to Harriet's conversational gambits but addressed no comments to Gil, except to respond to his direct questions to her, and even then only in monosyllables. Did she like the soup? *Yes.* Had she enjoyed exploring the grounds earlier? *Yes.* She stared at the table for much of the meal and ate very little. She needed feeding up, he thought.

Her gown, a pale blue satin in a dashing style that a fashionable young matron might wear, looked far too old for her. She looked even younger than usual tonight, like a schoolgirl permitted to dine with the grown-ups for the first time. Exhausted too, after the gruelling journey.

As they ate, Gil found himself sneaking glances at her. She didn't notice him looking. Since the wedding, he'd been trying his hardest to act as though she wasn't really there, but suddenly it was impossible to banish her from his thoughts. He kept seeing her as he'd left her the night before, a small, despairing figure in a large bed, face turned to the wall.

The wave of resentment that he had been riding since his father had confessed his own foolishness had petered out in that moment. Not that he was happy about his situation—and not that he still didn't think painfully of Tilly—but it was difficult to maintain the simmering anger when he remembered seeing her like that.

He found himself remembering the Rose of that first meeting in London. At first sight, she'd been quiet and self-conscious, but slowly, cautiously, her petals had unfurled as he'd talked to her. He'd made it his goal to make the sad-looking young girl laugh, and he'd succeeded too. It was second nature to him to draw people out of their shells, and within minutes he had coaxed a smile from her, then a giggle. By the end of the visit, she'd had a little sparkle in her eye and had made him laugh quite genuinely with a sly joke that had sailed over everyone else's heads. He'd been rather charmed by that, actually. It had almost made him forget that he'd been feeling sorry for her up till then.

Where was that girl now? Since their betrothal, he had only seen this silent mouse. He suspected the real Rose was not this mute, miserable girl. Suspected too that he might have scared the real Rose away. A week ago, that thought might have given him a certain twisted satisfaction. Not now.

Even so, it seemed to him there was no way to make the situation better. Rose must hate him after last night. The thought unsettled him. He had always believed himself to be friendly and likeable. He hadn't known he'd had it in him to be so angry or so cruel.

He started, realising Harriet had asked a question. Politely, he shifted his gaze from Rose. "My apologies, cousin. What were you saying?"

Harriet smiled at him indulgently. She had noted the direction of his gaze and no doubt thought he had been gazing at his wife out of an excess of romantic devotion.

While Harriet prattled cheerfully, Gil motioned to a footman to refill the wineglasses. He drank deeply, finding it impossible to follow Harriet's meandering story.

Rose was concentrating on her dinner, moving her cutlery industriously without seeming to actually use it to transfer any food to her mouth. She had that blank, careful expression on again. The one she'd worn in church when they exchanged their vows.

He wondered if she would expect him to come to her tonight? He hoped not. And yet... Part of him wanted a chance to make amends for the evening before. He decided that if she asked him again, he would go to her and do everything in his power to make her feel wanted. He would show her tenderness. He would make it good for her.

He could try at least.

After dinner, Harriet asked Rose if she would play the pianoforte for them.

"I didn't know you played," Gil said, attempting a smile in Rose's direction.

"I told you the first time we met," she answered in a flat

little voice. That made him feel foolish and thoughtless, and he found himself blustering something about how silly it was of him to have forgotten while Rose watched him with an unconvinced sort of look. Harriet interrupted the awkward conversation by suggesting they retire to the music room and asking the footman to arrange for a tea tray to be sent there.

When they reached the music room, Harriet excused herself to fetch her embroidery, leaving Gil and Rose alone. Gil began racking his brains for something to say, but it wasn't necessary. Rose ignored him, making straight for the piano. She picked up a sheaf of Antonia's sheet music and started leafing through it. After a dozen pages, her faint frown deepened, and he wondered if she was regretting agreeing to play. Perhaps the music was beyond her. Antonia, he recalled, was considered rather good.

"Don't feel obliged to perform if there's nothing suitable," he said kindly.

Her head swung round and she stared at him again. Although her expression was as calm as ever, he sensed that she was angry and wondered why.

"There's nothing here I want to play," she said in a clipped little voice, "but it's all right. I don't need music to play."

She turned, sat herself down on the piano stool and, without further ado, launched into a piece of such nimble-fingered, technical brilliance it took his breath away.

She was good. Very good. Much better than Antonia could ever hope to be. Slowly, he approached her, coming to a halt at her shoulder. He stood there and watched her play, fascinated by the swiftness of the fingers that flew over the keys, awed by the unerring certainty with which she hit the notes.

Halfway through, Harriet walked into the room, carrying her embroidery bag. She sent Gil a look of almost comical surprise, and no wonder. Rose was as good as any professional musician he'd ever heard play. Better than most.

She ended the piece with a great, flourishing sweep up the keys and turned round to face them. The echo of the final notes still hung in the air.

"I don't need the music for that piece," she said coolly. "I've played it scores of times."

"Goodness me!" Harriet exclaimed. "That was quite extraordinary! I've never heard a girl your age play like that. Antonia's very good but—don't you agree, Gilbert?—Rose is quite *exceptional!*"

"Yes, quite exceptional," he repeated dutifully. He meant it, though. Felt himself looking at his wife through new eyes.

"Play something else," Harriet begged.

At first he thought she'd refuse, but it was difficult for anyone to refuse Harriet, and at last, Rose relented. She launched into a series of pieces he recognised as Bach's Goldberg Variations. He'd heard Antonia play them, but in her case, all he'd heard was the difficulty of them and Antonia's better-than-average skill at mastering them.

Played by Rose, they were something else entirely. This time, he heard the simplicity of them, the ease. The ache of them. He heard the notes and the spaces between the notes too. Beneath those small, slender fingers, that music came to life.

And in the music, at last, he saw her. Her head was bent, her eyes turned from him, but the mask was gone, and he beheld her. Saw something in her that was resilient and brave and beautiful.

He felt a sudden and aching regret that found physical shape in the form of a lump in his throat.

He sat there, his big body crammed into a small, uncomfortable chair, a cup of tea going cold in his hands, and listened to Rose play.

When she finished, she gently closed the lid over the keys and turned around.

"I think I'll go to bed," she announced.

Harriet tried to press tea upon her. Rose refused, but Harriet only stopped when Gil announced that he would also be retiring. She wore a coy smile as they left the music room together, Rose's small hand resting on Gil's arm. Gil realised Harriet thought they were retiring early to be together. Well, perhaps they were. If that was what Rose wanted?

Rose did not speak to him as they walked up the long, winding staircase together. She did not look at him either, and her hand and forearm were very stiff where they rested on his own arm. When they reached her bedchamber, she quickly dropped her hand from his arm and opened the door, moving forward without even saying good night. It seemed she couldn't wait to get away from him.

He almost let her go. "Rose—"

She froze at the sound of his voice but didn't turn. "Yes?"

Gil paused, searching for the right thing to say. He didn't wish her to feel obliged to accept his company, but he wanted to make a kind of amends.

"Would you prefer me not to trouble you tonight?" he managed eventually.

To his surprise, her eyes flashed with anger.

"I would prefer," she said tightly, "for you to never trouble me again. I am aware that you married me for one reason only. And that it was nothing to do with the attractions of my person. You may rest assured that after last night, *I* will trouble *you* no further. There is no need for you to feel obliged to perform your marital duties again."

He stared at her, set back on his heels by this unexpected show of temper. She had been so meek until tonight.

"Rose, you don't mean that—" he began soothingly.

She looked at him then, eyes flashing. "I do! I do mean it! I wish to God I never had to set eyes on you again!"

Something about the venom in her voice, and her words, pricked at the sleeping dragon of his resentment. He felt wretched about last night, but still. He *had* been forced into marrying someone he didn't want. And giving up Tilly.

"Now, don't be childish," he said.

That seemed to rile her even more. "Oh, God, how I hate you!" she cried. "I can't believe that I *asked* you to come to me last night. I must've been mad."

He stared at her unlovely face for what felt like a long time, forcing himself to stay calm in the face of her anger. Her normally pale cheeks carried two splotches of scarlet, and a red wash was making its way up her neck. His gaze dropped to the sharp points of her collarbone. They seemed too prominent on her meagre chest. There was nothing of her at all, really. All skin and bone, but for all her size, she was practically vibrating with rage and passion.

When he felt he had himself under control he said, very calmly, "I realise that last night I was tactless—"

"Tactless?" She laughed at that, or rather half laughed, half sobbed. "Showing your disgust, you mean?"

Genuinely shocked, he immediately protested, "No! I didn't mean that. It's only—" And then he broke off, because how could he possibly explain? He frantically searched his brain for an explanation that wouldn't insult her. She saved him the bother.

"It's only that you didn't want to marry me—or bed me. That's it, isn't it?"

"Rose..." He trailed off. God, what could he say? It was true, and she'd worked it out easily. And now she probably hated him. Well, maybe that was for the best. He could never be what she wanted anyway.

She covered her face with her hands, and her shoulders began to shake. She was crying. He reached out a hand and touched her arm gently, uncertainly. Immediately, she thrust him off with a violent gesture. "Don't ever touch me again." This time, she didn't raise her voice. Instead, she spoke with a quiet emphasis that he couldn't mistake.

"I'm sorry," he said, and he was. She didn't respond. Just whirled round and yanked open her bedchamber door, slamming it behind her. The tumbling scrape of the key in the lock sounded somehow panicky.

At first, he just stood there, dumbfounded. Then, feeling foolish, he moved close to the door. "Rose," he said in a low voice. "Rose, are you all right?"

Silence was his answer. He knocked on the door and called her name again, louder this time. And again. Nothing. Eventually, feeling foolish and hoping no-one had overheard their exchange, he entered his own neighbouring bedchamber.

He could, of course, enter her bedchamber through the connecting door. He had a key. She could not deny him. He was her husband. Her lord.

But he knew there was no question of that happening. The least he could do was grant her privacy.

He lay awake for a long time. Not merely sleepless but waiting, though he knew not what he waited for. He didn't expect her to knock on his door, after all.

Perhaps he waited for the realisation that settled on him in the early hours of the morning: that he wasn't sure he *wanted* to be forgiven.

He regretted the pain he'd caused her, but she wasn't the only one nursing wounds. The memory of his last meeting with Tilly still hurt. He'd not told Tilly everything, but he'd said enough that she knew it was not his choice to marry. She'd been sweet and understanding, but she'd had tears in her eyes too.

No, Rose was not the only one who'd been hurt.

Rose said she never wanted him to touch her again. The sentiment mirrored his own feelings precisely. After a week of oppressive politeness, this sudden, raw honesty between them, painful as it was, was something of a relief. Perhaps it was better. Perhaps it was even worth his dishonour.

As the clock on the mantel rang three dull chimes, Gil made a decision. He wasn't going to wait at Weartham a week. He was going to go back to London tomorrow. Despite their differences, he and Rose were in perfect accord on the desirability of that course of action. He was going to save them both a lot of pain and trouble by leaving Rose alone, just as she wanted. Just as they both wanted.

Rose woke late the next morning. She glanced at the clock as she sat up and reached for the bell rope. Half past ten! It must have been the exhaustion of the long journey. She was normally awake long before now.

As she waited for Sarah to appear, the events of the previous evening came back to her. The mortifying argument with Gil. Her outburst. Lord, he'd looked shocked! She groaned, remembering her words. *"I wish to God I never had to set eyes on you again... I hate you... Don't ever touch me again..."* She regretted her outburst now. She'd been so determined not to let him see how much he'd wounded her, but last night, she'd showed him that soft, hurt, *raw* part of her, and now she felt naked and exposed. She was still groaning when Sarah entered the room, a pot of hot chocolate on a tray.

"Morning, your ladyship." The words were innocuous, but when Rose looked up, she saw that Sarah looked troubled.

"Is something wrong?" she asked calmly, cringing inside at the possibility that news of her argument with her husband had reached the servants.

"His lordship's man told me he's going back to London today, your ladyship. Did you know?"

"Going back to London?" Rose repeated stupidly.

The maid nodded, carefully looking away to pour the chocolate. "So his valet says, m'lady. His lordship's baggage is

65

being loaded, and the carriage is waiting outside the house with the horses all in their traces."

He is leaving me. He is leaving me after one day.

"Help me dress," Rose said, waving the chocolate away and rising from the bed. "Something quick, Sarah."

For once, she was grateful for her short hair, which needed no dressing before she left her bedchamber. Within minutes, she was on her way downstairs.

She found Waite pacing in the hall. He looked embarrassed to see her. All at once, she felt embarrassed too. Did he think she was running after him? That she would beg him not to go? She consciously schooled her features into a calm mask, aware she had already revealed too much to him last night.

"You're leaving?" she asked and was proud of the calm tone that emerged from her mouth.

"Yes." There was a long, uncomfortable silence; then he added, "After last night, I thought it best."

She wanted to say, *What do you mean?* but she stayed silent, watching him. Had he thought she was asking him to leave? She hadn't meant that, but the thought of saying *Please don't go* was unbearable. Impossible. She couldn't lose every bit of her pride this early in her marriage. Lord knew she had little enough of it left.

"All right," she said at length. "I'll wish you a pleasant journey then."

The strain in his expression relaxed minutely.

Relief. He was relieved.

She swallowed against a sudden clod in her throat, determined not to cry. She wasn't going to go and howl inconsolably over this. And she wasn't going to ask him when he intended to return or where their marriage went from here. Because she really wasn't sure if she wanted to hear the answers to those questions. It was easier all round just to let this happen. Easier to let him go.

"Good-bye, then," he said, tipping his hat at her.

She was married to this man, and that was how he took his leave of her. With a tip of his hat.

"Good-bye," she replied, her voice very cool.

And then she was gliding back up to her bedchamber again, while behind her, the front door opened and closed.

Back in her chamber, Rose watched from her window as the last items of luggage were loaded. Just before he got in the carriage, Waite shared a joke with the coachman and grooms, and they laughed, Waite most heartily of all.

Now that he was leaving her, that ready smile of his was back.

He climbed into the carriage looking happy and relaxed.

He didn't even glance up at her window once as he swept away.

Part Two:
Summer

And summer's lease hath all too short a date...
William Shakespeare
Sonnet 18

From the correspondence of the Earl and Countess of Stanhope, 1809-1813:

7th November, 1809

   Waite,

   I trust this letter finds you well.

   I am writing to enquire whether you will be coming to Weartham for Christmas. Please be assured that there is no need to attend on my account; however, Cousin Harriet has, quite properly, pointed out that arrangements must be made if you propose to be here for the festive season.

   I look forward to hearing from you with confirmation of your intentions.

   Regards,

   Rose

28th November, 1809

   Madam,

   Thank you for your letter of 7th inst. I do not propose to come to Weartham for Christmas. I regret to advise you that my father suffered a seizure a few weeks ago. He has recovered somewhat but I shall to be taking him to Stanhope Abbey as soon as he is well enough, where I expect to remain till the Spring.

   Should you require anything, please direct your correspondence to me there.

   Waite

27th September, 1810

Waite,

I hope this letter finds you well. Please pass on my regards to your father—I understand your sister found him much improved when she saw him over the summer.

Your cousin Harriet is in excellent spirits, and Weartham runs as smoothly as ever, thanks to the estimable Mr. Thomson and his new assistant, Mr. Anderson.

The purpose of my letter is to enquire whether you intend to visit us this year, perhaps for Christmas?

I look forward to hearing from you.

Regards,

Rose

29th October, 1810

Madam,

I write to inform you that my father died on 25th October. The funeral took place today. I hope you will understand that my brother and sister and I decided that it would be preferable for the funeral to take place without delay.

In the circumstances, I have no plans to visit Weartham in the foreseeable future.

This is the first letter I write in which I must sign myself as,

Stanhope

14th October, 1811

Dear Gilbert,

Would you like to join myself and Harriet for Christmas? If you say no this year, I think I shall have to assume you are avoiding me.

Rose

30th October, 1811

    Dear Lady Stanhope,

    His lordship asked me to convey to you his sincere regrets that he is unable to join you at Weartham Manor this festive season.

    He has also asked me to advise that if you require anything at all, whether funds or items that are difficult to source in Northumbria, then please write to myself. I am his lordship's personal secretary, and I will take whatever steps are necessary to attend to your wishes.

    I am,

    Your Very Obedient Servant,

    Ernest Andrews,

    Personal Secretary to the Earl of Stanhope

16th November, 1812

    Dear Mr. Andrews,

    Please advise my husband that his Cousin Harriet and I would be delighted if he could join us for the festive season. We have asked Mr. Posselthwaite (the Rector) and his wife, and Dr. and Mrs. Wright and the Misses Wrights for Christmas lunch. Unfortunately, there are very few genteel families in the immediate vicinity, but we can always rely upon the exhilarating company of the Posselthwaites and the Wrights. Indeed, we have quite a social whirl planned this year—I am sure it would compare favourably with the other house parties his lordship might be invited to attend. Why, as well as Christmas lunch, the Posselthwaites have invited us for refreshments and parlour games on Christmas Eve, and the Wrights are hosting a select party on the day after Boxing Day at which Miss Amy will play the pianoforte and Miss Catherine will sing—a treat indeed! I fear, Mr. Andrews, that after such exciting entertainments, I will require to take to my bed for a week to rest!

I look forward to hearing from you with my husband's usual response.

Rose Truman,

Countess of Stanhope.

2nd December, 1812

My Lady,

His lordship regrets that he is unable to accept your kind invitation to Weartham Manor for Christmas. He asks me to advise you that he is already engaged to spend the festive season elsewhere.

As ever, I am at your ladyship's disposal should you require anything.

Your Very Obedient Servant,

Ernest Andrews.

21st December, 1812

Dear Mr. Andrews,

Thank you for your letter of 2nd December. I enclose, by way of a Christmas gift, a lambswool scarf. I beg that you will wear this to keep off draughts. It will not do for you to neglect your health. My letters to my husband must not go unanswered.

In fulfilment of my wifely duties, I will send another invitation next year. You may wish to draft your reply now to save time.

Kind Regards

Rose Truman,

Countess of Stanhope.

18th October, 1813

Dear Mr. Andrews,

Can it really be October already? It is that time of year again—time to issue my annual Christmas invitation.

I have come to look forward to my husband's annual rejection. It is a point in the year as fixed as the seasons. It is soothing to know that some things in life never change.

I do hope that you have been untroubled by chills this year. As always, I am in excellent health.

I look forward to your very prompt and unfailingly polite reply.

Kind Regards,

Rose Truman,

Countess of Stanhope

29th October, 1813

Dear Lady Stanhope,

I deeply and sincerely regret to inform you that his lordship will be unable to attend Weartham this year as he has alternative plans.

I thank you for your kind comments regarding my health. You are very gracious, and I hope that one day I will have the very great honour of making your acquaintance.

Your Very Obedient Servant,

Ernest Andrews

Chapter Six

June 1814, London

Five years after the marriage of the Earl and Countess of Stanhope

"I wish I didn't have to leave you tomorrow, *cara*. You've only just got here."

Lottie's voice was unhappy, a frown drawing her brows together, but, despite a few silver strands in the glossy black hair that her maid was brushing out, she was as beautiful as ever.

Rose took another sip of chocolate—wickedly good chocolate—and tucked her bare feet up beside her. "Don't be silly," she said. "Coming here was an impulse. I should have checked with you first. But if all goes as it should, I won't need your hospitality longer than today anyway."

The maid began deftly plaiting Lottie's hair, slim fingers moving swiftly.

"*If* it all goes as it should? Do you think your husband would refuse to let you stay at the house?" Lottie turned in her chair to face Rose, her expression appalled. The maid shifted round, unperturbed, and continued to work.

Rose tried to smile reassuringly, but somehow the smile got caught up in her swallowing an inconvenient lump in her throat and went wobbly. "I don't know what he'll do," she said truthfully. "I barely know Gilbert."

"Is that why you came here last night instead of going straight to him? To gather yourself?"

Lottie's gaze was suddenly sharp—she saw too much

sometimes. Rose averted her eyes to stare down at her chocolate.

"It's a long journey, and I was tired by the time I got here. I just couldn't face him last night."

The maid fastened a final pin in place and stood back. Lottie nodded her satisfaction and dismissed the girl, then brought her own chocolate to the chaise longue, settling herself down next to Rose.

"I hate to think of you facing Waite alone, *cara*, but my boat leaves this afternoon. My carriage is already packed." She gestured helplessly with her free hand, her expression unhappy.

"Don't even think of it—"

"The concerts were arranged two years ago—"

"*Lottie.*" Rose put her hand on her friend's knee, stilling her. "It's fine. I just needed one good night's sleep before I saw him again. I feel quite up to it now. This meeting can only go one of two ways. Either Gilbert lets me stay, or he insists I return to Weartham. And I'm quite sure I can persuade him of the former option."

She did manage a smile this time, a bright one that hid all traces of her lingering despair. Lottie didn't need to know that when Rose had made her impulsive decision to come to London last week, she'd been feeling quite desperate. Oh, she'd made a life for herself in Northumbria, a good life with friends and occupation, but it was still the life of an exile. It was not the life she had expected when she had given her wedding vows.

Years ago, she had told her new husband that she never wanted to see him or be touched by him again. And she had lived with the consequences of those words for five long years. Now she had changed her mind. She had all the trappings of a brilliant marriage but with nothing to show for it. She rather thought she would lie with the devil himself to change her life. She wasn't sure that lying with Gilbert would be much better.

"Besides," she added, "you'll be seeing Papa. And I'm counting on you to persuade him to return to England."

Lottie made a scoffing noise. "Do not count on me for that, *cara*. I've never been able to persuade your papa to do anything. In his last letter, he was talking of a trip to Egypt."

Rose laughed, but inside she felt the old familiar sadness. Her father had left England within weeks of her marriage to Gilbert and had yet to return. Sometimes she wondered if she would ever see him again. It was as though, in marrying her off, he'd palmed off a responsibility he couldn't wait to be rid of. Well, she wouldn't be palmed off by her own husband. Not anymore.

"And your plan is still to beard the lion in his den?" Lottie asked, interrupting her thoughts. It took Rose a minute to realise she was talking about Gilbert.

"Yes. If I turn up at Stanhope House and ask to see my husband, what can he do but see me?" Rose asked lightly, though privately she'd been having visions of being turned away, another humiliation to add to the long list of humiliations culminating in the sly references to Gilbert's latest love affair in that scandal sheet of Harriet's that she'd so stupidly picked up and read last week.

The very next day, she'd been on her way to London, but the heat of her anger had worn off over the long journey, and now she was nervous of the confrontation to come.

"Are you quite sure this is the best course of action, *cara*?" Lottie asked carefully. "Your husband has refused to come to Weartham all these years, and while I'm sure he'll be gratified to see how beautiful you've grown—after all, the man is horribly shallow—I fear the shock of you turning up on his doorstep unannounced might cause him to do something foolish, like send you home before he's taken a good look at you."

Pathetically, Rose found herself seizing on the least relevant part of what Lottie had just said. "Do you think he will find me much changed?" she asked hesitantly, staring into her chocolate cup.

Lottie sighed. "*Cara,* I doubt he will know you."

"Really?"

Lottie rose and held out her hand. "Come here." She drew Rose over to the seat she'd recently vacated in front of the dressing table, facing the mirror, and sat her down. Then she lifted one of the silver-backed brushes and began to draw it through Rose's dark hair, still loose round her shoulders from being brushed out last night. After a brief silence, Lottie said, "Do you recall what your hair was like when you married?"

"Short," Rose replied.

"Yes, just a covering really; this long." Lottie held her finger and thumb an inch apart. Had it really been as short as all that? Rose touched her head as though to check, but of course, her hair was long now, long and thick and luxurious, dark brown tresses that spilled almost to her waist.

"I remember it well," Lottie went on, still brushing. "You were very poorly when I met you, and your hair was growing slowly. Your body had more important things to mend first." She looked up, meeting Rose's gaze in the mirror with those expressive black eyes that showed a depth of emotion that Rose hadn't been able to understand back then. "You almost died."

"Yes," Rose whispered. She remembered the worst of it not at all, and much of the rest only dimly. Seemingly interminable days of fever, the days and nights running into one another, the hallucinations more real to her than the world around her.

The physicians had glumly told her father she would die; and she would have done so if left to them.

"But you saved me, Lottie," she said, smiling at her friend in the mirror.

"Pshaw!" Lottie scoffed. "Anyone could see what you needed: rest, food, care. Those doctors would have had you in a coffin while you still breathed! But look at you now—so beautiful." She beamed. "No, he won't know you. On your wedding day, you weighed little more than a bag of feathers, and your skin was a mess. But look at you now! The marks are all gone!"

"Not quite," Rose countered lightly. "I have a few scars." Not merely physical ones either. She tried to dismiss the memory of a night in an inn long ago; a girl in a pink dress, a pink ribbon in her hair. A memory that still made her feel like that girl all over again.

"You call those scars?" Lottie retorted. "Those little moon-marks?"

There were hardly any scars on her face, which was amazing, considering how awful they had been. They'd been everywhere, even on her eyelids and inside her ears. But she'd been left with just three scars on her face, three little white circles at her left ear, her hairline and her chin. They were tiny, almost unnoticeable, the silvery scar tissue just a few shades lighter than her creamy skin.

There were a few more obvious battlefields on her body. A little ring of them on the back of her neck, like the interwoven links of a necklace; another clutch on the backs of her knees. A few other isolated ones here and there, on flank and thigh and arm. But none of them were unsightly, just little silver indentations in her flesh. They had long ago lost the power to make her feel ugly. Indeed, they made her feel proud now, to have survived.

Rose looked into the mirror and saw a woman who was beautiful. She saw her own beauty with satisfaction and joy and defiance. The gaunt, skeletal face of five years before had filled out to one of heart-shaped prettiness. The sad little cap of thin hair was now a thick, glossy mane. Her skin glowed, and her eyes shone with health.

"He won't know you," Lottie said again, but this time, the tone of her voice was almost wondering. "Not immediately. And certainly not masked."

"Masked?"

Lottie smiled, a wicked slashing smile. "Have you ever been to a masked ball, *cara*?"

"What? No, of course not. They're hardly *de rigueur* in deepest, darkest Northumbria."

"Would you like to go to one this evening? I'm sure your husband will be there. And don't you think that would be a much better place to meet him? Just think, instead of turning up as petitioner at his front door, asking for an audience, you set the time and place. And then you let him see your beauty, perhaps flirt with him a little—flirtation is the best language for your husband, *cara*, trust me. He responds to it better than English."

"You think I should meet him *in disguise*?"

"Oh, you'll reveal who you really are at the unmasking at midnight. But first you let him see your charms. Soften him up. Once you've caught his interest, everything else will be so much easier. Catch him with honey, *cara*."

"But what if recognises me straightaway?"

"He won't." Lottie shook her head, quite certain. "I have a mask and domino you can borrow—you won't even know yourself in them."

"Whose ball is this anyway?"

"The ball is being held by dear Nev, so of course he'll be delighted to have you attend. I'll send a note round to him now." Nev was an old friend of her father's and more recently of Lottie's.

"Does this mean it won't be a respectable occasion?" Rose asked. Nev was known as rather a rakish sort.

"Not *very* respectable," Lottie agreed. "Which is why I'm so sure your husband will be there. I always see him at Nev's affairs. I always give him a look, like this." She demonstrated an expression of scornful disdain.

Rose laughed, but she knew why Lottie gave him that look, and her laugh was hollow. "Because he always has a floozy on his arm, I suppose? He'll probably have his latest one with him tonight."

"If you're talking about Signora Meadows, their affair is at an end," Lottie said with a placid smile. "And if he is seeking her replacement, as he undoubtedly will be, he is going to find her: you. What could be more fitting?"

"Me?"

"Why not? That's what you want, isn't it? A real marriage?"

"I won't be able to attract him like that—"

"Of course you will. I have a few hours before I have to leave. First we'll dress you, and then I'll give you a flirting lesson. What's the worst that can happen, *cara*? Anything's better than just turning up at Stanhope House with a list of demands in your hand. That will get things off on entirely the wrong foot."

Rose thought of all the letters she'd sent Gilbert telling him about Weartham and her life there, the annual invitations to join her for Christmas. He'd never taken her up on any of them, demonstrating a single-minded determination to have nothing to do with her.

He was well known for having a weakness for pretty women, a fact that was tirelessly lampooned in the scandal sheets Harriet loved so much.

Well, Rose was now a pretty woman. The least she could do was turn that to her advantage.

Lottie turned away and went into the dressing room. A minute later, she was back with a dark green domino over her arm and a mask dangling from her fingers. Rose took the mask from her, turning the lovely thing over in her hands. It was made of feathers, emerald green and peacock blue, and strung with green velvet ribbons.

"How beautiful," she breathed.

"Try it on," Lottie smiled.

She did.

The mask followed the line of her brows and dipped down to her cheeks, leaving her nose uncovered. Behind the mask, her eyes glittered mysteriously.

She imagined seeing Gilbert like this. Not having to worry about his reaction—not straightaway, anyway. She could perhaps even try a little flirtation on him, try to ease things between them before confronting him. If they could just have a little time together being lighthearted, maybe he would see that a reconciliation mightn't be at all bad when she took the mask off. She imagined herself dancing with him, laughing with him. Smiling as she took the mask off.

She untied the ribbons and drew the mask away from her face, unveiling herself. The woman in the mirror looked hopeful, a little wary. It was an expression Rose didn't like the thought of Gilbert seeing.

She tried a smile out, made it warm and promising. Easy in front of the mirror. But in front of Gilbert?

"Well, *cara*? What do you think?"

Rose took a deep breath. "I'll go."

She would have an hour or two to win him over before she unmasked herself.

It had to be worth a try.

Chapter Seven

Gil rather liked masked balls. He enjoyed assuming a shadowy identity and finding some mysterious lovely to flirt with. And the annual masked ball held by Sir Neville Grayson was unbeatable entertainment. Grayson always had the most beautiful courtesans and actresses, the most wicked rakes and scoundrels, the most faithless husbands and wives. And having amicably parted with this latest paramour, Gil was in the mood for flirtation. He strolled through Sir Neville's elegant home, greeting acquaintances, the ones he recognised anyway, and eyeing ladies through his black velvet loo mask.

As this was not a particularly respectable affair, the ballroom was not as bright as one might usually expect, other than where the musicians played. Farther down, the candles were sparser, the relative dimness concealing the identities—and activities—of the numerous men and women thronging the place.

Gil wandered through the crowd, allowing his gaze to drift over the sea of people, waiting for someone to catch his eye. Ironic, then, that he was spied first. He felt her gaze, like a physical weight. The feel of it made him turn around, his spine prickling with awareness. And there she sat, staring at him, all her attention upon him. She sat half hidden, alone in a poorly lit corner of the ballroom.

Her gown was blue—green?—hard to tell in this light—and on her face, she wore a feathered mask. It left her small, straight nose and lovely, rather serious mouth uncovered. Her hair was dark and simply dressed at the nape of her neck. It gleamed in the candlelight.

When she saw him pause to look at her, she rose from her chair, smoothing the skirt of her gown. There was something utterly charming about that uncertain gesture. He smiled at her, testing the water, and she smiled back, though warily, he thought.

He closed the distance between them and made her his best bow. "Madam," he said as he rose to his full height again. "You are not dancing. That is something that ought to be remedied, I think."

She looked up at him. She was a full head shorter than he and had to tilt her head back to meet his gaze, exposing her pale throat. "Do you think so, sir?"

"I do. You are very beautiful and quite alone. Alone at a ball, no less, with dancing happening as we speak." He gestured at the dancers who took up the part of the ballroom nearest the musicians. The music would play constantly all night, and people would dance or not dance as they pleased, with whomever they pleased. It was nothing like a *Ton* ball, where the ladies doled themselves out in half-hour measures.

"Perhaps I am waiting for my husband?" the lovely woman said and smiled, a little twist of her lips that he noted with fascination.

"Are you?"

She shrugged. "Or perhaps I simply do not care to dance." She tilted her head, birdlike, which made the feathers on her mask seem curiously apt. He found that charming too. And her stature, which was small. And most especially her breasts, which looked to be delicious, the upper slopes very pale against the bluish iridescence of her gown, the lower curves lovingly outlined by the close-fitting bodice.

"Take pity on me, then." He grinned. "For I should dearly love to dance. Yet I don't know any ladies here at all."

"The ladies you do not know include my good self."

He laughed. "Ah, but that is very easily remedied, and once

we know one another, we can dance together all night. Provided your husband doesn't mind?" He raised an interrogatory eyebrow.

"Oh, he won't mind," she replied. "He didn't accompany me here, after all. Though dancing all night with you doesn't sound very proper, I must say."

"Well, it's not proper, of course. But this isn't a very proper affair. You do realise that, don't you?" He watched her carefully, curious. He wouldn't be surprised if she hadn't known till she'd got here. There was something deliciously innocent-looking about her. She hadn't seemed especially comfortable, sitting in her little corner, alone.

When she stayed silent, he smiled at her, adding coaxingly, "Come on, pretty lady. We can become acquainted while we dance. By the time we're finished, we'll be like old friends."

She gave a little laugh. "All right, then, but I warn you, I'm not much of a dancer."

"That can't be true," he retorted, offering his arm. "You look as though you were made to dance." She didn't answer but gave a snort of laughter as she laid her arm over his. It was an inelegant little sound of amusement that made him smile—then frown briefly as he wondered who it reminded him of.

He was distracted from that thought by the sight of her slender arm resting on his, gloved in white satin. As he led her to the dancing area, he imagined himself removing that glove and studying what lay beneath, memorising the shape and line of elbow and wrist, kissing each finger. It was just the sort of seductive assault women loved—risqué but not too wicked. Always time to call a halt and repossess your arm before it went too far.

The orchestra was playing a waltz. When they reached the edge of the dancing area, Gil turned his arm beneath her fingers, simultaneously bringing his body round to face her, capturing her satin-clad hand in one of his own and bringing his other hand up to draw her closer. Before she could speak, he was stepping forward and drawing her into the dance, sweeping her into the crowd. He heard her gasp and give a muttered protest. She stumbled once, but when he held her close and danced on, she quickly corrected her footing and was soon following him, her body beginning to respond to his signals.

"Don't look at your feet," he murmured in her ear after a few turns. "Look at me. I'll keep us upright and going in the right direction."

She looked up, and when their masked gazes met, he smiled again, a slower smile this time. She didn't smile back— she had that funny serious look again—but he couldn't mind. She looked too sweet with that grave, beautifully shaped mouth. She didn't need to smile to look lovely. He wanted to trace her lips with his fingertips. He wanted to kiss her.

"God, you're beautiful," he breathed, surprising himself with his honesty. He didn't normally like to give too much away at this stage. Light, expert compliments were one thing; a straight-from-the-heart confession was quite another.

"Do you think so?" she said, a tiny smile hitching her mouth at last.

He swept her deftly past a few other couples, feeling as though her smile had given his feet wings. "Yes, I do. But I want to see all of you, underneath the mask too." He peered at her. "What colour are your eyes?"

"What colour are my...? Oh, for goodness' sake!" She laughed. "They're grey, if you must know. Plain, dull grey."

"There is nothing the least bit plain or dull about you, pretty lady. Least of all your eyes."

He was holding her far closer than would be acceptable in an ordinary ballroom. Instead of maintaining a proper distance between them, he pressed her against him. The gentle curve of her waist beneath his hand was the most heavenly shape in the world. The soft brush of her bosom and the occasional press of

her thighs made him lightheaded. And the scent of her hair—
God! He wanted to dance with her forever, and he wanted to be
alone with her right now. She was like a tempting little sweet
that he didn't want to devour quite yet.

It was then he noticed the curtains on the far side of the
ballroom stirring and realised the doors to an outside terrace
must be open. How perfect.

Carefully, he swept her through a series of turns across the
ballroom and right through the curtains. They danced out onto
the narrow terrace—empty, thank God, of other guests—and
came to a sudden halt. She looked up at him, surprised and
apparently amused.

"That was neatly done," she said on a breathy little gust of
laughter. "You had me out here before I could protest."

He grinned at her. "Did you wish to protest? We can go
back inside if you'd prefer." His left hand still enclosed her
right, and his right hand rested at the dip of her waist, ready to
dance her away. But she shook her head, smiling.

"No, it's nice and cool out here," she said. "I could use a
breath of air."

He'd have kept holding her if he could, but she began to
move away from him, and he had to let her go. She leaned her
forearms on the stone balustrade and looked out into the night.

It was a beautiful night. Slightly warm, with a fat pearl of a
moon and a few stars dotting the velvet night like bright silver
pins.

"I don't feel like I'm in London at all," she said. "It's as quiet
as the country. Perhaps that's the Garden of Eden down there."

Gil joined her and looked down at Grayson's garden. It was
too dark to make out much other than the tops of the trees and
the shapes of a few shrubs.

"Do you think there might be a serpent about?"

She turned her head and smiled at him. "I think there
might be a few, actually."

He laughed and moved closer, his eyes eating up everything about her, the pleasing daintiness of her, the grave mouth that was even lovelier when it smiled. A lock of mahogany hair that tumbled over one creamy shoulder. He stepped forward and lifted the errant strand in his fingers. She shivered as his knuckles brushed her bare skin.

He wanted to see her without the mask so much he ached.

He lifted his hands and undid the ribbons of his own mask, tossing it aside and letting her see him first. She tilted her head to one side, eyes glittering through the feathers as she considered him. Although he felt faintly embarrassed by her perusal, he was warmed too by her attention. He did not consider himself to be particularly handsome, but he had learned over the years that women found him attractive; that for some strange reason, they liked his big body and his rough-hewn features.

"You look like a pirate," she said, very serious.

What on earth did that mean? Did she like the look of him or not?

Then she smiled. A slow, shy smile that transformed that grave beauty into something quite dazzling. "Wickedly handsome," she added softly.

That's more like it, he thought, grinning.

"Allow me to introduce myself properly," he said, making her his best bow. "Gilbert Truman, the seventh Earl of Stanhope, at your service. But seeing as this is a very improper sort of affair, you may as well call me Gil."

"Pleased to meet you, my lord," she said, sounding a little breathless. "Gil, I mean."

"Your turn," he said, gesturing at her mask.

She paused for a long moment.

He saw her swallow. Noted with curiosity that her hands were fisted in her lap. So nervous! This was not his usual sort of flirtation at all. He felt an odd pang of conscience. Perhaps he should take her back to the ballroom, masked and uncompromised?

But no. Not now. She was lifting her hands to the ribbons of her mask, and he was so desperate to see her face that he abandoned any thought of gallantry then and there. Even though he saw that her fingers trembled as she loosened the knot at the back of her head.

When finally she drew the mask away, he couldn't quite suppress an intake of breath. At the sound of his gasp, her eyes snapped up to meet his gaze. Wide, clear, troubled eyes. She wore an expression of such vulnerable—what? Hope? Fear? He found he couldn't put a name to it. And even as he wondered, his gaze was moving over the face she had bared to him, studying each detail in absorbed fascination.

She was...

...exquisite. As he gazed at her, his heart did an odd, aching thing in his chest and he suddenly wished he was still wearing his own mask. He wanted to hide his reaction to her. He wanted to gaze at her from shadows, unseen. He felt as though he'd been enchanted. No, more than that. As though she was the answer to something. His destiny, perhaps.

"You are so lovely," he murmured, unable to help himself uttering such trite words. Not that she seemed to find them trite. Her eyes widened, and he saw astonishment in her gaze. She opened her mouth as though to speak, but then she closed it again, saying nothing. For long moments, she just stared at him with an oddly anguished expression.

"I expect people tell you that all the time," he added. "Gentlemen, I mean."

"No," she said at last. "You are actually only the second gentleman who has ever commented on my looks."

Perhaps that accounted for her astonishment. And now he was the one feeling surprised. Had she been living on the moon? Perhaps her husband kept her hidden away? Gil wasn't sure he would entirely blame him if he did.

"Was your husband the first?"

She frowned at that. "No. My husband did not marry me for my looks."

"He sounds like a fool," Gil said, feeling aggrieved on her behalf.

"Yes. A great fool," she agreed, with another of those twisty smiles that made her look strangely unamused. Gil lifted his hand to cup the side of her face, unable to resist the temptation to touch her. She did not withdraw, and after a moment, he stroked her petal-soft skin with his thumb, relishing her faint shiver, wanting his lips there.

One thing first.

"What's your name, pretty lady?"

Rose knew she would remember this night forever. The night she unmasked herself to her husband—and he didn't recognise her. She would remember every detail: the instant at which the knot had released in her shaking fingers, the way the ribbons sagged at the sides of her head, the way they kissed her cheeks as she drew the mask away. But most of all, she would remember Gilbert's expression as he looked upon her for the first time in five long years.

She had prepared herself for the worst: horror, anger, disgust. But of course, she had hoped too. For interest, admiration, maybe even amusement. The one thing she had not prepared for was this.

Although his eyes had widened as she drew the mask away, they had not done so with any degree of recognition. Merely with wonder and pleasure. The sight of her pleased him, but not because of who she was. Because of how she looked. Because of a beauty she had lost and regained, and one day would lose again.

At first, she stared at him, not knowing what to say, how to tell him the truth. She had assumed he would recognise her. She opened her mouth to confess, but the words would not come.

And that was when he began to tell her how beautiful she was.

He thought her beautiful. The words were commonplace, but the way he looked at her was not. No one had ever looked at her like that before. As though she were the sun and moon and stars.

Her natural scepticism gave way to a slow, warming acceptance that began to spread right through her. He admired her. And not discreetly but boldly and without any attempt to hide or dissemble. His hazel eyes moved hungrily over her face, lingering on her mouth until she felt almost as though he'd kissed her.

The gazing was not a one-sided thing. The promising youth had transformed into a handsome man, and her eyes ate up the changes that five years had wrought. He wore his hair a little longer. It suited him. The dark-lashed hazel eyes were just as she remembered, but the creases at the corners when he smiled were new. And he'd filled out that big frame of his.

There was one difference between his perusal of her and hers of him. She remembered him very well, and he remembered her not at all.

"He won't know you," Lottie had said. How right she'd been.

He began to quiz her, and she answered almost automatically, still preoccupied. It was only when he touched her face with a whisper-light caress, only when he made her look at him and asked her, in a low, seductive voice, her name, that she returned to herself fully.

And in that long, endless moment, a dozen possible answers to his question crossed her mind.

For some reason, she found herself remembering the very last time she'd seen him before this night. Five years ago, in the hall of Weartham Manor. He'd been about to leave her. His face had been shuttered, polite, distant. Now he stared at her with eyes that glittered with desire. And God, but it was such a balm to that rejected girl she'd once been!

That was when she knew she couldn't do it, not tonight at least. She couldn't tell him the truth of who she was and watch his face change again. She glanced around, her heart beating fast, her mind seeking inspiration. And it came. From Nev's little Garden of Eden.

"Mrs. Adams," she said. "But since we're being informal, you can call me Eve."

Chapter Eight

"You said Mr. Adams did not accompany you this evening?" Gil asked carefully.

"No," Eve said. "We are not—" She broke off.

"You are not...?"

She took a deep breath. "I do not live with my husband."

Something eased inside him at that news.

She had turned to lean on the balustrade a few moments ago, and now he did the same, his shoulder brushing hers. They both looked out into the night.

"I do not live with my wife," he offered. He felt her turn to look at him but kept looking straight ahead. "Our marriage was a disaster."

"A disaster?"

"Yes. Yours?"

A pause. Then, "The same. A mistake."

He nodded, and they fell into a companionable silence.

"May I ask you something?" he asked at last.

"Of course."

"Have you ever bedded a man other than your husband?"

She huffed a laugh. "No."

"Kissed?"

He felt her eyes upon him.

"No," she said at last, her voice wistful.

"Really?" A quarter turn to his right brought him face-to-face with her. Her expression was wistful too. "What a terrible,

terrible waste." He smiled. "We should rectify that."

He closed the distance between them slowly, giving her ample time to pull away if she wanted to. Her eyes stayed open as he dipped his head. Their gazes met, and it felt like the kiss started right then, an instant before he touched his mouth to hers. Caught by her astonished grey gaze, he gathered her closer, one arm encircling her slender waist and the other cradling the back of her head as he pressed his mouth to hers.

God, but she tasted sweet. Like summer. Like strawberries. She wound her arms around his neck and pressed her body flush against his until he knew she must be able to feel for herself how hard he was for her. The luscious, pillowy softness of her breasts pressing against his body was making him frantic. He groaned against her mouth, raising his hand to cup a plump globe of flesh. It yielded beneath his gently kneading hand, the nipple grazing his palm, slight but insistent, the thin stuff of her evening gown the flimsiest of barriers. His cock throbbed painfully in his breeches, and he felt like a schoolboy, ready to come at touching a woman's breast for the first time. He tore his mouth from hers with effort and looked down at her upturned face, a face that looked as surprised as he thought his own must be.

"Eve," he said. "God. I've never—"

Felt like this before.

Wanted a woman the way I want you.

Fallen—

All the things he might say stuck in his throat, and he found himself simply staring down at her, heart racing. And so it was she who broke the silence, and with a comment that floored him. "Do you want to bed me, Gil?"

He gave a shocked huff of a laugh. "Isn't it obvious?"

"Indulge me."

"Then yes, Mrs. Adams, I want to bed you very much. Probably more than any woman I've ever met."

She closed her eyes for what felt like a very long moment. He began to think he'd said just exactly the wrong thing; that she was going to walk away from him then and there. But eventually, when she looked at him again, she smiled—a sad smile, he thought—and said, "Call for your carriage, then. I've danced enough this night."

Was there any danger that he was dreaming, Gil wondered, as he stared at Eve Adams, sitting on the opposite bench of his carriage less than half an hour later. He could barely make out her features in the darkness but he could see how demurely she sat. Knees pressed tightly together, gloved hands twisting in her lap. Her nervousness touched him. It was the reason he hadn't started making love to her already. The last thing he wanted to do was alarm her and cause her to change her mind.

It was a short drive, and very soon the carriage drew up outside Stanhope House. A groom opened the carriage door, and Gil jumped down first, offering his hand up while Eve stepped out. A footman had already opened the door, and Gil ushered her into the house, divesting her of her cloak before she thought to protest. Handing it to the footman, he asked for wine to be brought to his private sitting room and led Eve toward the stairs.

He ascended behind her, admiring her dainty curves. He felt like a big oaf next to her, truth be told. She was so diminutively graceful. A perfect package of feminine curves.

He led her into his sitting room and set about lighting candles as she settled herself on the small sofa. Before he could sit himself down, the footman was at the door with a decanter of wine on a silver tray.

"Have the fire in the bedchamber lit," Gil murmured to him as he relieved him of the tray. The footman nodded and departed, and Gil closed the door softly.

He poured two glasses of deep red wine and approached the sofa.

"What shall we drink to?" Eve asked as he handed her a wineglass and sat down beside her.

He considered for a moment, then lifted his glass. "To new beginnings?" he proposed, hoping that this was indeed the beginning of something.

"To new beginnings," she echoed and touched the edge of his glass with her own before taking a long swallow. She put her glass down on a little side table beside the sofa, and he stretched over her to do the same, thrilling even at the brief, brushing contact of his arm against her body.

"I want to kiss you very badly," he confessed once he'd pulled back. "May I?"

She nodded, wide-eyed, and he inched a little closer, leaning forward to cup her face in his hands, keeping his eyes open and watching the exact moment that hers closed. It happened just as his lips first brushed hers, just as he inhaled her intoxicating strawberry scent again. He closed his own eyes then and allowed his mouth to discover her, to explore the shape and softness of her lips. When she parted them on a breathy little sigh, he brought her more firmly against him, tunnelling his long fingers into the soft silk of her hair, feeling the pins holding it in place loosen and fall away.

Her hands were trapped between them, but she pushed them upwards, her fingers drifting into the hair at the nape of his neck as she opened herself up to his kiss, gasping at the first touch of his tongue, eager and nervous at once.

She responded to his kiss like a maid. He wondered if her husband had ever kissed her when they'd lived together. Surely he must have done? Surely the lucky devil must have wanted to worship her every night with his mouth?

He pulled back a little and watched as she opened her eyes in a dazed sort of a way. "Nice?"

She flushed and gave a little laugh. "Yes, very nice."

"More?"

Her smile faded, but she nodded. At the sight of her wary expression, he felt another of those unfamiliar pangs in his chest.

"Are you sure?" he asked. "You look as though you're about to go to your execution."

"I'm sure," she whispered, but she still looked nothing short of tragic, and Gil pulled farther back, frowning. The tragic look deepened. "What's wrong?" she asked, her tone bewildered.

"I don't want to bed an unwilling woman."

"I'm not unwilling!" she protested. "I want this."

"Do you?" He searched her face and still couldn't quite make her out. He saw hurt, fear, determination. No desire. "You look terrified."

"I am terrified," she admitted. She swallowed before she went on. "But I'm hoping you can make it all right. I'm hoping you can—make me enjoy this."

He paused, weighing her words. "Haven't you enjoyed it before?"

She flushed. "Not really."

He reached out and touched her cheek with his fingertips, feeling a wave of tenderness. "I see. Well, I'll try my best to make it good for you. And if you don't like it—anything about it at all—you must tell me, all right? And I'll stop."

She nodded, and a little of the tension went out of her face.

He leaned forward and kissed her again, taking his time. He made love to her lips, explored the soft crevice of her mouth, dipped his head to traverse the delicate line of her jaw and throat, making the journey in kisses. She leaned back against the couch as he seduced her with lips and hands and soft murmurs, gasping his name as he rained kisses on the upper slopes of her breasts.

When he reached for the fastenings of her gown, she went stiff. "Not here," she whispered. "Let's go to your bed."

He raised his head and saw that her colour was up, her mouth still plump from his long, thorough kisses. "As you wish."

In one smooth movement, he stood, slid an arm under her knees and swung her up into his arms. "Gil!" she laughed.

She was a lovely armful. His right hand curved against the swell of her breast, his left around the delicate crook of her knee. As he strode to the door, a strand of her hair tickled his face. He tried to blow it out of the way, twitching his nose theatrically.

"Do you want me to scratch your nose?" she enquired.

"Thank you, no," he replied gravely "I have another itch that is much more pressing." She laughed at that, but the husk of her laughter held a note of shock that amused him.

He strode to the door that connected his sitting room and bedchamber.

"Turn the handle, would you?" he said. Eve dutifully turned the doorknob, and Gil pushed the door open with his foot and carried her inside. It was well lit, since the footman had started the fire in the grate and lit some candles too.

Gil set Eve gently down on the floor, then stripped off his coat, throwing it aside with the sleeves inside out.

Eve looked around uncertainly. "It's very bright in here," she said.

"Do you mind?" he asked. "I can snuff the candles if you prefer, but speaking for myself, I very much want to look at you as we do this."

He could practically see her girding her loins. "All right," she whispered bravely.

"Good girl. Now, do you suppose you might help me off with this waistcoat?"

She stepped forward, lifting her trembling fingers to undo the buttons. He took the opportunity to stare at her creamy cleavage while she worked. When she'd undone all the buttons, she pushed her hands underneath the fabric of the waistcoat and slid it over his shoulders. Her small hands felt warm through the fine cambric of his shirt. He longed to feel them against his bare skin.

She turned around then, presenting him with a long row of buttons of her own to undo. He stepped forward, bringing his body up against her and pushed her hair over her shoulder. Having bared her neck, he set his teeth there, biting her nape gently, relishing her breathy moan and helpless shiver, before softening his mouth to a kiss while his hands worked down and down, his nimble fingers dispatching button after button.

Well, if there was one thing he did well, it was undressing a woman.

Within a minute, he was pushing her gown off her shoulders. It slithered to her feet with a whisper. He had her stays undone and her chemise off moments later. Now she was left with nothing on but stockings and garters, both of which he was more than happy for her to keep for now.

She was even lovelier with her clothes off, lush and feminine, the palette of her body so very pleasing—creamy white and rosy pink and glossy brown. Her garters were embroidered with little pink and green flowers and were tied just above her knees. He groaned at the sight of them.

"Lie on the bed," he whispered, and she moved obediently onto the mattress, lying down faceup. Her cheeks were very pink now.

With considerable effort, he managed to maintain a small distance between his clothed body and her almost naked one when he lay down beside her. He propped himself up on his elbow and allowed himself the luxury of staring at her. With one hand, he undid the knot in his neckcloth and tossed it aside. He watched the way her eyes immediately strayed to the exposed flesh of his throat.

"You really are a gorgeous creature," he murmured, his gaze travelling over her. And she was. A diminutive goddess with full breasts, rounded hips and slender legs. Delicate ankles. Small, delicious feet.

She said nothing in response to the compliment, and her eyes looked sad for a moment. He wanted to ask her why she looked like that, but he didn't. Instead, he let his hand drift over her body, his fingertips just barely caressing her, her collarbone, the swell of her breasts, her belly. When he grazed her nipples, he smiled to see they were already rigid with arousal. He glanced back at her face then and saw she had closed her eyes again. Her lips were parted, her breathing uneven. Gil's aching cock brushed painfully against the fabric of his breeches.

He let his hand drift down farther to slip between her legs, which were slightly open. The tops of her thighs were already gratifyingly damp. He was about to explore her more intimately when an unwelcome thought occurred to him.

He rested his hand on her thigh, halting his progress.

"Is there any chance you could fall pregnant?" he murmured.

"Don't worry," she whispered. "There is no chance of my conceiving an illegitimate child." And then she reached for him, pulling him down to her. He went to her with a groan.

As he kissed her, he parted the slippery folds of her quim with his long fingers. When he slid one of his fingers inside her, her wide grey eyes flew open; when he moved his thumb to her clitoris and began to slowly circle it, they closed again, and she murmured "Good Lord," in a faintly surprised tone that made him smile.

Leaning over her, he took her right nipple in his mouth, rolling his tongue around the stiff, puckered flesh. Her breasts were larger than he had expected. A lovely surprise, that—he liked generous breasts. She gasped and arched against him as he worked, a gratifying response that made him even harder and more eager for her. He did the same to her other breast, fascinated by her reaction. She responded as though this was all new to her, her eyes widening with surprise when he began to move his fingers inside her. He wondered if her husband was one of those men who simply did the deed, without any play beforehand. It certainly appeared so.

He treated her rigid nipples to long, languorous licks that made her writhe beneath him, and all the while, the fingers of his right hand delicately explored every fold and fissure of her quim while his thumb periodically nudged her clitoris.

She was beautifully responsive. She made uninhibited little noises of pleasure, impatiently shifting her hips beneath his hand, silently begging him to push his fingers farther inside her. She said not a word, and that odd mix of boldness and shyness touched him for some reason.

After just a few minutes of kissing and touching like this, she was thoroughly wet, the flesh of her quim swollen with desire. She did not try to reciprocate his caresses, merely lay beneath him, allowing him to bring her pleasure. He didn't mind in the least. He wanted to watch her come before he did, and concentrating on pleasuring her was a way of stopping himself coming first.

He lifted his head from her breasts and kissed his way upwards, past her collarbone and throat to her ear.

"Are you ready?" he murmured.

"I— Yes, I think so."

He dealt efficiently with the concealed buttons at the placket of his breeches, pushing them down with his drawers and settling himself between her spread thighs. It was hardly elegant to plough her almost fully dressed like this, but he couldn't wait another second to be inside her.

She shifted beneath him, her wet slit rubbing provocatively

against the head of his cock. *God, yes.* Gil gritted his teeth.

"I need to be inside you," he said helplessly.

"Yes," she moaned, burying her face in his neck, "do it." Her breath was hot against his skin.

He opened her with his fingers and pushed into her. Christ, but she was tight! Worried, he lifted his head to look at her, but she didn't seem to be uncomfortable in the least. Quite the opposite. Her expression was all concentrated bliss.

Somehow, Gil managed to rein in his instinct to wildly fuck. He closed his eyes and tried to think of something as far from erotic as he could manage while he established the sort of steady, driving rhythm that he had discovered was the key to pleasing women. After a minute or two, he opened his eyes again, drinking in the sight of Eve's abandoned expression. There was a moment when she tilted her pelvis, and he slid a quarter of an inch deeper into her. He groaned, stilling briefly, trying to hold himself back. Eve protested with a little incoherent noise of outrage.

"Don't stop!" she gasped almost angrily. He could tell from her frantic movements that she was close to her climax and felt, as he always did at such moments, boyishly elated.

He braced himself on his forearms and began fucking her in earnest, harder, faster, watching her flushed face with fascination. Her legs tightened around him, her heels digging into his buttocks, and then he felt her inner muscles clenching on his cock powerfully, rhythmically.

She muttered incoherently, "Oh God, I'm—this is—" while he watched her come apart beneath him. She kept her legs locked around his waist while the dying ripples of pleasure shuddered through her. When she opened her eyes, they held an expression of wonder.

It was that that undid him, beyond anything else. He began to ride her limp, satiated body again, this time giving vent to his own pleasure. His vision clouded in the midst of it, his head going back as he felt his cock pumping inside her, spurting his seed deep into her body. And it was beyond anything. Anything.

As the last pulses of his orgasm ebbed away, he lay on top of her small, warm body and kissed her damp forehead, relishing the brief illusion of a more profound intimacy. After a few minutes, he reluctantly rolled away. It was only then that he realised, mortifyingly, that he still had most of his clothing on, and that his breeches and drawers were at his knees. He quickly stripped, Eve watching all the time. She wore a languorous, satisfied expression that pleased him, and she watched him undress with eyes that gleamed with interest. When he was naked, he lay down again, pulling her toward him.

They lay facing one another, and he gazed at her with uncomplicated pleasure. She was beautiful, and he felt like a boy, bowled over by her. He was infatuated by her, certainly. Maybe even in love with her. He could almost feel his heart plummeting now, even though he knew it was ridiculous. He barely knew her! They had hardly spoken.

And yet he could say, quite honestly, that he'd never felt like this before, not even about Tilly. He knew himself lost. And knowing that, accepting it, he allowed himself the indulgence of lying back and drowning in her rain-clear eyes.

Chapter Nine

What time was it, Rose wondered? The clock in the adjoining sitting room had chimed once, perhaps half an hour ago. It was time to sleep. But it was rather difficult to sleep when you were lying beside your faithless, philandering husband for the first time in five long years.

The faithless, philandering husband who had entirely failed to recognise her, even when she removed her mask. Even when she lay naked in his bed.

It was mortifying but also horribly seductive. Because he didn't know who she was, she came to him new. With none of their history weighing her down. And he'd found her beautiful, had *wanted* her.

Even more miraculously, she'd wanted him too. When he took his mask off, she'd felt the same breathless admiration that had overcome her that day, years ago, when she'd watched him effortlessly mount his horse in the inn courtyard. In the face of that unexpectedly girlish response, she'd given in to the temptation to stay silent.

Now she hated herself.

All the way here in the carriage, she'd been steeling herself to confess. As he took her cloak and they walked upstairs, as he brought her wine and kissed her, she was thinking, *I'll tell him in a minute.* The trouble was, she knew as soon as he learned who she was, everything would change. So she'd been bargaining with herself all evening. *Just another minute, then I'll tell him.*

She would not allow the lie to continue any longer. As soon as he woke, she would tell him everything. But she would let herself have these last few minutes first. Just to lie here and watch him, like a real wife. It was a harmless enough thing, wasn't it?

Gil's long eyelashes brushed his cheekbones, quivering as he dreamed. His lips were faintly parted, and she could hear each soft breath he inhaled and released. She resisted the urge to touch his surprisingly soft dark hair.

He had grown into his looks, she thought. She had thought him handsome at twenty-two, but now she saw that he had been too young to carry off that piratical look of his. Now he looked rather magnificent. Big and fierce—when he wasn't smiling, anyway. His civilised clothing seemed to barely contain him. It was impossible to be unaware of the masculine body beneath all the expensive tailoring.

And he was not the cold, silent man she remembered from the last days of their honeymoon. His eyes glinted with humour, and he smiled often, a crooked, irrepressible sort of smile. A little self-conscious. Uniquely charming, especially when that surprising dimple showed. It was a smile that invited you in; that seemed to say, *You know what I mean, don't you?*

This was the man she had encountered at their first meeting in Stanhope House. Years ago, she had decided that she must have imagined him. But here he was! The very same. Charming and likeable and *warm*. And now devastating too.

She had to remember that this was only one side of Gil. He could be cold. Distant and cruel. He could change in a heartbeat. It was absurd that she had to remind herself of that, but it seemed she was something of a fool for him. She hadn't expected to be attracted to him when she saw him again. Not when five years of resentment had left her so bitter and angry that she bridled at the very mention of his name.

She had come to London not because she wanted to reconcile with him, but because she wanted her life—the life she was supposed to get when she stood up in church with Gil and promised to love, honour and obey him—and she'd known that to get that life, she was going to have to put her dislike of her husband to one side. It was something she had come to feel philosophical about. It wasn't as though she was the first wife in the world to have to disguise her loathing of her spouse.

She hadn't expected to be charmed by him; to take pleasure from him.

Gil made a small noise in his sleep, drawing her attention back to him. Her gaze travelled over his face, absorbing every detail; his well-shaped mouth, smiling even in sleep, his strong, slightly crooked nose; his thick, dark hair.

If he had been a stranger to her, would she have been fathoms in love with him by now? It would be very easy for a woman of her limited experience to mistake the sort of physical passion she had experienced tonight for something much more profound. After all, the only other man of marriageable age she knew was Will Anderson, the steward at Weartham Manor.

Thank God she knew what Gil was really like. Ruthlessly, Rose reminded herself that Gil had not troubled himself to exert his considerable charm upon the plain young girl he had married solely for her dowry. But it was difficult to reconcile this man, whose face lay inches from her own, with the man she had married; the man who had painfully taken her virginity and who only made love to her on their honeymoon with the most extreme reluctance. Tonight she had felt herself passionately desired. Tonight she had experienced intense pleasure. Five years ago, she had known only pain and humiliation. All at the same man's hands.

The pinnacle of her ambition tonight had been to warm him up to accepting her presence in his life. She'd had no hopes left of the sort of marriage she'd naively dreamed of at seventeen. But now, and for the first time, it occurred to her that maybe she *could* have more than a husband who merely tolerated her presence. It was a new and exciting thought, but it made her feel apprehensive too. She had learned the hard way how cruel hope could be.

The clock chimed twice. Two o'clock in the morning. Rose rolled away from Gil and onto her back.

She would not allow herself to think about the future anymore. Not until she had told him who she was.

Gil woke around dawn just as the sun began rise, its rays penetrating the cracks between the drapes and illuminating the bedchamber with dull, grey-washed light. He shifted onto his side, propping his head on his palm, and looked down at the woman sleeping at his side.

He wanted her again. And again. He wanted to keep her forever.

He knew he was being hasty. Yesterday morning, he'd have said that devoting himself to a single woman was an absurd idea. But now there was Eve, and meeting her had changed everything. Nothing would ever be the same again.

He wanted to tell her how he felt. He wanted her to know that she'd caused this revelation within him. Perhaps, when she woke, he'd try to broach the subject. Surely she felt this too?

He didn't know how long he watched her, but when she finally shifted and sighed, daylight was fairly streaming through drapes, the sun well and truly risen. She yawned and slowly opened eyes, her eyes widening almost comically when she realised he was staring down at her. He smiled warmly. "Good morning."

She recovered herself then, smiling back shyly. "Good morning."

He leaned down and kissed her, gently. She seemed taken aback for a moment; then the tension left her, and she gave herself up to his kiss, her mouth opening beneath his. His hand came up to brush her silky hair back from her face, exposing the tender column of her throat and the fine shape of her collarbone. Unable to resist the lure of those hollows, he moved his mouth to trace over the smooth, creamy skin.

"You are so beautiful," he murmured.

"So are you," she whispered.

He laughed lightly against her skin. "Beautiful? I'm no beauty, darling. More of a beast."

"You're blind," she said, and he laughed. She smiled sleepily and threaded her fingers through his hair, tugging him up to kiss him again.

He let her initiate that kiss, and it was...beguiling. Bold and tentative all at once. A study of his mouth. He moaned lightly as her lips drifted over his, and he felt her light, huffing laughter at his reaction, her slender fingers stroking the hair at the nape of his neck.

"Eve, Eve," he murmured against her lips. "Am I falling in love with you? Can it happen so quickly?"

In an instant, she went stiff, pushing him away and staring at him with wide, shocked eyes.

"Sorry," he whispered. That was a lie. He wasn't sorry. Disappointed at her horrified reaction, yes. Worried that his words might drive her away. But beneath that, there was an oddly joyous certainty and a passion for confession. He'd never felt so clear in his own mind about anything. He wanted to say the words again, and he felt almost sure of the answer to his own question. With difficulty, he remained silent and drew her down to rest against his body. She laid her head on his shoulder.

After a brief silence, he said, "Tell me about your husband."

She lifted her head, regarding him warily. "What do you want to know?"

"You said you were estranged. Do you never see him?"

"No," she said her voice clipped. "Never."

"And why is that? Has he ever—" He broke off. "Has he ever hurt you? Physically, I mean?"

She looked surprised by the question, staring at him for several long moments before she jerkily shook her head.

He wasn't sure he believed her. Her expression was guilty. But then she shook her head again, more definitely this time. "Not physically, no. He has never laid so much as laid a finger on me. I swear. He is merely—distant."

Gil shifted position, turning onto his side so they were face-to-face. "You needn't ever go back to him, you know. I could set you up. We wouldn't be able to marry, but I could get you a house of your own."

She stared at him, dumbfounded. "This is very sudden," she said at last. "What about your wife?"

"My wife and I do not live together," he replied. "We never have, and that's not going to change."

"Not ever?" Her voice came out in a thready whisper.

"No." The word emerged without the slightest hesitation.

"But you have no children," she pointed out weakly. "No heir."

"I have a younger brother," he said. "He is my heir."

Rose stared at her husband.

He'd rather die childless than come near me.

She knew that if she had more courage, this was the moment to tell him: *I am Rose. I am your wife.* But she found she could not do it. Instead, she whispered, with morbid curiosity, "Do you ever see her?"

"I haven't seen her since a few days after we wed."

"Why?"

"Because I don't want to." He said it in the reasonable tone of voice one might use to decline an extra helping of potatoes at dinner.

"But why?" she said again. Then, tormenting herself: "Is she so very awful?"

His mouth twisted. After a long pause, he sighed and said, "The truth is, it doesn't matter what she's like. She could look like Helen of Troy and have every accomplishment a woman should possess, and I still wouldn't want to see her."

He hates me that much?

The knowledge slid into her like a blade, shocking and sharp. Her chest felt full of something hot and thick. Not blood, but tears, or whatever tears are made of. Misery, maybe. Long moments passed before she had herself sufficiently under control to speak again.

"What happened?" she said. "What did she do to make you feel this way?"

"She didn't do anything. It's just that I was forced into the marriage. I didn't want to marry her, but it was that or ruin. And then, well, things got off to a bad start. I gave her a disgust of me, and it just seemed like the best thing was to leave her. She lives in Northumbria at one of my estates. I've not seen her since I took her there after our wedding."

He turned onto his back, looking up at the ceiling. She propped herself up on her elbow and looked down at him.

"Ruin? You had to marry her or be *ruined?*" That didn't sound right. Rose knew her dowry had been substantial, but there were far richer heiresses Gil could have married if the family coffers were empty.

Gil closed his eyes. "My father's doing. It's remarkable what a man can gamble away in just a year. After my mother died, he became reckless. I knew he was gaming deep but had no idea just how deep. Then, one night he played with a man who made his living at the tables. A respectable enough fellow, but a true gamester. The sort of man who could fleece a man like my father." He opened his eyes and looked at her, and his gaze was flat, unseeing. "He lost everything it was possible to lose that night. Not just money—land. Everything my father had that wasn't entailed. I think he must have been in some kind of mania."

A sense of dread began to creep up on Rose as she began to anticipate the revelation that was coming. She had to fight back an overwhelming desire to put her hand to his lips to stop him talking.

"And the man he lost it all to was my wife's father."

Rose swallowed against an impossible dryness in her throat. She didn't have to prompt him anymore; the story was flowing out of him.

"He offered all his winnings back, unconditionally, if I married his daughter."

So she had brought *nothing* to the marriage. Merely the writing off of his father's gaming debt to her own father. And to call it a debt! His father was a fool to have thrown away everything on a game of chance. Worse, her own was unscrupulous to have taken advantage of his idiocy. And Gil had gained nothing. To him, the marriage was merely the means of fixing his father's unforgivable error.

"You must have been furious," she whispered.

"I was not pleased when I was given the news," he admitted. He gave a dry little laugh and finally looked at her again, and this time, she saw something there she'd never seen before. Not anger. Not resentment. Pain. "The truth is, I wanted to marry someone else at that time," he said.

And that was the moment when her plan—such as it was— crumbled to dust.

She wanted to weep. "Oh God," she said. "No wonder."

"No wonder what?"

No wonder you hate me. No wonder you want nothing to do with me.

"No wonder you never see her."

Gil reached for her, pulling her back down to his shoulder, kissing the top of her head. She tried to relax into him, but she felt so traitorous. Yet she had to know it all. "Who was she? The woman you wanted to marry."

"Oh, a girl I'd known from boyhood. Her family lived near ours, though I only fell in love with her when she came up to London for her first season." He laughed. "She was very sweet, very innocent. I'd had a little experience with women by then— not much—but once I realised I was in love with her, I decided to keep myself pure for her. I could hardly wait to marry her." His voice was mocking, deriding the idealistic boy he'd once been.

"Did she know you wanted to marry her?"

"Yes. We weren't engaged, but I'd told her how I felt, and she knew I planned to ask her father for her hand."

Rose closed her eyes. The firm flesh of Gil's shoulder was warm under her cheek. "And what did she say when you told her you were marrying someone else?"

"She was understanding. She knew it wasn't my choice."

"Do you still see her?"

"Now and again. She married a friend of mine. She's happy." He sighed. "It was all a very long time ago."

"And you and she have never..."

"No," he said quickly. "Her husband is my friend, and anyway, she is not like that—she is the most faithful of wives—"

He broke off, and there was a lengthy, uncomfortable pause. Eventually, Rose gave a little laugh and said, awkwardly, "Unlike me."

He shifted beneath her, his shoulder rising under her cheek, urging her to look up. "Eve—"

She stayed stubbornly where she was.

"Eve, this is your first time with someone other than your husband, is it not? And you do not live with him anymore."

She ignored that. He wasn't to know she was being anything but unfaithful with him. "Why did you want to forget about the wedding?" she asked instead, determined to know the worst. "Was it so very dreadful?"

He did that humourless laugh again. She hated the sound of it. It was mirthless, a parody of laughter.

"Yes."

"What happened?"

Gil was silent for so long that she began to wonder if he was going to answer her at all. And then he said, his voice bleak, "My wife showed me what I really am."

It was so terribly unexpected that she lifted herself up to look down at him, too curious as to his expression to hide her own any longer. He met her searching gaze with eyes that were troubled. The wide, mobile mouth that had been smiling all last night was grim and unhappy. Unthinkingly, she brought a hand up to stroke the side of his face comfortingly. She had been ready to hear him say how ugly his wife was. How it had taken every bit of gall in him to bed her. Not this.

"What do you mean, she showed you what you are?"

He shook his head, smiling ruefully. "It doesn't matter," he said. "The truth is, I hate talking about her. I've spoken about her more to you than I have to anyone else in the last five years."

She stared at him, not understanding. Did he hate *her*, or just talking about her? Did talking about her just make him think about the woman he'd lost when he'd been forced to marry her? Or was it more personal than that, a physical disgust of how she'd looked then?

But what did it matter? She had learned enough to know that the chances of him agreeing to a reconciliation were nonexistent. And she didn't think she even wanted it now. Knowing the truth about her "dowry" changed everything.

"Have you had many lovers since your marriage?" she asked, returning the conversation to a strangely less painful topic.

"Enough," he said, and his gaze grew serious. "But I did not feel for any of them what I am feeling at this moment, Eve. For you. I didn't think I could feel like this ever again."

"I think you are mistaken," she muttered unhappily. "You don't know me."

"No, I don't. But I look at you and I feel as though I am two and twenty again. Full of hope and belief." His voice was wistful, and when he saw the expression on her own face, his mouth twisted self-mockingly. "Ridiculous, aren't I?"

She had been determined to tell him who she was. Have it all out with him. And now she couldn't bear to. His words gave her a power over him she didn't want, and she knew now that he would hate her if he learned the truth. Hate her even more, that was. She swallowed back the tears that threatened to fall.

"Not ridiculous," she said, smiling. "Just sudden. Surprising."

His expression softened, and she leaned down and kissed him.

"I want you again," he breathed against her mouth.

"Then have me," she sighed. "Once more before we rise."

Chapter Ten

The second time began slow and tender. Dreamy. Gil uncovered Eve's body in the soft dawn light and explored every dip and dale, every ridge and crevice. With lips. With fingertips.

Earlier, when she'd asked about Tilly, he'd thought of the contrast between them, Tilly's pink-and-gold perfection against Eve's subtler, darker beauty. And there had been no comparison. Not that he'd ever look back on his youthful love with anything but affection, but the draw of Eve was entirely different. Eve drew him with her own desire. Sweet, innocent Tilly had never displayed anything so vulgar.

He kissed his way up Eve's back, adoring her shivering response and the tiny moan of pleasure that escaped her. On her shoulder blade, she bore a small, round, white scar. More of them on her neck, under her hair. He kissed them too. Even her imperfections were delightful to him. She turned in his arms as he drew level with her and captured his lips with her own, murmuring passionate pleas into his mouth and wrapping her legs around him. And suddenly, his patience was gone.

He split the fruit of her sex, delving into her warm, welcoming depths, and she cried out, already close, it seemed. Within a minute, she was coming apart in his arms, her climax noisy and passionate. Her eagerness spurred him on, and he was close behind her, surprising himself with the speed and force of his second orgasm.

Afterwards, he drew her into his arms and fell asleep again, happier than he could remember feeling for a long, long time.

When he awoke, he was alone.

He sat up, puzzled and bereft. It took him a moment to

work out why.

Eve.

He rang for Crawford and pulled on a robe. By the time his valet appeared, he'd searched his bedchamber and sitting room and realised she wasn't there. Everything was gone except the feathered mask which had become wedged between the back of the sofa and the sofa cushions.

"My lord?"

"The woman who was here, where is she?"

Crawford blushed. He was a dreadful prude. "She left, my lord. Half an hour ago, at least."

"On foot?"

"I believe Mr. Timms arranged a hack for the lady."

"Why the devil didn't you wake me?" Gil shouted, his voice hoarse with disbelief.

Crawford quivered with indignation. "My lord, I did not realise you would wish to be woken. The lady assured us most firmly that you should be left to sleep."

"Did she leave a message? A note?"

"Nothing, my lord."

"God damn it all!" Gil hissed. "Call for my carriage and get me some clothes."

While Crawford scurried away to do his bidding, Gil turned her mask over between his hands and considered what to do. He would visit Sir Neville Grayson first. She had been Grayson's guest last night—he would surely know where Gil could find her.

Sir Neville Grayson was a tall, silver-haired man of around fifty. Despite the rumours of his endless dissipation, he showed no signs of overindulgence. His tall frame was lean and athletic, and his sharp blue gaze was shrewd. He leaned back in his chair and considered Gil, a faint smile playing around the corners of his mouth.

"I don't recognise the name," he said. "She must have accompanied another of my guests. I am no stickler, Stanhope. If someone I have invited to one of my entertainments brings a friend, they will be given entrance." He smiled. "Especially if the friend is a lovely woman. I assume Mrs. Adams was lovely?"

"Very," Gil said tautly. He found Grayson's sly humour irritating. He'd never much liked Grayson, who had been a friend of Miles Davenport's before Davenport had gone off on his travels.

"So you took this dove to your bed, and when you woke up in the morning, your bird had flown?"

Grayson's eyes sparkled with mischief. Gil felt like punching him. Instead, he feigned amusement at the jibe.

"Do you think you could find out who she is? If you ask around your friends?"

Grayson laughed. "Did you see how many people were here last night, Stanhope? That's a lot of people to ask. Some of them I mightn't see for months."

Gil felt himself colour. "Nevertheless, if you'd keep an eye and ear out, I'd be grateful," he said, rising from his chair, leaving the glass of Madeira he'd accepted untouched.

"Of course," Grayson said smoothly but his eyes sparkled with wicked amusement, and Gil had no doubt the gossip would be doing the rounds by this evening. Lord Lovehope, as one scandal sheet had dubbed him, had met a woman who wanted nothing to do with him. How very amusing.

He took his leave of Grayson and walked out into a day that was warm and golden. A perfect summer's day.

But it didn't feel like summer anymore to Gil.

Part Three: Autumn

The teeming autumn, big with rich increase...
William Shakespeare
Sonnet 97

Chapter Eleven

September 1814

Gil stared out of his bedchamber window. It had been raining all week, and those murky, swollen clouds suggested there was more to come.

"Bloody weather," he complained softly.

"Indeed, my lord." Crawford put the finishing touches to his master's neckcloth as he spoke. "It has been most vexing. Keeping your lordship's boots clean is quite impossible. The mud seems to get on everything. As for your lordship's new green coat—"

Gil turned away from the window with a sigh. "Do be quiet, Crawford. My head hurts like the very devil."

Ordinarily, Gil was tolerant of Crawford's verbosity. The old fellow had spent his life in Gil's household, having been his father's valet for almost thirty years—service that long earned one a few privileges. But right now, Gil felt as though he'd been hit over the head with an anvil, and his patience was all worn away.

Crawford pressed his lips together and assumed his martyred expression. His face had a naturally melancholy cast, thanks to a pair of eyes that turned down at the outer edges and a set of jowls that would put a purebred bloodhound to shame. When he was unhappy, as he was now, his whole face seemed to droop even further.

Even as he resented being made to feel like a brute, Gil found himself attempting to mollify the old man.

"I had planned to ride out to Hampstead Heath with Mr. Dudley this morning," he offered. "But it looks as though there's going to be another deluge, don't you think?"

Crawford generally leapt at the opportunity to voice an opinion. It was a measure of the depth of his wounded feelings that he merely sniffed.

"I'm sure I couldn't say, your lordship," he replied with great dignity.

A second attempt at peacemaking was beyond Gil—at that moment, his stomach roiled violently. He sat down on the end of the bed, a cold sweat breaking out on his face.

Crawford smoothly moved away, disappearing into the dressing room for a few moments and returning with a glass filled with a foul-looking brew. He offered it to Gil wordlessly.

Grimacing, Gil accepted the glass and drank the contents down. It smelled like a stagnant pond and tasted like one too. For a few moments after, he felt sure he was going to vomit and leaned over to put his head between his knees, breathing deeply. Eventually, though, the awful churning passed, and he straightened again, feeling oddly better.

"Where did you get that stuff?" he said faintly, handing the glass back to his valet. "It's vile."

"From Mr. Simpkins," Crawford replied. "Apparently, Lord James got the recipe from one of his friends and swears it's the very best cure for the aftermath of a night of drunkenness. I asked Simpkins to make an extra batch for your lordship this morning. Judging by the time you got home, I thought it likely you'd need it."

Crawford's voice held no hint of reproval, yet somehow Gil felt as though he'd been scolded. Bloody family retainers, he thought. He should've got rid of the old devil when his father died.

"You are nothing if not devoted, Crawford."

In response to that, Crawford merely sniffed again, turning away to brush down Gil's coat briskly before holding it out for Gil to slide his arms into.

Gil stood passively as Crawford buttoned and tweaked the garment until he was quite satisfied with the way it lay. Once the valet had moved away again, Gil went to the mirror and considered his reflection, smoothing down his hair with shaking fingers. He looked just as he normally did. A tall, well-dressed but not particularly fashionable gentleman. No one would have guessed that he'd only dragged himself home—from the lowest of gambling hells—at four o'clock this morning.

What had possessed him to stay out so late?

It had been the latest in a recent bout of late nights with James and James's rakish circle of friends. And, as usual, he woke up feeling regretful and full of self-loathing.

He'd fallen into some bad habits lately. Since that night with Eve Adams, and especially in the last week or so, when he'd finally had to accept that he wasn't going to be able to locate her. He wasn't sure why he was reacting this way—he wasn't usually the sort of man to seek oblivion at the bottom of a bottle. But for some reason, that episode, or rather the aftermath of it, had thrown him.

He was going to have to pull himself together.

"Do you require anything else, my lord?"

Gil shook his head. "I had better show my face at breakfast."

Crawford gave the barest of nods, still seemingly offended, and Gil left his bedchamber with a sigh.

He walked carefully down to the breakfast room, keeping very still so as not to jar his thumping head, standing still for one long, queasy moment before he pushed the door open.

James sat at the table, eating a huge plate of food with apparent relish. He'd probably drunk twice as much as Gil last night. It was galling to find him so jolly.

"Good morning," James said cheerily, looking up. "How are you feeling this morning, old man?"

"Like hell," Gil replied as he sank down into a chair. He

declined the footman's offer to bring him a plate, gesturing for coffee to be poured instead.

Having served the coffee, the footman bowed himself out of the room, closing the doors behind him.

"You should eat something," James said, slicing a devilled kidney in two. "Trust me, no matter how certain you are that you won't keep it down, you always feel better after eating."

Gil swallowed against the wash of saliva under his tongue that warned of imminent vomiting.

"Please don't talk about food," he muttered.

James merely grinned and set about his breakfast again.

After a few minutes of sitting still, Gil reached for the pile of post that awaited his attention. He sheafed through the letters idly, stopping suddenly when he reached one written in a familiar, flourishing hand. Rose's handwriting—loopy and flamboyant—had always struck him as somewhat out of character.

Cracking the seal, Gil unfolded the missive, frowning to note how short it was. Mere moments later, he cast it onto the table, shocked by what he had just read.

Gilbert,

I find I am with child. I would be grateful if you would come to Weartham to discuss the way forward.

Yours sincerely,

Rose

"Gil? What is it? What's wrong?"

Gil looked up dazedly. James's brow was creased with concern. "Who is the letter from?" he asked. "You look as though you've seen a ghost."

"Rose," Gil said. "It's from Rose."

"Your wife?" James sounded astonished. Gil never mentioned Rose by name. He'd conducted his life for the last five years as though she didn't exist.

"She writes with extraordinary news," Gil said, marvelling at how calm he sounded. "She says she's with child."

"*What?*" James dropped his coffee cup with a clatter, sloshing some of the hot brown liquid into his saucer. "When were you up at Weartham?"

Gil looked at him squarely. "I haven't been up there in years."

"What? You can't mean..."

Gil felt calmer than he'd have thought possible when he met his brother's incredulous gaze. "I can only assume she has taken a lover," he said.

James gaped at him. "What are you going to do?"

"Go up there, I suppose. Talk to her." He paused before adding, almost as an afterthought, "Obviously, I can't allow another man's bastard to inherit the earldom."

"Do you mean to divorce her?"

Gil just stared at his brother.

Divorce.

It shamed him that the word caused a wave of hope to crash over his heart.

"It's a possibility, I suppose," he said at last. "And there are other ways..." He left the sentence hanging, unfinished, as the possibilities crowded in on him. None of them seemed anything other than appalling. He shrank from the very idea of taking a child from its mother to grow up with strangers. But perhaps Rose would want that. All these things would have to be discussed.

"When do you mean to go?"

Distantly, he heard himself say, "I'll set off today." His mind raced ahead, thinking that it would only take an hour to get packed, and he could easily get one leg of the long journey done by nightfall. It was almost funny that after five years of avoiding Rose like the plague, suddenly he couldn't wait even a day to set off on this journey.

"I could come with you, if you'd like." James's tone was diffident, but when Gil's gaze jerked up at those words, he saw that James was very serious in the offer, his blue eyes uncharacteristically grave. Gil felt a lurch of gratitude toward his brother, even as he knew he'd have to refuse.

"Thank you," he said. "But I should go alone."

"Very well. Is there anything else I can do?"

Somehow Gil managed to dredge up a wan smile. "Have your valet make another batch of that vile brew I had this morning. I have a feeling I'll need another dose of it before the day is out."

"Robert White is behind on his rent again," Will said.

Rose frowned at him. They usually conducted their business in the library, but the library was dark and stuffy, and at the moment, she felt perpetually sick. She had decided to use the old countess's sitting room instead. If Will thought it was odd that she had opened the room up to the chilly breeze, he did not comment upon it.

"His wife just lost a child," she murmured. "Another one." Beneath the desk—a spindly legged French thing—her hand fluttered to her stomach. No one knew about her pregnancy, except her maid. And possibly, by now, Gil.

"He's been behind before. Several times. You need to take action."

Rose was silent.

"He drinks the rent money away," Will added patiently. "Do you imagine that helps his wife?"

She knew he was right. Nevertheless, she wanted to cry at the thought of the lost child. How mortifying. This pregnancy had turned her into a watering pot.

"All right," she said. "But speak to him first. Give him the chance to sort it out."

"I always do," Will said as he made a brief note in his book.

"What else?" she asked briskly.

"That's all for today," Will said. He shut his notebook and placed it on the desk in front of him. He glanced at her quickly, then away again. He lifted his teacup to his mouth and carefully looked at a painting on the opposite wall over the rim, avoiding her gaze.

A few weeks ago, she'd thought of Will Anderson as a friend. But when she'd come back from London five weeks ago, everything had changed. Their old intimacy was gone, and Rose couldn't seem to retrieve it. At first, Will had looked at her with the same old warmth, but he had stopped after a while, probably wounded by her swiftly averted gaze. She hadn't been able to help herself. For some reason, their easy intimacy had made her feel guilty, as though she was betraying Gil, which was ludicrous given how faithless Gil had been and how old this friendship was. Nevertheless, she was helpless to prevent her own withdrawal.

The trouble was, now she knew how it really was between a man and a woman. She remembered the times when she'd caught Will gazing at her when he thought she wasn't looking. Worse, she remembered the times she'd looked at him. The times she'd wondered how it would feel to have his strong male arms around her, what his kiss would be like. It was hardly surprising. He was the handsomest man in the county and the only young man in her vicinity. Of course he had been the focus of her girlish curiosity. But now those innocent musings made her feel wretched, especially if she'd misled Will. And it wasn't just Will. It was Weartham itself. She'd come back here a changed woman, and suddenly she saw that Weartham was even more limited than she'd realised. Even more devoid of society. Even more remote.

She lived in a house of women, and the only men she knew were married or servants. Little wonder she had managed to live so chastely for the last five years.

"Will you be joining us this evening?" she asked. Will usually dined with her and Harriet on Thursdays.

"Yes, thank you, my lady," he replied civilly. She winced inwardly at his formal tone and that *my lady*. It felt like a reproach.

"Good," she replied heartily. Too heartily. "Seven o'clock, as usual."

She rose then, anxious to close the interview. She felt so sick, both physically and at heart. Every time she saw Will, she felt sorry and sad.

"Very good, my lady," Will replied, standing up. With the utmost formality, he executed a bow worthy of a duke and withdrew. Will had the most beautiful manners of any man Rose had ever known, despite his humble origins. And somehow, that made her feel even sadder, witnessing the perfection of his address.

Once he had gone, Rose crossed to the open window and breathed in lungfuls of fresh air until her nausea faded.

Gil must surely have her letter by now.

The first draft had confessed who she really was, and what she had done in great detail. It had been by turns abject and shrill. She had torn it up and tried again. And again. After several more attempts, she had realised that this was not something one could explain in a note.

So she had written another letter. It was nothing more than a bald announcement of her pregnancy and a request that he come to Weartham to discuss matters.

If he didn't come, she would have to go to London again.

She hoped he would come, even as she dreaded his arrival. She wanted to be on her own territory when she confessed.

Not that she would have to say much. As soon as he saw her—Eve Adams sitting in the drawing room at Weartham—he would know the truth.

She wondered how he would feel when he read her letter. Would he work out the truth on his own? Or would he simply assume she had cuckolded him? Would he be angry? Or relieved at the thought that he might finally be rid of her? A pregnancy caused by another man would give him grounds for divorce, although it would be scandalous and take years.

She had wanted to leave him with his memory of Eve Adams intact and untainted. She had not *wanted* him to discover that Eve was, in truth, the woman he despised most in the world. In the end, she had not wanted to be found out.

But running away had been stupid. It had been cowardly. This confrontation with Gil had to come. She accepted that now. Still, she dreaded it.

Rose leaned her head against the window frame. She knew she needed to prepare herself for the worst. Gil might try to divorce her over this. If he could find a man who would swear he'd lain with Rose, it could be done.

The trouble was, that was not even the worst possibility. The worst was that he might decide to take the child away from her entirely. To be raised by nursemaids.

She did not think he would do such a thing. She did not think he was wantonly cruel. But he was bound to be angry and humiliated. And perhaps he would not be prepared to believe anything she said. Perhaps he would always wonder if the child was his, even if he accepted it.

Anger might make him impetuous. She would have to be prepared to placate him, to reason with him. Even to beg his forgiveness if necessary. Now was not the time to indulge her wounded pride.

She placed her hand on her stomach and thought about the child inside her. Her child.

And Gil's.

Chapter Twelve

Gil had been riding for several hours. The muscles of his thighs ached, but he was near the end of his journey now. In half an hour, probably less, he would turn into the gates of Weartham Manor for the first time in five years.

It was a grey-skied autumn day, bleak and windy. The road was banked on either side with great mounds of crisp, bronze beech leaves. Every now and again, a gust of wind would blow a little flurry of them into his path.

His carriage, containing his luggage and Crawford, were some way behind. Gil had left Crawford to organise everything at the inn this morning and had ridden on ahead. He disliked travelling in closed carriages; hated the forced indolence. It was too bumpy to read or do much of anything. And the scenery was better enjoyed on horseback.

Although he did not look forward to the confrontation with Rose, he couldn't help but look forward to seeing Weartham itself. It had been a long time, and he was fond of the place. Odd to think that this was the first time he had come to Weartham as its master. When he had last been here, only a few nights after his wedding, his father had still been alive.

He intended to bathe and rest in his rooms before he saw Rose. It would be better to see her dressed in fresh clothes, rather than like this, caked in mud and smelling—well, like a man smelled after riding for several hours.

As for Rose, how would she look? For the hundredth time, Gil tried to bring his wife's image to mind, but, as ever, all he could summon up was a vague recollection of a slender girl with short hair and sadly marked features. He remembered the features a great deal less well than the marks. He couldn't even have said what colour her eyes were.

He knew her hair was brown. That her skin had been very pale and her body painfully thin when last he saw her. Beyond that, his visual memory faltered. Yet he could still recall, from their two nights together, the feel of her small, birdlike bones beneath his hands and the surprising softness of her small breasts against his chest. Odd that.

He wondered who the father of her baby was. He wondered if Rose was in love with the father or if their tryst had been a terrible mistake. Or worse, a rape. Would she be hoping for a divorce or horrified at the inevitable ruin that would bring? Her letter had given him no clue whatsoever. It had been brief and to the point, just like all her others. Or most of them.

Unexpectedly, Gil's lips twitched as he remembered the letters she had taken to writing to Andrews after Gil refused to correspond with her directly any longer. She had blackened him forever in Andrews's eyes. The man thought she was wonderful because she sent him inconsequential gifts and chatty notes asking after his health. Chatty notes filled with sly humour at Gil's expense, revealing that same humour he'd liked when first they met. Before he'd discovered the truth about her.

He'd read her letters. Every one. That was the irony of it. He might have refused to write back, but he hadn't been able to resist reading her prickly missives. Each one was brought to him with Andrews's reply already drafted. His secretary would be wearing his tight-lipped expression when he handed them over, exuding as much disapproval as his deferential nature allowed.

"A letter from her ladyship," he would say. *"With my reply for your approval."* His replies had been defiantly full of good wishes and obsequious thanks, almost as entertaining as Rose's letters.

Whenever he read one of her letters, he always pictured his

mother's old sitting room at Weartham. The spindly legged writing desk in front of the window. He would imagine her there, a small, thin woman with short hair, the bare, vulnerable nape of her neck exposed as she bent over her letter.

But of course that was not how she would look anymore. Harriet had written to him with news of Rose getting better, putting on weight, growing her hair. *She's turning into quite the beauty,* one letter had said. He couldn't quite believe that, but certainly she would not look like the girl he had left at Weartham anymore. She was two or three and twenty now, fully a woman.

After one more bend in the road, the gates of the manor hoved into view, surprisingly small and domestic. Weartham was nothing to Stanhope Abbey, less than a quarter as large, but it charmed all who went there. The house itself was big enough to entertain a number of guests but small enough to feel cosy. The gardens were a delight, the nearby coastline bleakly dramatic. No wonder it had been his mother's favourite escape from London.

As he trotted through the gates, Gil was struck by a wave of nostalgia for all those careless summers he'd spent here with his family. He and James had been hellions then, galloping along the beach on horseback and losing poor little Tonia in the woods; blackberry picking and tickling for trout; sneaking down to the secret, forbidden swimming hole. They had been allowed an amazing degree of freedom here, a world away from Stanhope Abbey and school and society's expectations. When they were older, they had taken to loitering around the home farm. Gil had shared his first proper kiss with a bold dairymaid called Mary. Even now, a dozen years later, he could vividly remember the surprising slide of the girl's eager tongue into his mouth and the press of her thighs against his own. It had been shocking and wonderful. She was probably married with half a dozen children by now.

Suddenly, the house was before him. Gil smiled to himself.

It looked just as it always had: the solid, quietly impressive hall of a country squire. He almost expected his mother to be waiting for him in the drawing room, sewing or writing a letter.

He dismounted before the large front doors, handing his horse to a groom to take to the stables. The door was opened before he could knock by a tall, thin man with a beaky nose who wore an expression of polite enquiry upon his face. His intelligent gaze swiftly took in the quality of Gil's tailoring and the large, glossy chestnut that was being led away. His tone, when he spoke, was deferential. "Good afternoon, sir. May I enquire who is calling?"

"Good afternoon," Gil replied pleasantly. "Lord Stanhope, calling on his wife."

The butler's hastily disguised astonishment was almost comical. Gil adopted an expression of perfect unconcern and walked past him into the house. By the time he turned around, the butler's unruffled look was back in place.

"I will advise her ladyship of your arrival. Your lordship's baggage...?"

"Is following. My carriage and my man should be here in an hour or two. My rooms will need to be made ready."

The butler noticeably pinkened.

"I'm afraid," the man said, in a voice tight with embarrassment, "that your lordship's rooms are already taken."

Gil frowned. "My wife has visitors?"

"Ah—no. It's just that her ladyship took over the earl's apartments some years ago." The man flushed even pinker. As though he felt he should have prevented such a travesty.

"I see," Gil said. He felt slightly foolish and unaccountably annoyed. It was absurd of him, he well knew. He had made it very clear he would not be visiting Weartham at any time, so why should she *not* take the largest and most advantageously positioned rooms?

And yet it felt like a deliberate insult.

For a moment, he considered instructing the butler to have his wife's things moved back to the countess's apartments. But that would be ridiculous. Petty. He would not sink to that level. What he *would* do was see her now.

"Very well. Make me up one of the guest bedchambers," Gil said calmly, as though it didn't matter to him at all. "And while you get it ready, I'll see my wife in the library. Be good enough to inform her I will be waiting for her there." He began to walk toward the library.

"Ah, my lord...?"

Gil turned around again, impatient at this further interruption. "Yes?"

The man looked embarrassed. "Her ladyship is, ah, in the library already. Going over the accounts."

It was idiotic to feel so wrong-footed. As though Rose had planned to be in the library when he arrived. She hadn't even known when to expect him! If he hadn't been so irritated he might have laughed. So far, she was running rings round him, and he hadn't even glimpsed her yet.

"I see," he said. "Well, I'll announce myself. Thank you...?"

"Lennox, my lord."

Gil nodded. "Thank you, Lennox."

He would have a brief advantage, he thought, as he walked to the library. A moment or two while she took in his sudden and unannounced arrival.

He wasn't sure what he would say to her. He was prepared to be reasonable. Generous even. But it depended on her. How she dealt with him in these next few minutes would determine everything.

He paused briefly before the closed library door. Then he took the door handle in a firm grip and entered without knocking.

His mouth opened to say "Good afternoon, Rose," the only words he had rehearsed, but they died on his lips, withering there unspoken as a dark, familiar head lifted from the enormous accounts book on the desk.

He stared; then his mouth opened, and a single word emerged.

"Eve?"

For a brief moment, he felt the sharpest, brightest joy he'd ever known. His heart clenched almost painfully in his chest, and he took a step toward her. It was Eve Adams sitting at his father's library desk; Eve pouring over the accounts of Weartham.

In the same instant, comprehension dawned.

"Eve." His hand dropped to his side as he said it again, realising simultaneously that that was not her name at all.

She looked stricken, her grey eyes anxious, her face blanched. Her lips formed his name, but no sound came out. And in that moment, before the full horror of it dawned on him, he wanted nothing more than to go to her and take her in his arms; smooth out the furrow between her brows with his fingertips. Tell her it would be all right.

It was the flicker of her eyes to her left that distracted him from that thought; that drew his attention to the fact that the room had another occupant, a man, standing at the window holding a sheaf of papers in his hand. A man whose keen blue eyes had narrowed upon Gil.

"What do you mean, bursting in here upon Lady Stanhope?" the man said, frowning. He was shorter than Gil and more slender but there was an air about him of quiet authority.

"Get out," Gil replied flatly. And then his eyes returned to the woman at the desk, not sparing his interrogator another glance.

Rose spoke then, her words addressed to the other man but her gaze fastened on Gil. "Will, this is my husband, Lord Stanhope. Would you be good enough to leave us?"

The man—Will—didn't move. He was staring at Rose with a concerned expression. "Are you quite sure you wouldn't prefer me to stay?"

Rose turned her head and sent him a strained smile. "Quite sure. Thank you, Will."

Her companion frowned, but he protested no further, turning on his heel and walking out without another word.

Gil ignored the sounds of his departure. His whole attention was fixed on the woman who sat at the desk before him.

"Am I falling in love with you?"

The memory of him speaking those words to her flashed, unwanted, into his mind, and a wave of shame washed through him, thick and hot. She must have been laughing herself sick as he said those words, the wife he'd refused to see for five years. And all along she'd known exactly who and what he was. Christ, he'd almost convinced himself that she'd returned his feelings; that it was just that she couldn't say the actual words.

He half turned from her and ran a hand roughly over his face. Reaction was beginning to set in. A building anger fed from the pain and bewilderment within him.

"Why did you do it?" he asked from between clenched teeth. He thought it was a remarkably restrained opening gambit in the circumstances, but he saw that she flinched at his tone.

"I wanted our marriage to be real," she said, "but you refused. You rejected every overture I made. Since you wouldn't come to me, I decided to go to London."

He gave a mirthless laugh. "And pretended to be someone else entirely. What a marvellous joke, Rose!"

She flushed. "I did not intend to deceive you."

"Really? So when you introduced yourself as Eve Adams, you were being *honest* with me?" His voice dripped sarcasm, but he thanked God for his anger, because he knew that after this first blaze of rage, there was something far worse to come.

She looked away from him. "I only wanted to speak with you for a little while before revealing who I was. I thought that when I unmasked myself, you would recognise me. When you did not—" She broke off, looking at him with a pleading expression.

"You decided to lie," he completed for her.

"I meant to tell you who I was, eventually."

"Then why didn't you?" he cried, a raw plea that seemed to come from somewhere deep inside him.

She stared at him with wide, shocked eyes that held a hint of fear. "I'm sorry," she whispered.

"Why, Rose?"

He saw her swallow, saw her nervous fear of him, and he wished he could take any kind of satisfaction from it, but he couldn't.

"The things you told me about the circumstances of our marriage shocked me. I hadn't known about your father's gaming debt to mine. I had thought my father had provided a real dowry. Rather than just foregoing his winnings, I mean."

He fixed her with an unforgiving look. "I see. You didn't realise that your father blackmailed me into marrying you against my will. "

Rose's flush deepened, but her eyes glittered. "In fairness, I doubt he'd have seen it like that. To my father, a gaming debt is a debt of honour. And I am quite sure he did not know you were so reluctant. I do not think he would have wished to marry me to a man who was unwilling."

"You believe he thought me *willing*, then? Willing to marry you as you were then?"

She flinched minutely at that, and he felt a pinprick of remorse even in the midst of his anger. Could she really still be hurt by the memory of how she used to look? Now that she was so lovely?

"Yes," she said, her voice calm and controlled. "I believe he

138

thought you were willing. As did I, until our second night together. Do you remember? We were staying at an inn, and I knocked on your bedchamber door, and you—"

Now it was Gil's turn to flinch, though he tried to disguise his reaction by interrupting her with a drawled "I recall consummating our marriage once or twice, yes." He hated himself even as the words fell from his lips.

Rose stared at him, expressionless. And God, but there she was at last: the girl he'd married. He remembered that bland look very well.

"I realised that night that you did not wish to be married to me," she said mildly. "Your distaste for my person was very evident."

He knew he'd hurt her that night. But he said nothing, turning away from her and walking to the window to stare out at the well-kept lawns of the formal garden, feeling hollowed out, his anger dying in the empty space inside him.

"I felt no distaste for you," he said with his back to her. "But I did not wish to marry you."

There was a long pause, then he heard her sigh, and she said, "It is the same thing. You did not want me."

"It is not the same thing," he said tautly. "But you are right—I did not want you."

"You married me solely to retrieve the properties your father lost to mine."

"Yes."

He heard her moving behind him. A moment later, she was standing beside him. He felt her eyes on him and turned his head to meet her gaze. She wore a pleading expression that he hardened his heart against. "Gil," she said. "You must understand that I believed you were willingly entering into a real marriage with me, in return for a real dowry. Had I known what the arrangement was, I would never have consented. Especially if I'd known you loved someone else—"

"Do *not* speak of her to me!"

"But—"

"I would never have told you *any* of it, if I had known who you were," he hissed, his anger riled again as he recalled how he'd opened her heart to Eve Adams. "And I *especially* wouldn't have spoken of her." He cringed to think of what he'd revealed to her of the young man he'd once been. The idealistic boy.

"I'm sorry."

"Are you? Why don't you admit that you enjoyed it," he said bitterly. "Having me in your power? Grovelling at your feet like a—" He stopped himself. She was staring at him, horrified.

"I—no! Gil, *no!* I truly meant to tell you, but then you talked about the past, and the more that came out, the more I realised things were different from how I'd always believed. In the end, I just couldn't do it. I decided not to tell you at all. I waited till you fell asleep and slipped away, and the very next day, I came back here." She sighed. "But then I found out about the baby—"

He stared at her with cold, angry eyes.

"I don't believe you," he said at last. "I think you planned it all. You always intended to get pregnant, didn't you?"

"No," she whispered. "I didn't."

"*Stop lying to me!*" His fist slammed into the wall, six inches from her head, the pain of the blow blooming sharp in his knuckles and radiating down his arm. Rose cried out and shrank from him, one hand going protectively to her belly.

Her plain fear made him rear away from her, empty desperation mingling with self-loathing now. He turned again, sagging against the window frame to stare out unseeingly at the iron-grey sky.

After several minutes of silence, he faced her again. "You are sure the babe is mine?"

"Yes, I'm quite sure," she said bitterly. "*I've* never done— that with anyone else."

"Unlike me, you mean?" he said, investing his words with ice. She looked away and shrugged carelessly, but he saw the betraying movement of her throat as she swallowed.

God, what a mess.

He gave a weary sigh. "When I got your letter, I was curious as to who the father of my wife's child would be," he said. "I didn't imagine it would be me."

"Well, it is you," she replied flatly.

"How can I be sure? Perhaps it is that fellow who was just here."

"Oh, you are a pig!" she blurted out. "The babe is yours!"

He said nothing to that. He did believe her, but he wasn't sure why. He knew he oughtn't to trust a word she said.

She twisted her fingers together. "So what now, Gil?"

"The fact that you may be carrying the next Earl of Stanhope changes everything. You will understand that I cannot allow any speculation about the paternity of the child?"

"Yes, I see that," she said miserably.

"We'll put on a display of wedded bliss for a while," he said. "Go to Town and let it be known that we're been reconciled. Then Stanhope Abbey. I want my child to be born and raised there. You may live where you please once the babe is born."

She went white. "I want to stay with the baby."

Her voice was raw. It hurt to listen to it, but he made his own cold. "Is that so?"

"Yes, it is." She firmed her jaw and looked him in the eye, but he could see her chest rising and falling with rapid, panicky breaths. It brought him no satisfaction to see her like this, a supplicant to his whims. It almost made everything worse.

He shrugged. "Well, that's up to you," he said, then despised himself for giving in to the need to offer her relief. When he next spoke, his voice was brusque and icy. "It's time I bathed and dressed."

She nodded. "I'll arrange for your bedchamber to be prepared," she said.

"No need," he replied. "It's being attended to. I asked Lennox to have one of the guest bedchambers made up. I gather you are in my rooms, and I have no wish to disturb you."

She flushed. "I can easily remove—"

"No. I wish us to leave for Town as soon as possible. Moving rooms is entirely pointless in the circumstances."

"Very well," she said politely. "Is there anything else I can do for you, then? You must be hungry after the journey."

"I'm perfectly capable of giving instructions to my servants directly, thank you," he replied tautly, noting her flinch again. He strolled to the door but turned back to her, hand on the doorknob. "What about Harriet? Does she know?"

"She knows I went to London to see you. She doesn't know what happened there—or about the baby."

"Ah, well, we can practice the tale of our reconciliation upon Harriet at dinner tonight, can't we?" he drawled, and he bowed with mocking courtesy before leaving the room.

He maintained his façade of calm control for the next half hour, until he was finally alone in his room, in his bath, scrubbing away the dust and dirt of the long ride here.

And then it hit him. He dropped his head into his hands. He felt scoured out and empty. Somehow, in these last months, Eve Adams had become a talisman of something, something important. He thought they had chosen each other. Now it turned out there had been no choice at all.

Neither for him nor her.

Chapter Thirteen

Rose sank into the chair behind the desk and looked down at the neat column of figures she'd been going through with Will when Gil had come in. There was a large black ink blot on the last entry where her pen had rested too long and a spatter of ink across the rest of the page. In a moment, the whole page had been ruined. It was irretrievable.

She had managed to stay largely dry-eyed throughout that awful interview with Gil, but somehow this stupid mess of ink brought a flood of tears to her eyes, and now she found herself crying, really crying. Tears streamed down her face, and her diaphragm was racked by sobs that came from deep inside her. It was horrible, ugly crying, the sounds that came out of her animal-like, her nose and eyes streaming. She pressed her fists up against her mouth to try to muffle the noise, but it did no good.

After a while, the sobs died down in intensity and frequency. She found a handkerchief in the desk drawer and blew her nose. She couldn't yet stop the slow slide of tears from her eyes, but the worst of it was over.

There was a soft knock at the door.

"Who is it?" she called out, her voice wavery.

"It's Will. May I come in?"

She hesitated, then wiped her face again. "Yes, all right."

The door opened, and he stepped inside, his handsome face worried.

"Rose," he said, walking slowly toward her, as though to avoid alarming her. "Is everything all right?"

He had never called her Rose before, and she was oddly touched by his lapse. He was such a proud, formal man.

She tried to smile but knew somehow the result of her efforts was tragic. "I'm fine."

He sat down in his usual chair. "I heard Lord Stanhope shouting. And then he left, and you were crying." He swallowed. "I was worried. I shouldn't have left you."

She leaned forward and touched his hand gently. "Don't be silly. He is my husband, and anyway, you had no need to worry. We had a row, it is true, and I was upset, but he did not so much as lay a finger on me."

Will slid his hand out from under hers, covering hers instead in a protective gesture. "If he ever hurt you—"

"He wouldn't, Will."

"But if he did. I hope you know you could come to me. And that I would—I would take you away."

She felt like crying again at that. "Oh, Will."

"I could keep you safe," he insisted. "If it came to that."

She smiled at him, more touched than she could say. And guilty too, that she'd made him feel that way.

"Thank you," she said. "But there is no need for you to offer your protection, Will, I promise you."

It was the gentlest of rejections, and she saw him comprehend her. He nodded and withdrew his hand.

Rose picked up her pen and dipped it in the ink. Slowly and carefully, she scored through the ruined page with a series of diagonal lines. When she was finished, she looked at Will. "Now, where were we?"

She didn't see Gil again until dinner that evening. She slept the rest of the afternoon away, wiped out by the desperate tiredness that sometimes assailed her these days. One of the symptoms of her pregnancy.

If she could've got away with a tray in her room, she'd have done so. But it was Gil's first night here and—well, she had asked him to come, hadn't she?

She dressed for dinner with more care than usual, selecting a violet gown she particularly liked and having Sarah dress her hair carefully. She looked very well when she was ready, but that didn't make her feel any less nervous when she finally descended the stairs.

Gil and Harriet were already in the drawing room, and Gil stood politely when she entered. His immaculately cut coat drew attention to his wide shoulders and lean torso. Skin-tight breeches hugged his long, muscled legs. He should look elegantly modern in his evening clothes, but as soon as she saw him, she thought of a warrior. Everything about him was hard and powerful. A rigid tension gripped his shoulders, and there was a stony expression in his eyes that she fancied was for her alone.

"Good evening, Rose," he said evenly. "You look very fetching this evening." He forced a smile, and it looked wrong; too civilised and polite, unnatural. His eyes were not warm; they remained hard and watchful.

She greeted him and thanked him, equally civil and polite despite her churning stomach and dry mouth, then turned her attention to Harriet, who was watching them. "Harriet, you must think me quite dreadful to have given you no warning of Gil's arrival. I'm sorry. I had no idea he would get here so soon."

Harriet ignored the apology. "Oh, Rose, Gilbert's been telling me all about how you're going back to London with him, and then on to Stanhope Abbey! What wonderful news!" She beamed, including them both in her happy gaze.

"I'm glad you're pleased, cousin," Gil replied smoothly. "Rose was not looking forward to telling you. I know she will miss you."

"Oh, and I will miss Rose, but this is—this is *just* as it should be!" The older woman's smile was incandescent.

Rose smiled back weakly but was saved from having to reply by the entrance of Tom the footman, who announced that dinner was served.

They trooped dutifully into the dining room and made their way through five courses, though later Rose couldn't remember one thing that she ate. Nor what they spoke about, though the conversation flowed along, an endless stream of news. News about Weartham, news about Stanhope Abbey, about Gil's brother and sister and about Rose's father's travels abroad. The latest *on dits*, of which Rose and Harriet had read in Harriet's beloved scandal sheets but of which Gil, of course, had firsthand knowledge.

Rose contributed to the conversation, but later, in her bedchamber, she couldn't remember any of it. She only remembered how Gil looked.

She lay in bed, staring into the dark, and saw him again as he'd looked across the table. Subdued, polite, civil. Nothing about him offensive. Nothing warm either. And no hope, she thought bleakly, of more than that from him ever again.

She wished, oh, she *wished*—but just what she could wish for that would make it better, she didn't know. None of it could be undone, after all. And if it could be mended, she didn't see how. The only hope was the baby. When Gil saw his son, his heir, perhaps he would feel differently? Perhaps he would feel differently even if the baby was a girl?

"My wife and I do not live together. We never have, and that's not going to change."

The desire for an heir was strong in men, was it not? That primordial need to pass on to the next generation?

"I have a younger brother. He is my heir."

Under the bed covers, she lifted the hem of her nightgown to her waist and slid her hands over her naked belly. She could feel a slight, unfamiliar roundness there but nothing more. She explored her abdomen with her hands, poking gently, looking for she knew not what. There was nothing to discern yet, no matter how desperately she wanted to feel her baby.

Suddenly, she knew what she wished for. She wished she was months from now, swollen with the child. She wished that she could feel the babe turning and kicking inside her. She wished to touch her body and know her child was there.

She wished not to be alone anymore.

On the third morning after his arrival at Weartham, Gil breakfasted alone. Again. Rose was taking breakfast in her room. Apparently, she was too ill in the mornings to eat much of anything. Gil suspected that the real reason for her non-appearance was that she was avoiding him.

Although she had been quarrelsome and challenging during their first encounter, in the two days that followed she had mostly been coolly polite. Deferential. The very essence of a good and dutiful wife, at least on the rare occasions when she was in his presence.

They were leaving for London tomorrow. That gave Rose plenty of excuses to evade him. There were numerous visits to be paid, friends to be bid farewell, discussions to be had with Will Anderson about the running of the estate for the rest of the year. To Rose's obvious irritation, Gil had insisted on sitting in on those discussions, claiming he was interested in how Weartham had been run over the last five years. He knew she was dying to point out that he'd had no interest in the estate until now, but she managed to resist, merely murmuring her agreement.

He sat behind the desk as they talked, forcing Rose to sit on the other side with Anderson. He noticed that when Anderson addressed any remarks to him first, it made Rose irritable, and so he played up to it, directing all his questions at the other man, even though Rose was plainly capable of answering them all. He derived a strange satisfaction from angering her with his refusal to acknowledge her part in running Weartham.

Apart from the meetings with Anderson, he left her to do as she pleased.

Pathetically, he was starving for the sight of her. But he refused to dog her footsteps. And besides, the desire to see her and be with her was at war with another part of him, a part of him that wanted to thrust her violently away from him, that wanted to repudiate her, fiercely, and with every fibre of his being.

She was Eve, and she was not Eve. She was the perfect wife: beautiful, accomplished and pregnant with his heir. And every time he looked at her, he felt sick to his stomach to remember how he had all but declared his love to her. He reminded himself of it several times a day. And of his foolish, excruciating belief that she had reciprocated his feelings.

It seemed as though his body remembered her as Eve. It yearned toward her. When she walked into a room, his eyes sought her out. Once or twice, he had raised his hand to touch her in some small way, and then he would remember and would have to put his hand in his pocket or let it drop uselessly to his side. It was disorienting, like waking from a dream.

Altogether it was just easier to let her avoid him and to occupy himself with other things. He had not been to Weartham in five years. There were account books to be gone through and the estate to be ridden over. His questions during Rose's discussions with Will Anderson were not entirely idle.

When he had finished breakfast, Gil went to the library. The account books for the previous year were sitting on the desk where he had left them yesterday afternoon. He opened them, trying to concentrate on the painstakingly recorded figures and entries. But somehow, this morning, he found it difficult to think about anything other than Rose. She was distant with him, and he was the same with her. How could they live together like this? He wanted her in his bed, wanted her with a fierce ache, but he had not been to her bedchamber, not that first night nor either of the two following. Instead, he had retired to his own guest bedchamber and lain awake, staring at the ceiling. Remembering.

It was odd how well he remembered his bride now. He'd been watching her, on and off, and to his amazement, he *had* been able to detect the girl she had once been. That girl had been a pale, colourless shadow of the woman she now was, but she had the same soft grey eyes, the same facial structure. It was true she had changed a great deal, but even so, it seemed incredible to him now that he hadn't recognised her at all.

When he had tried to picture Rose on his journey up to Weartham a few days ago, he had been unable to recall precisely what she looked like. But now that his memory had been prodded, he found he could remember the seventeen-year-old reasonably well, her sad little face, pale under a dullish cap of short brown hair. And those distracting marks—livid then but all gone now. Except for the odd, puckish little scars. He remembered kissing one on her shoulder blade...

He had not expected Rose to alter. Nor Weartham, for that matter. But Weartham had changed just as its mistress had. Two days ago, he had turned into its gates and felt soothed by its familiarity, but that familiarity had been an illusion. In numerous small and subtle ways, it had been transformed. And Rose was its undisputed monarch. The servants treated Gil like a deeply honoured but not quite trustworthy guest. One who might pocket the silverware if not carefully watched.

Whilst at first glance little had altered at Weartham, the changes were everywhere. New farm buildings, renovations to the tenants' cottages, wholesale changes to the crops being planted. Even the gardens had been tampered with. These changes were disconcerting, causing him to misstep and lose himself several times a day. Rose's appropriation of the earl's rooms was particularly irritating.

She ruled the small principality of Weartham as regally as a queen. And the nearest thing she had to a consort was her steward and favourite, Will Anderson. It was plain to Gil there was something more than friendship between them. From his travels around the estate, his discussions with his tenants, his review of the account books, he knew that they spent a great deal of time together. Will's crabbed handwriting alternated with Rose's elegant loops in the accounts books. Yesterday, when he'd been rifling in the drawers of his father's desk, he had found another small notebook that seemed to record Rose's daily thoughts.

Speak to Will tomorrow about the north meadow.

Ask Will to speak to the grooms about the horses' feed.

Will and the Misses Wright for dinner Thursday evening.

Wherever Gil looked in the books, he saw Anderson's writing or his name. And Rose almost spoke to him as if he were master here. Or rather, as if to spare him the awkwardness of pointing out he was not master, while Anderson himself was formal and slightly aloof. A man on his dignity.

Had anything occurred between his wife and Will Anderson? Although he was sure they had not lain together, Gil wondered endlessly if they had been intimate, and if so, how intimate. After just two days, it seemed to him that the question had been circling round and round his brain forever.

He had brought this on himself, and he well knew it. He had stayed away from Weartham determinedly for five years and allowed his young wife to run the estate. He had given her free hand to choose her own steward. He would look ludicrous if he objected to her spending time with Will Anderson now, and he had no intention of behaving ludicrously.

But that didn't mean he had to allow them to be alone together.

Not for the first time, Gil wondered if Rose had feelings for Anderson. He would not ask her, but he knew there was *something*. He could sense it. Rose's manner toward Anderson was careful, Anderson's coolly distant. Even very slightly affronted...

He was interrupted from his reverie by Rose herself when she appeared in the doorway of the library. He looked up from the account books with an expression of polite enquiry when she said his name. From behind his façade of disinterest, he took the opportunity to stare at her. His gaze travelled over her without any noticeable reaction, but as he looked, he stored every tiny detail away. She wore a sprigged muslin gown. She looked fresh and summery despite the steely grey of the autumnal sky. Her breasts looked rounder and fuller than before. Probably a result of her pregnancy, he told himself. It was an effort to put the too-fascinating thought of her breasts from his mind.

She had reddened slightly under his gaze. "I hope I am not interrupting you? I just wanted to ask you something." She smiled uncertainly, her tone apologetic. Part of him felt like a monster to see her so tentative. Another part of him felt it was only right.

"Yes?" He disguised his discomfiture with terseness.

"I wanted to know when will I—we, that is—return to Weartham from London?"

He frowned at her. "I don't know, Rose. Perhaps not for a long time. Why do you ask?"

She walked fully into the room then, closing the heavy door behind her. "I had wanted to let Will know," she said. "I need to speak with him about next year. We had planned a number of small improvements, but we will have to see how the next few months go. I had been planning to discuss these matters with him in more detail after Christmas, but I'm conscious I may not be here."

For a moment, Gil merely stared at her disbelievingly. *Will*

151

Anderson again! He was all Rose seemed to think about! Gil could feel a slow, hot anger beginning to build inside him. He almost welcomed it after the suffocating politeness of the last two days. He let it permeate his whole body, clenching his fists as he stared at her with hard eyes.

"I presume," he said tightly, "that when you say *Will*, you are referring to Mr. Anderson?"

She flushed several degrees more scarlet. "Of—of course I am," she stammered awkwardly.

"But *you* call him Will," Gil pointed out in a deadly voice. He paused for several moments, staring at her fixedly before he added, even more quietly, "and what does he call you?"

Rose looked appalled. "I can assure you that he addresses me quite properly! I suppose I think of him as Will because—" She floundered to a halt, and the silence between them swelled uncomfortably.

"Because?"

She looked at him beseechingly. "Because he's been a good friend to me, Gil. Can't you understand that?"

He stood up and walked around the desk, closing the distance between them. He did not touch her. He was too angry to touch her.

"From this moment, you will put Mr. Anderson out of your mind."

Her brows drew together at his dictatorial tone, and her lips thinned. "For goodness' sake, Gil! Whatever has brought this on?"

"What has brought this on?" he repeated, his voice rising with disbelief. "*Your* behaviour over the last two days has brought this on! The soulful glances directed at Mr. Anderson. The way you tiptoe around his quite irrelevant feelings."

"What? You *cannot* be serious?"

He laughed humourlessly. "I am quite serious. This languishing you've been doing after your chivalrous knight of

152

the turnip field—it has to stop. Now." He ignored her sharp gasp of outrage. "If you want to be my wife in more than name, I expect you to behave like a wife."

"*Languishing!*" she exclaimed. "I have *not* been languishing over Will Anderson!"

"No? I sat with you both yesterday for two hours. You were making eyes at one another over your damned seed catalogue like Pyramus and Thisbe!"

"We were not! What errant nonsense!" she retorted hotly, but he thought he saw a flash of guilt in her eyes. "Where did you get such ridiculous ideas? I can't—"

He interrupted her, in no mood for her protests. "You are too friendly with him," he continued implacably. "You spend far more time on estate business than is warranted, and you must know it. Mr. Anderson is a first-rate steward, well able to deal with it all himself. You call him Will as though he is an intimate of yours. It is inappropriate! I have no doubt the whole village gossips about it."

Rose stared at him, her cheeks hectic with colour, her grey eyes sparking with anger. "I cannot believe," she cried, "that you are throwing an innocent friendship in my teeth when you have been throwing up the skirts of practically every woman of your acquaintance for the last five years!"

"Is that what this is, then? This *friendship* of yours? Revenge for what I've been doing?"

"Revenge?" Every trace of the quiet, biddable female was gone now. Her face was flushed, and her eyes glittered. "Do you think I *cared* that you were tupping all those stupid women?" she asked bitingly. "Do you think it *hurt* me to think of you with them?" He looked up to encounter eyes that were bright and sharp with malice. "Of course it didn't," she hissed. "It was just embarrassing." She filled the last word with scorn, and he took her meaning: *he* was embarrassing. An absurd, philandering peacock. He felt his face heat.

"As for Will," she went on, more calmly, "he has been a true friend. And I will not allow you to cheapen that with your nasty insinuations."

He laughed out loud at that, a coarse, masculine laugh that mocked those fine feelings of hers. "Do you think that's how he sees you, Rose?" he asked. "As his dear friend? I can tell you now that he does not."

He stepped right up to her, taking her chin between his thumb and forefinger and turning her face up to his. He felt her body stiffen in shock and rejection, but she did not pull her chin away. She stared at him, her grey eyes hard with hate.

It was astonishing how he felt so drawn to her even as he wanted to thrust her away from him. He stroked her jawline with his finger as he stared down into her pretty, mutinous face.

"Will Anderson wants to take your clothes off," he said, slowly and deliberately, "and stick his cock in you."

Something flickered in her eyes. Revulsion; denial. But she determinedly pressed her lips together and said nothing, her face stiff with loathing.

"Just as I do," he added, unable to stop himself. Her eyes widened at that, and he thought perhaps his own did too. They stared at one another, both surprised. They were breathing heavily, their gazes locked, his hand lightly touching her face. It seemed to him that her face was a question. Impulsively, he lowered his head and captured her lips with his own.

His eyes were open, as were hers. There was a fraction of a second when she might have pushed him away; when he might have pulled back. His pride warred with his desire and lost resoundingly when he saw excitement flicker in her eyes.

He let himself take what he wanted.

At first, her mouth was immobile beneath his. Not resistant but cool and still. He moved his lips over hers, plucking at her mouth coaxingly, drawing her lips into the shape of the kiss, persuading her to meet his desire. Gradually, he felt her mouth begin to move, becoming as pliable as warmed wax. She began to kiss him back, tentatively at first, and then her mouth opened with a sigh, and she tilted her head farther back, giving him access to her lips, her mouth, her throat.

With a groan, he slid his arm around her waist and pulled her body up against his. Lord, but she felt good, familiar and intoxicatingly feminine. As he pulled her even closer, she wound her arms around his neck, fractionally deepening the kiss, and all he could think was, *at last*. She was in his arms again, and it felt so right and so easy. Everything else, all the lies and the history between them, melted away. And now there was just this, this closeness, her soft mouth under his and her pliant body in his arms. And soon there would be more. He thought about taking her here, on the desk. He might not trust her, but he wanted her with a relentless ache that demanded satisfaction.

Even as he ground his hips against her, his rational mind thought, *No, not like this*. She was his wife, after all. The least he could do was to make love to her in a bed.

Reluctantly, he lifted his mouth from hers, and she opened her eyes dreamily as though waking from a deep sleep. She blinked at him.

"Shall we go to your chamber?" he asked, smiling.

Something happened to her eyes. They seemed to go flat. The dreamy look left her, and she stared at him in silence. His exuberance fell abruptly away. She lowered her arms from his neck and stepped back a pace, breaking his gentle hold on her. A moment ago, she had felt like part of him. Now they were apart again.

"Yes, of course," she said in a cool voice. "You might have done before if you wished. You are my husband—I'll hardly deny you."

Her grudging acceptance stung.

"Very well," he said, shrugging. "I'll come to you tonight."

He turned and walked back to the chair behind the desk, back to his account books. But Rose did not leave.

"I thought you meant that you wanted to come to my bedchamber now." Her cheeks were flushed with what looked like mingled embarrassment and anger.

"You are my husband—I'll hardly deny you."

Those words had killed his passion as surely as a bucket of cold water. The thought of her tolerating him was horrifying. He wanted her to *desire* him, as he desired her.

Even as these thoughts clamoured to be spoken aloud, it felt as though they were stuck in his throat. He stared at Rose for several moments, on the cusp of blurting it all out, but he couldn't do it. The habits his father had taught him were too ingrained to do anything other than shove his feelings behind the dam of his pride. And so, in the end all he said was, "Tonight will be fine."

His gaze lingered long enough to see her flush deepen to crimson before he turned back to the ledgers, staring unseeingly at the columns of numbers until Rose finally turned and left the room.

Chapter Fourteen

When Gil went down to the drawing room before dinner that evening, he found Harriet sitting quietly by the fire, embroidering. She looked up at his entrance and smiled at him, setting her sewing aside.

"Well now," she said, sounding pleased.

"Cousin," he murmured. It was the first time he'd been alone with Harriet since the day he'd arrived. He'd been hoping to avoid an interview with her, having had one or two rather frank letters from her over the last few years which he suspected she might want to reprise verbally. He remembered those letters still, the measured, reasonable words of censure.

"Gilbert," she began. "I cannot tell you how happy I am that you are taking Rose back to London with you. I don't pretend to understand how things are between you..." She hesitated awkwardly. "I sense some strain between you still, but I'm sure that, given time, you will make a good marriage of it."

"I certainly hope so," he replied. He tried to look remote, but it was difficult to be remote with a woman who had dandled one on her knee in infancy. She did not appear to be put off by his distant tone.

"Rose is such a special young woman," she went on, clasping her hands together earnestly. "I hope you realise what a treasure you have in her, my dear."

Oh, I do.

"You cannot know," Harriet went on, "how difficult it was for her when she came here. And what a—success, yes, really, a *success* she has made of her life here. When I think! My goodness, Gilbert, she was only seventeen years old when she came here. To be mistress of a house like this at seventeen. She has done wonderfully well. Weartham thrives. But of course, you must know. You've seen the estate and the books since you came."

"She has done very well," Gil replied, his tone suggesting a distinct lack of interest. Harriet frowned.

"She has done more than that," she said, and her tone was gently chiding. "She has made friends of your neighbours. She has improved the lives of your workers. Did you notice the new roofs on the cottages on the home farm? And the new well? And the schoolroom?"

It was impossible to stay cool with Harriet badgering him.

"Yes, of course," he said. "And you are right, cousin, she has managed exceptionally well."

Harriet beamed, but her smile quickly faded. "She will be missed," she said. "By everyone, but by me especially."

"Well, why don't you come to London with us? You will always have a home at Stanhope House—or at the Abbey, if you prefer. My father always said so; you know that." He didn't even think about it before he spoke. He'd always been fond of Harriet, even during these last few years when she'd made it plain how she disapproved of him. Perhaps especially then.

She beamed again, at him, this time, quite in her old way. "Oh my dear!" she exclaimed, her voice a little surprised sounding. "What a kind thing to say! As it happens, I've thought a great deal about this, and I *do* wish to remain here. And Honeysuckle Cottage is absolutely perfect for me, I must say. But how *very* decent you are, Gilbert!" Her warm brown eyes searched his face, and he felt his cheeks warming.

"It is such a relief to see you have not changed as much as I had feared! But I can't understand why you and Rose—" Her eyes slid past him, and she stopped mid-sentence. "Ah, well, never mind. Here is Rose come to join us."

He turned to see Rose entering the room, and his heart

leapt. He felt as though he'd been transported back months to Grayson's ball. She wore a green gown, and her hair was dressed just as it had been that night. It was as though his heart thought, *Eve*, the sight of her gave him such a leap of unexpected joy.

She must have seen something in his face in that instant. A smile began to animate the corners of her grave mouth, tremulous and eager. But then his mind caught up with his stupid heart, and he scowled and watched her tentative smile fade and die away.

Somehow, his mouth spoke conventional words of greeting, and Rose replied in kind, walking toward him. A sudden and overwhelming need to put space between them assailed him. He turned and strode to the fireplace, lifting the poker from its stand and stirring the coals. Once he'd invigorated the fire, he lingered there, staring down at the flames, while Harriet began telling Rose the day's news, which seemed to involve the betrothal of one of the vicar's daughters.

He gazed into the glowing embers of the fire until the heat made his eyes smart. Until the physical discomfort distracted and centred him. Only then did he turn back, a polite smile pasted on his face, to join their conversation.

He reminded himself, as he half listened to Harriet, that he had said he would be going to Rose's bedchamber tonight. To partake of his marital rights.

Why had he done it?

Why had he imagined he could bear to touch her?

He stole a look at her then. She was listening intently to Harriet, her lips parted in a half smile, her eyes sparkling with humour. She was lovely. He felt the full force of her loveliness in his gut, in his hardening cock. Yes, he remembered exactly why he had asked to go to her. Even as he resented her bitterly, he remembered exactly why he had smiled and looked down at her and said, *"Shall we go to your chamber?"*

Joanna Chambers

God, what fools men were.

To distract Harriet's attention from her poor appetite, Rose kept up a constant stream of chatter over dinner. Gil didn't say much, merely maintained the same façade of polite attentiveness he'd been wearing since she walked into the drawing room earlier.

Eventually, the two women fell into reminiscing about their years together at Weartham. Rose wondered what Gil thought of the life they described as they spoke; such a quiet, unsophisticated life. And yet she felt happy to remember it all, in a melancholy sort of way. When the last of the dinner had been cleared away, a deeper sadness settled on her. This life was over now. Harriet would be living here at Weartham, hundreds of miles away from Rose's new home. And Rose hardly knew anyone in London. She would have to start all over again.

After dinner, Harriet asked her to play the pianoforte. She was glad to comply—she didn't feel like talking anymore. She played pieces she knew inside out, so well that she simply had to let her fingers begin, and they unerringly found the right notes. It was a competent enough performance, but she knew herself; she was not playing with her heart. All she could think of was the night ahead of her. Of Gil coming to her chamber.

Harriet embroidered while she played, but Gil simply watched. She had her back to him, but she felt his gaze upon her, his attention making the tiny hairs on the back of her neck lift. She wondered what he was thinking as her fingers drifted over the keys. She didn't ask, though. Just played. Piece after piece.

After over an hour of playing, she stood and said that she was tired and intended to retire for the evening.

Harriet chattered on for a little while about how long the

journey to London was and how of course Rose must get her rest. And then she embraced Rose, and her eyes were damp. And Rose knew that hers were too.

"We'll say good-bye properly tomorrow," Rose whispered.

She had spent the last few years longing to be elsewhere, and now that she was leaving for good, she didn't want to go. She wouldn't only miss Harriet. She would miss Will, her friends at the vicarage, everyone. She would miss the house, and the sea, she realised. The open, windy landscape. London was miles from any coast. There was no room there, no space. Ever since she had become pregnant, she had had the strongest yearning for fresh air. She kept opening windows to breathe in lungfuls of it, cold and clear. The air here was good. In London, where there was all the industry and waste of a million teeming souls, the air was stale and used.

Rose embraced Harriet again and bid her a fond good night. On her way to the door, she nodded at Gil.

"Good night, Stanhope," she said, all formality. She'd taken to calling him Stanhope in front of others. It seemed the countess-like thing to do. Privately, though, she thought of him as Gil.

"I'll be up shortly," he replied.

She looked away in confusion, embarrassed in front of Harriet, who'd sat down again and was pretending to peer at her embroidery.

"Yes, well, good night," Rose said again and hurried out of the room.

Her face was hot as she climbed the stairs. He was angry with her still, she knew. He would be angry for a long time, perhaps forever. And yet after he'd kissed her in the library this afternoon, he'd smiled at her with sleepy eyes and told her he'd come to her tonight. It had astonished her. And enraged her. He had been brooding around the house in silent hostility for three days, but he was willing to put his resentment aside for a tumble between the sheets!

Sarah was waiting for her when she reached her bedchamber. The maid helped her out of her gown and took it to the dressing room.

"I'll pack this away just now, your ladyship," she said.

"Very well. Then you'd better go to bed, Sarah. We have a long journey ahead of us tomorrow."

"Yes, m'lady."

Rose took off her shift and got into her nightgown, brushed out her hair and cleaned her teeth. The routine of it did nothing to settle her. Her stomach was in knots.

She knew she should be pleased he was coming to her tonight. She wanted their marriage to be as amicable and fruitful as it could be—she did!—and naturally, that meant welcoming him to her bed. Gil was earthy and passionate, and even though he was furious with her now, she knew he wanted her in bed. It was the one decent card she still held.

And yet she felt sick at him. Disappointed and angry. Was he really so shallow that the towering resentment he had been advertising so publicly since he'd arrived could be soothed simply by throwing her skirts up?

But the fact of the matter was that that was going to have to be enough in this marriage. If they could at least recapture the excitement of the night when she'd been Eve Adams—well, it would be something, wouldn't it? Not exactly the pinnacle of all her girlish dreams, but *something*.

She tried to recapture how she'd felt that night, walking up the staircase to his bedchamber. The tingling excitement, the delicious anticipation. And then what came after. Shared pleasure and quiet intimacy.

If she could have that again, despite everything, it might be enough.

It was more than many people had, wasn't it?

Rose was sitting at her dressing table when Gil walked into her bedchamber. He entered without knocking, not wanting to seem tentative. With the same intention, he closed the door firmly behind him and began to remove his coat. Neither of them spoke.

She was brushing her hair with brisk strokes. It cascaded down her back in dark, shining waves. He remembered that night in London, waking with her in his arms, her hair streaming across the pillow beside him, its fresh, summery fragrance teasing his senses.

She was in her nightgown. He was used to sophisticated women who wore pretty confections of lace and silk to bed, not nightgowns like this—of high-necked white linen. The sort of thing nuns probably wore, he thought sourly.

Or virgins on their wedding nights.

At that thought, he was struck with a startling visual memory of their wedding night, of standing over her in her dim bedchamber, looking at her as she slept in just such a nightgown. Disturbed, he banished that image from his mind determinedly and set to work removing the rest of his clothes.

With mistresses, undressing for bed had tended to be an enjoyably mutual effort. This silent, solitary approach felt horribly formal, as though they were about to embark on some archaic ritual. *Christ, is this marriage?* He had no stomach for it.

He pulled off his cravat and shirt and placed them on a nearby chair. When he turned around again, he discovered Rose was standing, facing him—was staring at him, in fact, her hairbrush forgotten in her hand. He was clad only in his drawers now, and as he watched, her gaze travelled over his body, lingering at his crotch before jerking self-consciously back to his face. He felt his cock stir at the unexpected perusal.

Well then. Perhaps I do have the stomach for marriage?

163

Gil kept his eyes on Rose as he slowly untied his drawers and pushed them down, kicking them away to stand before her quite naked. She was looking at him with what looked like hungry fascination, and he discovered that he liked to have her eyes upon him like that. He stood with his arms relaxed at his sides, wondering how she would react if he did nothing at all. Would she approach him of her own volition?

They faced one another without moving for perhaps a minute. Then, just as Gil was thinking of walking toward her, Rose closed the distance between them. She came to a halt just out of arms' reach and raised her hands to the buttons of her nightgown. Her nimble fingers unfastened, unfastened, unfastened, ten, fifteen, twenty little buttons until the gown gaped open almost to her waist, allowing him a shadowy view of her body. She shrugged her shoulders out of the gown, and it felt to her waist.

Gil stared at her, lustful and fascinated. His cock bobbed in front of him, undeniable evidence of her appeal, as his eyes devoured the picture she presented. Her nipples were larger and darker than before, her breasts fuller. She pushed the gown down over her hips, and it fell to the floor. He saw then that her previously trim waist was slightly thickened, and there was a slight roundness to her belly there hadn't been before. There was not much sign of a baby yet, but she was different. Fruitful, fertile.

She took one more step forward and lifted her face to look at him. Her expression was grave. "Well. Here I am," she said.

It was an offer that he did not want to take, grudging and dutiful.

After this afternoon in the library, he'd wondered if he'd imagined the taste of desire in her kiss, but now he saw a hint of it again—in her eyes this time—and he wanted more.

He sat on the bed, leaning back on his elbows, and looked up at her. "And here am I," he countered.

She frowned very slightly, but eventually she moved

164

forward again, till her knees hit the side of the bed and she stood over him. Slowly, Gil levered himself forward. When he was sitting straight, her delectable breasts were right in front of him. But though his mouth fairly watered to taste her and his hands itched to touch her, he made no further move. Instead, he let his hands rest on his thighs and waited. If she was waiting for a cue from him, she would get none.

Her grey eyes were puzzled and stormy. They searched his face but apparently found no answers there.

After a long time, she lifted her hands and placed them on his shoulders lightly. Her palms shaped themselves to the roundness of his muscles, her fingers fluttering uncertainly. Just as he thought she was about to withdraw, she let her palms graze their way up his throat until her hands cradled his jaw on both sides. She drew him to her and moved toward him too, closing the little distance between their mouths until she'd stoppered it with a kiss.

God, but her lips were the softest he'd ever known, her scent the sweetest. She was all around him, her small hands clasping his face and now drifting into his hair, her fascinating, newly rounded body pressed to his, her hair loose, the scent of it in his nostrils now. And he was lost.

For a moment, less than a moment, he thought *Eve*. And then, *no*. But Eve—Rose—it didn't matter right now. It was *her*, and he was drunk on her, drowning in her. She murmured his own name, his full name, against his lips. *Gilbert*, the "b" a puckering little kiss of its own, and then her mouth was drifting down, her hands pushing his head back to give her access to his throat.

He groaned as she bit him softly there, soothing the tiny sting with a damp, openmouthed kiss that drifted to his collarbone, then up again to his mouth. And then she was climbing onto his lap, straddling him, a thigh on either side of him, her already damp quim pressed against his aching cock.

She tilted his head back and kissed him greedily, just as

she'd kissed him that night. His hands went helplessly to her hips, pulling her closer, and his hips bucked as his cock searched for a way to penetrate her. She moved over him maddeningly, exciting herself by rubbing against his hard length, the wetness of her slick against him. It was as gratifying as it was infuriating. He no longer doubted that she wanted him, and when her hands went diving down between their bodies to seize his cock, he let her be the one to guide him into her tightness.

He watched her take him in, her pretty face transfigured by desire. Brow damp, lips parted and cheeks flushed. He let her glide onto him, a small gasp escaping her as she hilted him in her.

"Ah, Rose," he groaned. "Take it, then; take what you want."

And she did, rising and falling on his cock, her eyes closed as she focused on her goal. He watched her, hungry for her need, holding himself back as she took and took and took, her muscles clenching on him rhythmically, milking him, binding him.

I'm just ploughing her, he told himself, trying to make it basic and easy. But it was impossible to fool his treacherous heart. It seemed to swell in him when she came, crying out her pleasure. It seemed to swell with a kind of cosmic gratitude because he was with her again. *Eve. Rose.* And then he was coming too, with her, their cries and groans mingling and echoing and dying away into the night.

They remained where they were for a long while in their strange embrace. He rested his head against her breast, trying to ignore the tangled emotions that threatened to overwhelm him: keen joy, helpless sorrow, bleak disillusionment.

Part Four:
Winter

What freezings have I felt, what dark days seen!
William Shakespeare
Sonnet 97

Chapter Fifteen

October 1814, London

Every morning when she woke up, Rose knew immediately that she was back in London. It was the noise. Stanhope House was in Mayfair and somewhat removed from the grimmer realities of life in the capital, but even here there were sounds that reminded her she was no longer in the countryside: the clatter of horses' hooves on cobbles, the rumble of carriages, the quick step of servants sent on errands.

She noticed the absence of sounds too. Birdsong in particular. There were some pigeons on the square, but their citified cooings were nothing like the birds at home. She missed the reedy song of the skylarks and the peep-peep of the song thrushes. She missed home.

She sat up slowly in bed and considered carefully how she felt. Fine. That was the truth of it. She was four months gone now, and the worst of the sickness seemed to have passed. Her breasts, which had felt tender at the beginning, felt better now. She was lucky, the doctor said. "Some ladies suffer terribly," he'd told her. "Be glad you are not one of them."

As she arranged her pillows behind her, she glanced at the rumpled space to her right. Gil had lain there last night. For a while. He'd risen and left as soon as he thought her asleep. He came to her every night now. She hardly saw him during the day, but they came together in the quietest hours of the night. There was passion between them, and, more surprisingly, tenderness, though it did not find its expression in words. Only in the kisses of silent lips and the blind questing of hands in the darkness. There were times, during the night, when she thought about saying something; times when she thought her words might even reach him if she could only think what to say. *I'm sorry? Can you forgive me? I want to forgive you. Can we begin again?*

Impossible.

In the morning, it was difficult to believe he had ever been in her bed, except for the disturbed sheets. The man who came to her at night was very different from the one she saw after she had risen in the morning. He was so very withdrawn in the daytime. He always had somewhere to go or something to do that took him out of her orbit. He was, in fact, as absent as he had always been. During the day.

A knock at the door heralded the arrival of her morning chocolate.

"Good morning, m'lady." Sarah smoothly entered the room, deposited the tray on her mistress's lap and walked over to the window to open the curtains.

"Good morning." Rose sipped the chocolate and lay back against her pillows.

"Which gown would you like to wear today, milady?"

"You choose." Always the same answer these days. Sarah tutted disapprovingly and walked into the dressing room. She emerged after a few minutes with a primrose-yellow morning gown. Rose nodded uninterestedly.

Once she'd finished her chocolate, she got up and let Sarah bustle her into her shift and stays and button up her gown. Then she sat down in front of the dressing table to watch the maid put up her hair. She felt aimless, sitting idly while Sarah made the braids for her coronet. But there was not a thing she needed to do until her morning callers arrived. She could lie abed the whole morning if she wanted.

She could not enjoy her leisure, though. Unlike most ladies of fashion, she was used to a life of activity. Over the last few years, she had thrown herself into the running of Weartham with vigour. Here she was expected to do as little as possible. The housekeeper reported to her each day, but it took all of half an hour to approve her exceedingly sensible suggestions and peruse her flawless menus. Rose was usually twiddling her thumbs by eleven o'clock. And this was only her second week in London.

Her first week had been taken up with her presentation to the Queen, a necessity before she could enter society. The dressmaker had made her elaborate court dress—convention demanded a full-skirted gown in the style of the last century—within just a few days, and Gil's aunt Leven had sponsored her. Once that was over, the invitations had begun to trickle in, and now there was a steady flow every day. Balls, musicales, routs. It was the little season. The last hurrah of the top ten thousand before they returned to their estates for winter.

Now each afternoon brought a rash of fresh callers to Stanhope House. Rose was an object of considerable curiosity: Lord Stanhope's hitherto invisible wife. They came to stare and wonder, and sometimes to ask sly questions. *Why had she not come to London before now? Was it true she had only just been presented? At her age and married these five years?*

She was a mermaid. A bearded lady. Freakish and fascinating. The latest *on dit*. She was the neglected wife of that notorious lothario, Lord Stanhope. It was difficult not to feel gratified by the surprised expressions on the ladies' faces and the admiration in the gentlemen's eyes when she stepped forward to meet them. They had assumed she was ugly. Perhaps they had been *told* she was ugly. A galling thought, that.

Gil had been present during the first two days but since then had been conspicuously absent. Three afternoons in a row now, she had faced the callers alone. He didn't explain his absences to her, just took himself off in the mornings, returning for dinner in the evening. And it wasn't as though there was anyone else in the house. Gil's sister was staying with cousins in Bath, and his brother James was rarely to be seen, though he too lived at Stanhope House. James's existence seemed to revolve around sporting events, drinking and gambling, and he kept hours that rarely brought him into contact with Rose.

Rose had never felt more alone in her life than she had these last few days. Even when Gil had first abandoned her at Weartham, she'd at least had Harriet. Here she had no one. And every day, a dozen curious callers. There was nothing to do but to paste a smile upon her face and parry the questions and stares as best she could. Put a brave face on it, even when one of Gil's former lovers, Lady Cairn, appeared. A pretty woman, Rose had to admit, but unlikeable. She'd gravitated to the only gentleman present, ignoring the ladies for the most part. And she'd smiled like a cat with a fish when Rose had admitted she didn't know where Gil was.

"Are you looking forward to the ball tomorrow, milady?" Sarah asked, interrupting her train of thought.

"Yes, I am," she surprised herself by replying. For some childish reason, she was excited at the thought of going to a ball—her first official ball. She didn't count Nev's masked one.

She wondered if Gil would deign to dance with her. She knew she wasn't an especially good dancer, not having had much practice. Just with the dancing master and the other girls at the seminary. Oh, and Will, of course, at the annual village dance—though only country dances were danced there.

Sarah's voice was dreamy. "Which gown will you wear, milady?"

"The blue, I thought," Rose replied distractedly.

Sarah stared at her, aghast. "Not the silver?"

"You think the silver more suitable?"

"Infinitely, milady."

"Then I shall bow to your superior judgment."

Sarah smiled complacently, satisfied with the outcome of their discussion. She went back to the braiding of Rose's hair.

And Rose went back to wondering what callers this afternoon would bring.

"Lord and Lady Stanhope," a footman announced.

Gil stepped forward, Rose's arm on his, to greet Lord and Lady Clive, the hosts of Rose's first ball.

Gil bowed, Rose curtseyed, and after Lord and Lady Clive had reciprocated, Gil performed the introductions. Lord and Lady Clive's expressions, when they looked at Rose, were avid with curiosity. And, in Lord Clive's case, admiration. His eyes swept down the length of Rose's silvery gown and up again, lingering on her bosom, then her mouth.

Gil discovered he wanted to punch Lord Clive on the nose, although, rather inconsistently, he also discovered that the man's reaction gave him a strange thrill of somewhat masochistic pleasure.

And what was that all about?

What did it matter to him what anyone thought of Rose?

It was a thought he had plenty of time to contemplate that evening. Forced to introduce Rose to dozens of friends and acquaintances, he then watched her proceed to dance her slippers off with everyone but him.

He really ought not to mind. He was the one who had suggested they go about in society together for a few weeks. The very purpose of coming to this ball was to introduce Rose to the *Ton*, wasn't it?

So why, every time some grinning fool approached them to enquire who Gil's lovely companion was, did he feel like frog-marching her out the door and back to Stanhope House?

It was ridiculous. *He* was ridiculous.

Gil heaved a sigh and leaned his shoulder against the pillar that he was half hiding behind. There were plenty of people he could talk to if he chose, but he wanted to be alone for a while, and he'd found this quiet nook from which to watch Rose dance the quadrille. She was dancing with some young pup called Thorpe, who affected the most absurd poetical airs, like a third-rate Lord Byron. Thorpe was gazing soulfully at Rose. Making a cake of himself, Gil thought irritably.

He turned his attention back to his wife. Her movements were graceful, though obviously unpractised. He could see that she needed to think about the steps as she performed the passes and turns of the dance with her overeager partner.

Lord, but she was beautiful tonight. Her silver gauze gown glittered under the blazing chandeliers, making her look like a fairy. Titania maybe, with that regal pose of hers. A serious sort of fairy. The sort that would be running fairyland, he thought, and smiled to himself, thinking of her poring over golden accounts books in her silver finery.

He'd been watching her for only a few minutes when a female voice spoke behind him. "Hello, Gil."

He turned, a smile already growing at those unmistakable soft tones. "Tilly—"

Eyes twinkling, she offered her hand, and he lifted it to his lips, grazing her gloved knuckles with his lips. "You look wonderful," he said. And she did, in a diaphanous gown that enhanced her pink-and-gold beauty, a beauty that looked more mature now.

"Thank you." She blushed becomingly. Still that quiet, modest nature. "You're very kind, Gil."

"Hardly. Merely pointing out the obvious. And how is Dray? And the children?"

She was plainly pleased to be off the subject of her own looks, launching into an animated monologue about her family, how busy Dray was with his politics and how the twins had had mumps but were quite recovered now. Tilly was a domestic creature at heart, and Gil smiled at her indulgently as she talked, not especially interested in her news but soothed by her easy contentment.

"And what about you, Gil?" she said at last. "I see that your wife is with you this evening. Is she—that is, is everything...?" She trailed off hopefully, gazing at him with wide blue eyes. He shouldn't have been surprised by her question, but Rose had never been mentioned between them before. He found himself wondering why Tilly had asked. Had she seen him staring at Rose? Had he looked infatuated? The thought of other people guessing his innermost feelings made him queasy.

"Rose came down to London a couple of weeks ago," he replied. "We are—that is, we plan to try to live together." He gave an uncomfortable laugh, an attempt at lightness that didn't come off.

"Really?" Tilly said, blue eyes suddenly glittering with what looked suspiciously like tears. "Oh Gil! I—I'm so very pleased for you. I'd been thinking, you know, what a—well, a perfect *waste* you've been making of your life. So, I'm glad. Truly." She gave a little sniff and smiled in a wobbly way, and he found himself gazing at her, surprised by her little display of emotion. She was always so full of her husband and children and her home. He was amazed she'd even given him a thought.

After a moment, Tilly tore her gaze away from his and looked at the dancers. "She's very pretty, I see."

Gil stared at Tilly's averted profile, wondering how to respond to that.

"I—well, yes," he mumbled eventually and followed her gaze. His eyes immediately found Rose amongst the dancers, turning in silver splendor, her gown glimmering with the reflected flames of a thousand shivering candles. She was the most beautiful woman in the room, he thought, though it seemed ungallant to say so to another woman, even Tilly.

"Well, goodness, how things have changed!" Tilly said brightly. Then she looked up at him and smiled the old Tilly smile. "You must bring her to see us, Gil. I want to extend the hand of friendship, of course. It must be so difficult for her, entering society for the first time."

He returned her familiar smile with one of his own, fond and indulgent. "That's very kind. I'd be grateful, and I'm sure Rose will be too."

She beamed, like a schoolgirl given praise. "A dinner," she decided. "I was planning one soon anyway and can easily make it larger. You can be the guests of honour."

"I wouldn't want to put you out."

"Don't be silly. It'll be a pleasure!"

"Then, thank you. We will be delighted to come."

Her attention was snared then, by something across the room. "Oh, bother," she said, though she smiled. "Dray wants me."

Gil glanced in the direction of her gaze, and sure enough, Dray was beckoning her. He tipped his head at Gil when their eyes met and smiled a greeting but then beckoned Tilly again.

"I'd better go," she said. "Dray and I have to look in at Lady Lennox's rout before we go home, and it looks as though our carriage is waiting. But perhaps I'll call on your wife tomorrow? I really ought to be introduced to her before I invite you both for dinner."

"She'll be pleased to make your acquaintance, I'm sure." Gil smiled.

It was only a minute or two after Tilly took her leave that Rose returned to his side. She had young Thorpe in tow and they made a striking couple, being of a similar height and build, both dark-haired and fair-skinned. Rose rested her arm on Thorpe's as they walked. He was talking animatedly, and she was smiling at him. Gil gritted his teeth. By the time they came to a halt beside him, Thorpe was beside himself, all puffed up from her attention. He bowed over her hand with a flourish.

"My lady's hand is as white as the new-fallen snow," he declared, even though said hand was encased in a silver satin glove that went all the way up to her elbow.

Gil glared at him. "*Your* lady?" he muttered irritably.

Thorpe glanced nervously at him and quickly let go of Rose's hand. The puffed-up look vanished.

"Would you excuse me, Lady Stanhope?" he said quickly. "Miss D'Aubney has promised the next set to me."

"Of course, Mr. Thorpe." Rose smiled, and he hurried away as though he had a pack of foxhounds at his back.

"Did you have to be quite so rude?" Rose asked mildly once he was out of earshot.

"All that damned poetry," Gil grumbled. Then he looked at her narrowly. "I thought you hated poetry."

A reluctant laugh burst from her. "I do," she confessed and then laughed again, more freely this time. God, she was lovely when she laughed, with her clear, bright eyes dancing and her mouth quirking up like that. It was good to see her smile again, and smiling *at him*. It was like being in the sunshine after a long, bleak winter.

"Oh, he went on and on," Rose said. "I don't think he said one sentence that wasn't in iambic pentameter."

Gil laughed at that, and so did she. When their eyes met, it seemed to him that she was all lit up from within, and all at once, he felt so *close* to her. He wanted to stretch his hand out and touch her. Just a brushing little contact. Nothing at all compared to what they did in bed together each night—but he didn't feel he had permission for that sort of public intimacy.

Just then, the orchestra took up their instruments again, and couples began to take their places on the floor. When the music began, Gil realised it was a waltz—and that no partner had come to claim Rose. Well, perhaps there was a way to touch her after all?

He turned his gaze back to her. "May I have the pleasure of this dance?"

Her face fell a little. "I promised this waltz to that tall red-haired fellow whose name I've forgotten."

George Latimer.

"To my way of thinking, the gentleman has lost his chance," Gil replied. "He should have arrived before the music started."

"He's probably been looking for me. We are a little out of the way over here—"

Gil glanced over Rose's shoulder and saw Latimer bearing down on them. When the man saw Gil notice him, he raised his hand and gave a smile, as if to say, *I'm just coming.*

Gil knew he should tell Rose.

But he didn't.

Instead, he shrugged apologetically at the other man, took Rose in his arms and danced her onto the floor, leaving Latimer staring angrily after him.

Rose didn't notice, thank God. She just looked up at Gil with sparkling eyes and said, "Sweeping me off my feet?"

"It's a speciality of mine. Keep your eyes peeled for a terrace, won't you?"

A shadow passed over her face at his reference to Grayson's ball, but there was a gleam in her eyes too, and he couldn't regret mentioning it. For all the lies between them, that night was still a precious memory, if a bittersweet one now.

He turned her again—a mistake. "Oh no, look, Gil!" she cried "There's that red-haired chap! How mortifying! You should take me back."

"Absolutely not," Gil replied, unrepentant. "If I take you back, I shan't get another chance to dance with you tonight. And he *was* late, Rose. It really doesn't do to keep a lady waiting."

It was only when the words were out that he realised how very foolish they were. He half expected her to say something— *You should know,* or maybe, *At least he didn't keep me waiting for five years*—but she said nothing. And after an awkward pause, the uncomfortable moment passed.

"Dancing's easier with you," she observed after another circuit of the floor.

"Is it?" He felt absurdly pleased by that, and celebrated by sweeping her round in a flashy turn that made her laugh again. He thought—again—how lovely she was when she laughed and wished it could be like this always between them. "Perhaps," he mused, "it's because your body knows me."

"My body knows you?" she repeated dubiously.

His mouth quirked. "Our bodies have more than a passing acquaintance by now." He leaned closer and murmured in her ear, "All those nighttime encounters they've been having."

She shivered at his breath in her ear, and when he lifted his head, she was blushing fetchingly. He felt himself grow hard at her reaction and drew her body closer, indecently so, to hide his predicament.

"Let me show you what I mean," he said. "For example, when I do this"—he pressed his hand against hers to indicate the direction of their next turn and swept her round—"you know exactly what to do, don't you?"

She peeped up at him from under her lashes. "Yes, I see what you mean." Her eyes brimmed with laughter as she added, "And I rather think *your* body has decided it's bedtime again."

He grinned. "Are you referring to the unexpected guest that I've been pressing against your skirts, my lady?"

She gave a little snort of a laugh—it was a most unladylike laugh and one that he recognised as uniquely hers. He remembered James deriding it all those years ago, but the familiar, irrepressible sound of it delighted him.

"I'd have thought you'd grown another leg, my lord, *if* my body didn't know yours so well."

He laughed again, a shocked, happy laugh that made the dancers around them turn and stare, some with curiosity, others with disapproval. Gil didn't care. He couldn't give a damn what anyone thought right now when she was looking at him with that carefree expression.

"I want to kiss you very badly," he confided in her ear. "Right here, in the middle of the ballroom."

"Now that you mustn't do," Rose whispered back, eyes sparkling. "By all means, rub against my skirts for relief, my lord, but a public kiss would be truly scandalous."

They kept up the same silly nonsense all the way round the ballroom, right up to the end of the dance, and when he led Rose from the floor, Gil felt more lighthearted than he'd felt in months.

"Who is your next partner?" he asked, casting an eye around the assembled guests.

"Actually, I do not have a partner for the next dance."

He felt like cheering at that but limited himself to a small smile as he lowered his head and spoke in her ear. "Shall we take a walk round the gardens, then?"

She grinned up at him and opened her mouth to speak, but before a word emerged, another voice interjected.

"Good God! Is this Lady Stanhope I see before me?"

They turned simultaneously to face the owner of the voice.

"Nev!" Rose cried and stepped forward.

It was Sir Neville Grayson. The thin, handsome face that usually wore an expression of utter weariness wore an expression of fond indulgence now.

"Darling!" he said. He took the two hands that Rose held out to him and kissed them before turning his gaze to Gil.

"Good evening, Stanhope," he said with cool politeness. "I see you've brought your wife to town. Not before time, old man."

Gil bristled. Grayson must have known about Rose's disguise at his masque that night. "I fail to see what business that is of yours, Grayson," Gil replied rudely. He laid a proprietary hand at Rose's waist.

"Gil." Rose frowned at him, pulling away slightly. "Didn't you know that Sir Neville is an old friend of my father's? I've known him since I was in leading strings."

Sir Neville pulled a face at her. "My dear, it's not *quite* that long. Your father—excellent man that he is—has a few years on me. And I'm certainly sprightly enough to beg a dance from you. Are you free?"

"I—yes, of course, Nev." She sent Gil an apologetic look, and since she'd already accepted, he couldn't even protest. Just had to watch as Grayson executed the most exquisite bow Gil thought he'd ever seen and stretched his arm out to Rose to escort her to the floor of the ballroom. She walked away with him, smiling and chattering, her face animated. When they took their places on the floor, Grayson murmured something in her ear that made her laugh and raise her hand to her mouth as though he'd ever so slightly shocked her.

Gil bristled with aggression. Damned coxcomb, making up to Rose, and him old enough to be her father! There was nothing he could do but watch as Grayson danced and flirted and laughed with his wife, and she flirted right back.

All of a sudden, he felt like an idiot. An idiot for forgetting that Rose was only here tonight because she'd plotted with Grayson to deceive and seduce him. Now she was doing it again, twisting him round her little finger with a few smiles. And he, like a fool, had been lapping it up.

He watched her skip down the line of gentlemen in her set, smiling happily. As she passed Grayson, she whispered something in his ear, and he laughed.

He wondered if she was laughing at him, even now as he watched.

Chapter Sixteen

"Does Stanhope know Lottie and I visited you at Weartham, dear heart?" Nev asked as they met to execute a brief turn.

"Not exactly," Rose replied before the dance parted them again for a while.

"Is it a secret?" he asked when they were reunited.

She considered carefully. "Not as such, but it's perhaps best not mentioned."

He nodded. "All right. That's diplomatic."

They linked hands, holding them above their heads and stepping toward one another, their faces very close for a moment. For a heartbeat, no more, Nev looked uncharacteristically serious. "Is he treating you right, poppet?"

"Of course!" she replied. She looked away, pretending she was having to think about the steps of the dance. After a few seconds, she looked up with a bright smile. "Do you imagine he locks me up with nothing but stale bread and water? Don't be ludicrous, Nev. I'm well looked after."

He frowned at her. "He can't have been too pleased when he found out who you really were."

No point lying.

"He wasn't." She smiled in what she hoped was a reassuring manner. "But he's fine now. Truly. It's all sorted out."

Nev looked over her shoulder. "He certainly looks smitten. He couldn't take his eyes off you when you were dancing with all those other gentlemen, and he's still glaring at me now!" He grinned at her, amused. "Makes me feel young again, having a husband after my blood. It's been a while since I engendered such jealousy."

She frowned. *Jealousy?* Hardly that.

"You'll be pleased about Miles, then," Nev said, abruptly changing the subject.

She frowned at him, puzzled. "Pleased how?"

Nev's look of dawning horror was almost comical. She saw the precise moment at which he realised he had spoken out of turn.

"What is it?" she pressed.

"Nothing. Really, it's nothing." They parted again, and she went down the line, executing a turn with each of the gentlemen in their set. When she reached Nev she gave him her gimlet look.

"You were about to tell me something about my father, Nev; don't bother to deny it."

"Don't be absurd," he said airily, but his eyes slid away from hers.

"Tell me. I won't leave it alone. I'll hound you till you confess."

"Oh, damnation, Rose! I wasn't supposed to tell you. It was supposed to be a surprise."

"A surprise? What surprise?"

He stared at her for a moment more, then shrugged, giving up the game finally. "Your father's coming home. His ship's due to arrive in England in three weeks."

Gil was silent and moody in the carriage on the way home. He'd been like this since her dance with Nev. It was disappointing, after their waltz and the good humour between them. It had been so unexpected. The first moment of amity they'd shared out of the bedroom. But now he was sitting opposite her, a frown on his face and his mouth all closed up and grim, fast as a trap. Back to normal, in other words.

Even on their wedding day all those years ago, he hadn't been quite so morose as he was now. He'd been remote and cold then, but this atmospheric sullenness was worse, a state of being he'd perfected over the last few weeks.

At first she'd felt chastened by his obvious displeasure— she had brought this situation about, after all, with her stupid lie—but as the days went by, she found herself growing weary of his relentlessly unforgiving mien. Since they'd arrived in London, she'd tried to do everything he wanted of her, and nothing seemed to please him. And when they were alone, like this, he just lapsed into a tense silence that was becoming more and more difficult to ignore.

She wished they hadn't had that lovely dance now. It was cruel to let her think things were getting better, only to have to go back to this. Like pushing a boulder up a hill and watching it roll back down again.

She rested her head against the carriage window. *To err is human, to forgive divine.* She should tell Gil that. Give him something to chew on. Was that Shakespeare? Or Bacon? Or Pope? The trouble with detesting poetry was that one could never ascribe quotations properly. And in any event, she didn't think Gil would be impressed by the sentiment. So she left the words unsaid and instead watched a raindrop meander down the carriage window, tracking its halting descent with bored fascination, ignoring the black, velvety night beyond the glass.

It was annoying, she reflected, how even when she was staring at her raindrop with rapt attention, she was still fully aware of the shape and presence of Gil occupying the opposite seat of the carriage; still aware of every tiny movement of his big body. She watched her small, innocent raindrop and wondered whether he intended to come to her bedchamber tonight. Part of her wanted him to. At night, it was almost possible to pretend everything was all right. Almost. But tonight, the other part of

•

her resented the thought of him following her to her room; resented that he would sit here now, practically vibrating with tension, then calmly appear in her bedchamber later to take his pleasure of her body. She swallowed hard.

She was beginning to realise she couldn't just live for the nights, as good as they were. She'd planned to stay quiet and patient for as long as it took for him to get over her betrayal—forever if necessary, she'd naïvely thought. Now she realised it wasn't in her to do it. Here she was after just three weeks, and already she felt rebellious and angry with him. Already it was an effort to bite back the sarcastic comments her tongue longed to utter.

"Are you aware of Grayson's reputation?"

She was so deeply sunk in her own thoughts that she jumped at the sound of his voice, her hand going to her throat. She turned to face him and made herself smile politely, refusing to acknowledge his belligerent tone.

"I believe he's accounted something of a rogue," she replied lightly.

"You underestimate him," Gil said flatly. "He is a scoundrel. I don't want you associating with him."

She stared at him for a moment before she spoke. "Sir Neville is a friend of my family. I've known him since I was a child. Good Lord, I only stopped calling him *Uncle* Nev a few years ago! I am not going to refuse to see him!"

"He's been embroiled in numerous scandals. Duels, even. It is rumored that he killed a man in France."

Rose shrugged. "And that is all it is. Rumour. He is accepted by polite society."

"He's a roué. A despoiler of women and a—a libertine."

She would have laughed if she hadn't been so angry. Coming from Gil, this was rich!

"Well," she said tightly, "it takes one to know one."

Gil glared at her. "I am not like him, Rose."

She stared at him in sheer disbelief. She couldn't believe his gall. How many women had he had?

He looked annoyed as he waited for her response. Annoyed and puzzled. As though she were speaking nonsense.

"You," she said, very precisely, "are a philandering, faithless, despicable lothario." All of a sudden, she was full of trembling rage. "Since I arrived in London a *fortnight* ago, I've met no less than three of your former paramours. One of them even had the gall to come calling on me! The streets are littered with your cast-offs!"

Even in the dimness of the carriage, she saw his eyes glitter. "Do not be ridiculous," he bit out. "That's all in the past now."

Ironically, she hadn't even considered he might betray her again with another woman until she heard this abrupt denial. Now uncertainty bloomed in her gut. Impatiently, she shook her head as though to dislodge this new, unwelcome thought. "And so what if it is in the past? That doesn't change how people look at me. The day Lady Cairn called, I had at least half a dozen other callers, and they were all watching like hawks to see how I reacted to her. They were delighted to witness my humiliation." She sucked in a ragged breath. "Not that you care. You disappear after breakfast. This is the first evening I've seen you in a week!" She wished immediately she could unsay those last few words, cringing at the whine in her voice. Lord, it wasn't as if she even *wanted* to see him.

He let out a humorless laugh. "Well, you wanted to come to town, Rose, and here you are. This is how it is in London."

"When I came to London, it was to *talk* to you. I certainly didn't come here to flit from party to party, or to sit in a stuffy drawing room all afternoon, day after day, making idle chitchat with people I don't know and don't care to know. I only ever wanted to take my place as your wife, but you'll never let that happen, will you, Gil? You had no choice about marrying that ugly girl, and I'll never be allowed to forget that! And it's going to be like this forever, isn't it? You *hating* me and making me pay, even—even when you're sharing m-my b-bed!" She halted abruptly, shamed by her rising hysteria, by the tremor in her voice and the sudden flooding of her eyes. She slumped against the side of the carriage, hiding her face in her hands as she began to sob.

"Rose—" Gil uttered her name into the silence, a shocked plea that she ignored. She felt him stand, then move his body into the seat beside her. He leaned over her, brushing aside a few tendrils that had come loose from her coiffure and tugging her hands from her face. She turned farther away from him, toward the window. "Rose, please—" He sighed. "Please stop crying. I don't hate you. I truly don't."

"Well, you certainly don't *like* me," she sobbed.

"That's not true," he replied softly. But she thought he sounded uncertain, and when she glanced at him, he looked thoughtful and serious.

For a while, they sat there silently. He rubbed her back awkwardly while she finished crying, the silence between them punctuated by her stuttering breaths and sniffles. When she finally got herself back under control, she felt like an idiot. She'd never been one for fits of tears. It must be the baby, she decided.

She felt stupid now, and transparently desperate. It was childish to crave love and affection from him. She should sit up and talk rationally. But she didn't want to. It was easier to stay where she was, her head leaning against the side of the carriage, her body obedient to its lurching rhythm. There was something oddly soothing about it.

She must have fallen asleep. When she next opened her eyes, it was to encounter Gil's shoulder. He was carrying her into the house, a footman with a branch of candles lighting the way. Gil looked down at her, unsmiling.

"You fell asleep," he explained. "I'm taking you to bed."

She shifted in his arms. "Let me down. I can walk now."

"Stay where you are. We'll be there in a minute, and I'll help you out of your gown. Save you waking your maid."

She didn't want to wake Sarah, and she needed help with her buttons, so she let him carry her. When they got to the bedchamber, the footman withdrew, and Gil put her down. He began to tackle the delicate fastenings of her gown with quite as much skill as Sarah would have shown. Must be all that practice, she reflected bitterly. Then, pathetically, she felt a fluttering of excitement as his fingers brushed her bare flesh.

He peeled away her gown and petticoat, her stays and her shift. He sat her on the bed and removed her evening slippers and garters. He rolled her stockings briskly down her legs. When she was quite naked, he only said, "Nightgown?"

"Nightgown?" she repeated stupidly. By then he was already rifling through the drawers of the armoire. He brought out a delicate thing of silk and lace that she'd only just bought and never worn. When he handed it to her, she blushed but took it and put it on, shivering when the delicate fabric whispered against her skin. It revealed more than it concealed, and she looked up at him, embarrassed but hoping, against all sense, to see interest warming in his gaze.

He wasn't even looking at her. He was picking up the silver-backed hairbrush from the armoire, apparently quite genuine in his stated intention to act the part of her maid. She'd already pulled the pins out, letting the mass of her hair fall to her waist, and he therefore applied himself straightaway to the task of brushing it out. Long strokes of the brush, from the top of her head all the way down. Slow, soothing strokes, one hand pulling the brush, the other smoothing down her hair after.

Such an innocent intimacy. The palm of that smoothing hand was warm and broad, and it gentled her till she felt quite boneless. Little by little, she relaxed against him, until her back was against his chest and the silver hairbrush lay discarded on the mattress beside him. His arms came round her, and she felt something—his cheek?—rubbing against the top of her head. She sighed.

After a while, he murmured, "Ready to go to sleep?"

The pang of disappointment that assailed her dismayed her. She shoved the feeling determinedly aside and nodded.

"In you get, then." He shifted as he spoke, and she obediently stood, watching as he pulled the covers back for her. The sheets were cool and clean, and she felt her whole body relax as she slid between them and Gil tucked her in. Only then did she realise how absurdly tired she felt.

Gil sat down on top of the bedcovers, still fully dressed. After a minute, he said, "I don't hate you. And I don't dislike you. I think you're quite bewitching, actually, which is half the trouble—" He broke off and frowned at the mattress, then sighed heavily. "I'm sorry, Rose. I realise that we can't go on like this, that I need to put the past behind me. There will be a baby soon, after all."

"In five months," she agreed softly.

"We're going to be a family," he said, and it sounded like a resolution. If only he would stop frowning and smile, she might even feel hopeful about that concession. But he didn't smile, and the furrow between his brows did not ease.

After a brief silence, he stood. "You're tired. I'll see you in the morning." He turned and walked to the door.

"Good night, Gil," she said, willing him to turn round. Turn around and smile at her, or *something*. Something that would give her one little scrap of hope that everything would be all right.

"Good night."

The door closed behind him with a quiet click.

First thing the next morning, Gil sent round a note of

apology to Ferdy, having decided to stay at home instead of going riding with his old friend. It was time he stopped avoiding Rose, time he let go of his resentment. When he remembered her tears in the carriage last night, he felt ashamed, knowing he was the cause of her heartbreaking sobs. They'd been getting on so well till he'd seen her with Grayson. But that reminder of her deception had made him angry all over again.

That anger had faltered, though, in the face of her tears and her insistence that he hated her. When he realised she believed he would come to her bed, hating her; that he would use her body, *hating* her, he'd felt sick. What kind of a man did she think he was? He saw the nights they'd shared since Weartham completely differently now. Those hours that for him had been the only peace between them had been a battleground for her, and he hadn't even known.

He accepted too that he'd behaved poorly since they'd come to Town, abandoning her to the whims of the *Ton*. Leaving her to cope with the likes of Isobel Cairn waltzing into her drawing room. To think that Rose had known exactly who Isobel was— he cringed at the thought. She was worth ten Izzy Cairns. A hundred. Lord, the two of them weren't remotely comparable! What must Rose think of him that he'd spent months bedding a woman like Isobel? How could he explain to her that he'd chosen Isobel because it was easier to dally with someone you had no feelings for?

Well, everything was going to be different now. As of today, he was going to put the past behind him. As of today, he was going to show Rose he was committed to their future.

He'd planned to kick off this new start with a civilised breakfast at which he would be pleasant, smiling, and would announce his intention to spend the day with Rose. However, after kicking his heels for almost two hours in the breakfast room waiting for her to appear, he realised she wasn't going to show. He might as well have gone riding with Ferdy after all.

Was she still angry with him? Still tearful? He'd hoped

they'd got over the worst last night, but perhaps not. Unable to bear waiting any longer, he went up to her rooms and knocked on the door.

"Rose, it's Gil. May I come in?"

There was a pause, then her voice, slightly surprised. "Of course."

She was dressed, though her hair was loose around her shoulders, and sitting at her desk, writing a letter. He wondered who she was writing to.

"Good morning," she said. Her pen was poised in her hand, an enquiring look on her pretty face.

His wife was exceedingly pretty. He knew it was shallow to be moved by that but still, the sight of her each day made his heart skip a beat.

"I wondered how you were," he said. "You didn't come down to breakfast."

She looked puzzled, as well she might since he'd made a point of avoiding her at breakfast since they'd come here. "I never come down for breakfast. I just have coffee and rolls up here in the mornings." She paused. "Were you waiting for me?"

He felt faintly foolish. "I had thought we could spend the day together," he said airily.

"Oh!" Her surprise couldn't have been more obvious, and he felt the need to backtrack.

"We need to be seen together," he pointed out. "I shouldn't have left you to receive so many callers alone. People will think it odd."

"I see." Her expression went slightly flat. She turned away from him to put her pen down on the ink blotter. When she turned back, she was matter-of-fact.

"Well," she said, "I am glad that you will be here to see our callers today."

He hadn't intended this. He had intended to suggest they

spend the day together. Alone. But now he didn't want to say so. Suddenly, it seemed too large a gesture, and he wasn't sure how it would be received. It seemed that every word he spoke to her came out wrong, smaller and less generous than he'd intended.

They stared at one another for a long, awkward moment.

"Well, I suppose I'd better let you finish your letter," he said.

She smiled at him, her hand already creeping to her pen. He felt stupidly hurt. Was she so eager for him to leave? It was as though she couldn't wait to get back to her letter.

"I'll see you downstairs once you've finished then," he added.

"Yes, of course," she replied absently, but it seemed she'd already forgotten him. By the time he closed the door behind him, she was bent over the letter again.

Chapter Seventeen

It was not Gil's habit to receive morning callers, a tedious business he'd left to his sister in recent years. Today, it took up the whole afternoon.

It was a cold day, and the fire had been banked up, making the drawing room overly warm and stuffy whilst the callers streamed in and out, making stifling small talk.

A number of the guests from last night's ball decided to call. Their number included Mrs. Mills, an attractive widow in her middle years; Mr. Preston, her escort; Lady Gressingham, an old dragon; Lady Gressingham's two perpetually unmarried daughters, and, of course, Tilly. Gil introduced Tilly to Rose as the wife of an old school friend—which was perfectly true, of course. Rose greeted her cordially, and the two women chatted pleasantly while Gil suffered through one of Lady Gressingham's famous lectures.

Charles Thorpe arrived next, bearing a nosegay of violets and a poem—a verse, he informed Rose earnestly, that he'd written in her honour.

Once Thorpe had handed over the violets, he pulled the poem from his pocket and presented it to Rose with a flourish. He'd rolled the paper up and tied it with a blue ribbon that exactly matched his coat. And the violets. All in all, he cut quite the ludicrous figure.

Gil watched the little dance between Rose and Thorpe with fascination. Everything about Thorpe drew attention to his person, from his outlandish blue coat to the elaborate bow he executed as he handed Rose the poem. He really was the most ridiculous boy.

Mr. Preston sniggered audibly and whispered something to Mrs. Mills.

Rose pulled the ribbon off and unrolled the paper. Her eyes scanned it for a full minute, her expression serious. When she'd finished reading, she smiled at Thorpe.

"It's lovely, Mr. Thorpe," she said earnestly. Then she began to roll the paper up again and retie the ribbon.

"Oh no, Lady Stanhope!" Mrs. Mills protested, sending Mr. Preston a mischievous look. "Do read it! We all so love to hear poetry recited, do we not, Mrs. Drayton?" She turned to Tilly, begging her to join in the joke and plainly looking forward to mocking Thorpe's efforts.

At first, Tilly said nothing, looking uncomfortable, but when Mrs. Mills nudged her, she joined in with the other voices—Mr. Preston and the two Gressingham girls, and yes, even Lady Gressingham—all urging Rose to read the poem out.

Rose looked around the room, her eyes resting momentarily on each guest, measuring them. Then she turned her attention back to Thorpe, smiling gently.

"Do you mind awfully if I do not, Mr. Thorpe? I have never had a poem composed in my honour before, and I should rather keep it to myself, if you do not think that terribly selfish."

She hated poetry.

Thorpe, who had plainly been hoping for a public reading, fool that he was, softened. His self-satisfied expression transformed into one of rather touching pleasure that made him look very young. Really, he was a mere pup, and Gil felt unworthy, suddenly, for his hostility to the boy.

Rose was much kinder than he was. Much kinder than anyone else in this room. And braver, he thought, thinking of Tilly's accession to Mrs. Marsh's stronger personality.

Rose gave the rolled and beribboned poem to a footman, who bore it away as though it were a precious jewel, Then she turned back to Thorpe, and they began to converse, Rose

194

listening, with every appearance of interest, to the young man as he held forth with.

She didn't need to be kind to Thorpe. The other guests would have preferred if she had not been, and Thorpe probably wouldn't have noticed either way. But she had.

And really, *why* did that make him feel so damned wretched? As though he'd lost something?

Because... whispered a voice inside him... *it means...*

What?

For weeks, he'd been reminding himself over and over that he didn't know Rose. The woman he'd met at Grayson's ball, his perfect woman, had been a chimera. The real Rose was a liar. A cheat. She had made a fool of him.

But even pretending to be someone else, there had been something about her that was real and true. And it was *this*; this thing that made her defy her malicious guests merely to be kind to a boy who didn't even really deserve her kindness. It was this thing that made her bright and determined and so very *alive*. And all at once, in this ordinary little drawing-room moment, it was as though Gil had caught a glimpse of something rather profound. He wanted to go away and puzzle at the thought. But his drawing room was full of guests, and one of them—Lady Gressingham—was demanding his attention with a question about his great-aunt's health.

Soon after, Tilly took her leave, promising an invitation to a dinner very soon. Then Mrs. Marsh and Preston made their farewells, just as Neville Grayson was announced. Rose glanced at Gil when the footman came in with Grayson's card on a tray, and Gil deliberately kept his expression bland. After a moment's hesitation, Rose walked forward to greet the new guest, wearing her brightest smile. The hothouse blooms Grayson presented put Thorpe's violets to utter shame.

The man proceeded to monopolise Rose for twenty minutes, maneuvering her neatly onto a small sofa and leaving Gil to entertain Lady Gressingham, her daughters and the now monosyllabic Thorpe.

The fire fairly blazed in the grate as Lady Gressingham delivered a strident lecture on the need to keep servants in their place. Gil's eyelids began to droop, from weariness, as well as the sheer heat of the room. He felt like groaning, or begging for mercy, when the drawing room doors opened yet again. Happily this time, it was a friendly face. Ferdy, with his sister Gertrude. Gil stood up with tactless haste while Lady Gressingham was still mid-flow and made his way over to his friend. Ferdy looked shifty and apologetic.

"Hello, old man!" Gil said, grinning at his friend. "And Gertie, always a pleasure!" He bowed formally over her hand.

"Don't you Gertie me!" she hissed under her breath. "You've been neglecting that poor little wife of yours. Leaving her to the mercy of all the tabbies in London while you gallivant round London with your friends." She bestowed a look of purest scorn on her brother as she spoke the last word, and Ferdy blushed like a schoolboy.

"She made me come," Ferdy mumbled with a sidelong glance at his sister. Twenty-nine years old, Ferdy was. The Honourable Ferdinand Dudley. But Gertie would always be two years older.

Gertie ignored him. "Still, you're here now," she continued in a slightly less hostile tone. "So that's something. You'd better introduce me to her."

Gil didn't bother protesting but simply led Gertie and Ferdy over to Rose and performed the demanded introduction. Within two minutes, the indomitable Gertie had displaced a stunned Grayson from the sofa next to Rose, delivered a subtle but effective put-down to Lady Gressingham and extracted a promise from Rose to become involved in her latest charity venture. Something to do with fallen women that made Lady Gressingham flush with indignation. Even more pleasingly, the displaced Grayson was cornered by Lady Gressingham and was forced to listen to the remainder of her lecture. He sat, meekly listening, an uncharacteristically hunted look on his handsome face.

"Amazing woman, your sister," Gil said to Ferdy as he pondered this satisfactory turn of events. When Ferdy was silent, he turned to look at him. It seemed as though Ferdy hadn't heard him. He was staring at Rose with an expression of mild astonishment on his face. When he realised Gil was watching him, he started guiltily.

"Sorry, old man," he mumbled. "Frightfully rude of me. Staring at Lady Stanhope. Not done. 'Pologies. But it's true what they say, what?"

"I don't know, Ferdy," Gil said. He forced a smile. "What do they say?"

"Oh—nothing." He blushed deeply. "You know me, Gil. Mouth. Always running away with me. Stupid."

"I know that Rose and I are the subject of gossip at the moment. I'd rather know the worst of it," Gil replied.

"It's really not bad!" Ferdy protested.

"What, then?"

"Oh, it's just that everyone's saying how dashed pretty Lady Stanhope is and wondering why you kept her up in the wilds so long. Must say—trifle surprised m'self, Gil! I always thought she was supposed to be an antidote!"

"Did you? I never said so, Ferd!"

Ferdy's brow crumpled as he considered this. "No, don't believe you did, old man," he agreed at last. "Might have been James who told me. Or maybe Dray. Can't recall. Anyway, it's what everyone thought, what with your lady always being up north and never coming to Town." He blinked at Gil with innocent good humour.

Gil felt sick. He'd prided himself on never actively maligning Rose after their marriage—not even to James. As far as he was concerned, what lay between them was private, and the full truth of his resentment was unknown to anyone else. His friends had never spoken of Rose to him—nor had anyone else. She'd never been to Town, was completely unknown to the *Ton.* But *of course* they'd wondered about her. Even Ferdy—blinkered, horse-mad, oblivious Ferdy—had wondered about her.

And now they were turning up in their droves to find out why he'd exiled her for so long. He realised Ferdy was looking at him with a worried expression.

"Have I spoken out of turn, old man?"

Gil smiled tightly. It was an effort, but he did it. "Not at all. Aren't you going to tell me about that pair of greys you bought last week?"

Ferdy needed no more encouragement. He launched into a horsey monologue, a paean to the virtues of his matched greys. It wasn't long before Gil found his attention wandering back to his wife.

It was far too easy to look at her. She was perfectly in his eye line, sitting beside Gertie on a small sofa, talking and laughing.

She looked delightful when she laughed. She looked delightful when she did many things, of course: when she danced, when she looked up at him from her writing desk with a distracted expression, when she was kind to untalented would-be poets. But he did especially love the way she laughed. He loved the way she was hiding her laugh behind her hand as she listened to Gertie, her merry silver eyes sparkling above. Loved the beautiful quirk of her lips. Loved her—

Loved her.

He loved her.

Chapter Eighteen

November 1814

"Are you ready, Rose?"

Gil walked into his wife's bedchamber to find the maid fastening a pearl pendant around Rose's neck and Rose herself fiddling with an earring.

"Almost."

He sat in the chair by the fire to wait. A few moments later, the maid stepped back, and Rose dropped her arms to her sides. Both women stared at her reflection in the mirror critically. Gil was rather less objective. He thought she looked delicious. Her satin gown was the colour of clotted cream with some sort of gauzy gold overdress. Creamy pearls bobbed at her ears and kissed the tops of her breasts. Another of those fairy queen ensembles, he thought.

"The pearls look very well, milady," the maid said after a moment. "Much better than the other."

Rose nodded. "Yes, you're right. Would you put the others away before you go, Sarah?"

Sarah lifted a number of other pieces from the dressing table and took them away. Then, with a curtsey, she quietly withdrew from the chamber. Rose wasn't quite finished, though. She touched scent to her throat and wrists, subtly rouged her cheeks and lips, fiddled with a hair comb.

Gil enjoyed watching her get ready like this. Her ordinary little movements were bewitching and seductive to him. And it was, after all, the only intimacy he enjoyed these days.

Lord, but he was feeling frustrated. It was weeks since he'd shared her bed. Rose had given him no sign that he was welcome to return, and he would make no assumptions about that again. The next time he came to her—if there was a next time—he wanted to be sure she was willing. He would wait to be invited.

He would happily forgo this evening's entertainment. They'd been inundated with invitations these last weeks and had been out every evening—he longed for a night without small talk. But tonight's invitation was one that could not be declined. It was the dinner Dray and Tilly were holding in their honour. He wished he could spend the evening peeling away Rose's gown instead. Tasting those delicious breasts...

"There is something I've been meaning to mention to you, Gil," Rose said, her voice distracting him from his pleasant thoughts. He tore his gaze away from the expanse of creamy bosom revealed by her gown and looked up to meet her gaze, suddenly aware that his enjoyment of the view was very visible. He crossed one leg over the other to disguise his erection. But it didn't appear Rose had noticed. In fact, she was looking rather preoccupied, stroking the underside of her wedding ring with her left thumb, a nervous habit he'd recently noticed.

"Oh yes?"

"It's to do with my father."

Gil went very still. Miles Davenport had not been spoken of by either of them for months, but still, the mere mention of him made Gil's gut tighten. Words could not do justice to the level of antipathy he felt toward the man.

He glanced at Rose and saw she had noticed his reaction and was dismayed. He was sorry for that, but not so sorry he could hide his feelings.

"Papa is coming back to England," she said.

Miles Davenport had been obliging enough to leave England mere weeks after Gil's wedding to Rose, but Gil had always known he'd be back one day.

"When will he arrive?" he asked, and his calm voice was deceptive. Inside, he could feel all the pent-up anger he had against the man beginning to roil.

Rose took a deep breath. "His ship is expected to dock on Monday."

"The day after tomorrow!"

"Yes." She studied his left shoulder.

"How long have you known?"

Her cheeks pinkened, and she avoided his gaze. "Not long—I'm not supposed to know at all. It's meant to be a surprise. Nev told me by mistake."

"Oh, how lovely!" Gil bit out, his voice tight with fury. "Dear old Uncle Nev, eh?"

Rose looked wounded. "I thought you didn't mind him visiting anymore?" she said. "You haven't said anything about his calling on me."

"Mind? Why should I mind a scoundrel with a reputation like his visiting my house and monopolising my wife?"

"He doesn't monopolise me!" Rose protested, then added, "Oh, Gil, let's not argue about Nev. He's really not important." She looked miserable, and Gil felt slightly guilty about his schoolboy jealousy, and for making this task that she'd probably dreaded even harder for her.

"Papa's going to be staying with Nev to begin with—" she continued. She let the unspoken remainder of that sentence hang in the air hopefully. But Gil didn't pick it up. He didn't want Miles Davenport in this house. He just didn't. He knew it would be considered very odd indeed if Miles did not stay with his daughter and her husband when he had no establishment of his own in town, but Gil really couldn't bear the alternative. Making bland small talk with the man over his dining table. Trying to put on a show of amiability in front of the servants.

"That's good," he said firmly. "He'll get on very well with Grayson. They're old friends, after all."

"Perhaps for a short visit, but I really do feel he should come to us for—"

"No, Rose." His voice, when it emerged, was colder than he'd intended, and Rose stared at him, lips slightly parted, grey eyes troubled.

After a tense moment, she said, "You can't mean that. He's my *father.*"

Distantly, Gil was amazed that she *wanted* the man to stay here. After all, Gil was not the only one with reason to resent the man. Did it not occur to Rose that her father had acquired a husband for her in the worst way? That he had let her hitch herself to a man who was seething with anger and resentment and then waltzed off on his travels for five years, leaving her to sink or swim? The fact she had swum owed nothing to Miles Davenport. Or to himself, admittedly.

"I do mean it," he said, more calmly. "It will be much better for your father to stay with Grayson."

"Better for who? Not for me!"

"Yes. Better for you. And for everyone. If he stays here, we are bound to argue. I will not be able to stay silent about the past if he is here."

When he saw the hurt expression his comment provoked, he almost asked her to ignore everything he'd just said. Almost.

"You cannot even *try,*" she whispered.

"You shouldn't ask it of me," he replied implacably. "It is not fair. Your father—what he did..."

She stared at him in silence for several beats, looking utterly defeated. "We're never going to get past this," she said at last, almost more to herself than to him. "I was stupid. I thought we could overcome it. I thought that eventually, given time, you could put the past aside, if I could." She looked at him squarely. Her expression was an odd mix of anger and disappointment. "But you can't, can you?"

Gil met her gaze and shook his head. "I can't have him

202

living here under my roof."

"And I can't not," she replied flatly. "So where does that leave us?"

How could she not *see* what her father was? The man was an immoral, unfeeling cad who had shown about as much regard for his daughter as for a brood mare.

"It is my house," he said grimly. "I will decide who may and who may not set foot in it."

Her eyes glittered with sudden anger, and her cheeks flushed. "Yes, this is *your* house. And I am *your* wife," she said, her voice beginning to rise. "I am only too aware that I have nothing of my own anymore! I gave up my life at Weartham, my independence—for, for *this*! A life of pointless bloody entertainments that bore me tears. And I can't even invite my own father to stay with me! My God! I must have been mad!"

She was shouting by the end, her voice cracking with emotion. She whirled away from him, dashing tears from her eyes. Within two strides, he had her wrist in his hand and was pulling her round to face him.

"Rose—"

"Let me go, you big brute!" she cried, hitting out at his shoulder with her free hand.

He kept hold of her wrist, his grip firm but careful. "Rose, please, just listen."

"No! I won't listen to you anymore!" she cried wildly. "I know you hate him—you don't have to explain that to me again! I understand why you feel wronged. But he is my father, and despite everything, I love him. And I've *missed* him. I haven't seen him for five years. God, don't you know what it is—" She broke off, staring up at him with wet eyes, then looked away and said, "Don't you know what it is to be lonely?"

He felt like he'd been punched. Like all the air had been knocked out of him.

Slowly, he unfurled the fingers around her wrist, releasing

her. He wanted to say, *Sorry*. Or, *Yes, I'm lonely now*. But he stayed silent, and she turned away from him, going to the mirror to shakily smooth her coiffure.

"We should go," she said, and when she turned back, she looked like a fairy queen again. "We are the guests of honour, after all. It would be rude to be late."

Chapter Nineteen

Thank God she wasn't sitting with Gil, Rose thought. They couldn't have been farther apart, in fact. Rose was next to Mr. Drayton at one end of the long table and Gil was at the other, next to Mrs. Drayton.

Mr. Drayton was an attentive host, but he had another lady on his left to entertain while the middle-aged gentleman on Rose's right had little to say for himself. She had ample opportunity, therefore, to observe her husband talking with Mrs. Drayton. It did not appear that he felt similarly compelled to check on her.

Mrs. Drayton looked ethereally lovely in pale blue silk, her golden hair dressed simply. Gil gave her all his attention, listening to every word she spoke with apparent fascination and laughing aloud several times. As for Mrs. Drayton, she beamed back at Gil, her expression fond.

Rose pushed her resentment determinedly aside. Gil was friends with Mr. Drayton—of course he would be friendly with Mrs. Drayton too. And it was no wonder he was making the most of Mrs. Drayton's smiling, happy company after their bitter row earlier.

It was no wonder either that he couldn't bear her father. She knew he had some justification. Even now, though, she felt *wronged*. Why should she keep paying for the sins of her father? Indeed, why did she have to keep paying for her own sin, that stupid—all right, downright *egregious*—error she'd made in pretending to be someone else? Yes, it had been wrong, but hadn't she paid enough? And after all, her stupid, impulsive, *egregious* decision had been brought about by Gil's neglect of her for five long years. The sense of being wronged burned within her, side by side with the regret she couldn't rid herself of in relation to her own behaviour.

Her depressing thoughts were interrupted when the lady across the table caught her eye. Mrs. Hornby, Rose recalled, from the introductions earlier.

The woman flicked her gaze at Gil and back again. "Your husband is a great favourite with the ladies, Lady Stanhope." The words were very faintly slurred, and she immediately lifted her wineglass and drank deeply.

Rose glanced around self-consciously, but no one else appeared to be listening.

"My husband is an amiable man," she replied and looked down, giving her plate her close attention.

"Oh yes," Mrs. Hornby replied. "Lady Cairn certainly found him to be so."

Rose couldn't stop herself looking up, the words leaving her lips before she could stop them. "And did you...?" She broke off, but Mrs. Hornby understood her.

"Not I, no. I've been as faithful to Captain Hornby as the day is long." She raised her glass again in a silent toast and drained it, setting it on the table noisily. "More fool me."

Mrs. Hornby's voice had begun to rise and become belligerent, seeking out a wider audience. To Rose's horror, the other guests began to stir. They continued their individual conversations with their neighbors, but there was a discreet watchfulness about them now, an awareness that something was happening at Rose's end of the table no one wanted to miss. Rose glanced quickly at Gil. He could hear nothing of what had been said by Mrs. Hornby from where he sat, but he looked at her quizzically, clearly realising something was going on. Rose looked away.

Mrs. Hornby gestured to a footman to pour more wine for her. A stern-looking man on Mrs. Hornby's left—Captain

Hornby, presumably—leaned toward her and muttered something in her ear, dismissing the footman with a wave of his hand. Mrs. Hornby hissed something back at him, and when he pulled away, his cheekbones were stained with red. His wife took another gulp of wine and fixed her gaze on Mr. Drayton.

"Mr. Drayton," she called out in a strident voice. All eyes turned to her, glasses and forks halted mid-motion. "Aren't you going to propose a toast to Lord and Lady Stanhope? Are we not here to celebrate their—" She broke off for a moment, befuddled and frowning. "Indeed, Mr. Drayton, pray tell, what *are* we celebrating?" She looked around the table at the other guests. There was an awful silence that was broken by a nervous titter. Rose felt her cheeks burning but kept her gaze defiantly up, her fingers crushing her napkin in her lap.

"An excellent notion—" Mr. Drayton began in a determinedly cheerful voice. He scraped his chair backward to stand up, holding his wineglass half aloft, but before he could say more, Mrs. Hornby interjected again.

"Oh, I know!" she cried. "Let us drink to Lady Stanhope's *remarkable* forbearance. Such a fine quality in a lady!" She stood abruptly, and her own chair fell back, landing on the floor with a loud clatter. She staggered slightly, sloshing wine over herself and the table. The same footman rushed forward to lift her chair.

"Lydia!" Captain Hornby was standing now too, his expression quite furious, his colour high. "Stop this at once! You are embarrassing Mr. and Mrs. Drayton and their guests."

"Oh, am I?" she cried. It was a cry of anger and disbelief, but then she looked around the table, at the faces of the guests, and said it again, this time in a faintly horrified tone. "Am I?" Everyone looked away, embarrassed by her display of emotion.

The captain ignored her. He turned to Mr. Drayton. "I beg your pardon, but I believe my wife is unwell. I must take her home." He took her arm, and she sagged against him. "Mrs. Drayton," the captain added with a nod in his hostess's

Joanna Chambers

direction. "My sincerest apologies."

Mr. Drayton rose from the table to see the Hornbys out. It was only when the door closed behind them that Rose finally looked at Gil. He was staring at her, a haunted expression on his face. Their eyes met for barely a moment before she looked away.

Gradually, the tinkle of cutlery against plates and the swell of muted conversation brought the room back to life. When Mr. Drayton rejoined his guests, he initiated a spirited conversation about a production of *MacBeth* he and his wife had seen the previous evening. Several others at Rose's end of the table had also seen it, and a lively debate ensued of its merits and flaws. Mr. Drayton sought Rose's opinion on both Shakespeare and the play, despite the fact she hadn't seen the performance under discussion. She was grateful to him, even though part of her would much rather have sunk through the floor. Her involvement in the conversation was halfhearted at best, and soon she'd lost the thread of it. All she could think about was that all the world knew her husband had had scores of other women since his marriage to her.

It was no surprise Gil's actions were common knowledge. She'd read the scandal sheets herself, hadn't she? But it was one thing to know it. It was quite another to have someone point it out publicly; to really understand the degree and depth of that universal knowledge.

It felt like hours until the meal finally came to an end and Mrs. Drayton rose to lead the ladies to the drawing room for tea, leaving the gentlemen to their port. Rose couldn't bear to even glance at Gil on her way out. She walked past him, staring straight ahead, aware of his eyes upon her even as she resolutely ignored him.

In the drawing room, she drank tea and joined in the chitchat about the latest fashions. It was torture. All she wanted was to go home. After a while, she drifted away from the other ladies and made her way to the pianoforte. She began sheafing through the music, seeking something to play. Preferably something familiar. Her fingers were still trembling. After a few minutes, one of the other ladies joined her. She was a pretty, plump woman, married to a forgettable baronet. Lady Charlotte something or other.

"I felt so sorry for you at dinner, Lady Stanhope," the woman murmured in a low voice, too quiet for the other ladies to hear, "being subjected to that awful display by Mrs. Hornby. Like as not she has just found out her husband has been friendly with a certain actress for some months now!" Lady Charlotte's blue eyes shone bright as she shared this nugget. Rose felt sick.

"The poor lady was perhaps unwell," Rose murmured noncommittally. Lady Charlotte snorted.

"She must be five and thirty and has been married to Captain Hornby for a dozen years. It has taken her a great deal of time to discover what most of us learn very early in marriage. Men are faithless creatures." She shrugged. "But there is nothing to be done about it."

Rose gripped the sheaf of music between her hands while the other woman prattled on and on.

"I am lucky, I suppose," she mused complacently. "With my husband, there has only been one other woman. A mistress he has had since before we married three years ago." She paused and laid her hand on Rose's arm, her expression sympathetic. "I can't even imagine what it must have been like for you, my dear." When Rose stayed silent, Lady Charlotte's hand fell away, and her smile gradually died, to be replaced by a look of anxious concern.

Rose couldn't move, couldn't speak. Everything in her was given over to fighting back the tears that had risen to clog her throat and prick her eyes.

"Oh dear!" Lady Charlotte whispered, palpably dismayed. "I do apologise, Lady Stanhope. Joshua is always saying I have a tendency to prattle on."

Just at that moment, the gentlemen entered, and Lady Charlotte hurriedly excused herself. She joined her faithless husband, a man who looked like a bemused sheep. Rose stayed where she was, next to the pianoforte. When she looked back at the music sheets in her hands, they were too blurry to make out, just something to direct her hot, aching eyes at so no one would see the tears that threatened to fall. Eventually, Mrs. Drayton came to her rescue.

"Gilbert tells me you play the pianoforte, Lady Stanhope," she said in a friendly way. "Would you be good enough to entertain us? I am afraid I am a woeful musician."

"Yes, of course. I love to play. And this is a lovely instrument." She smiled her thanks at Mrs. Drayton and settled herself on the piano stool, her back to the room, safe from the curious eyes of the other guests, her lowered head excusable now.

She flexed her fingers. In the background, the conversation murmured.

Bach's Goldberg Variations. So well-known to her she didn't need the music; her fingers found the notes of the opening aria unerringly. She let herself linger over the notes and pauses of the music, playing it the way she did at home, more slowly than was conventional, the melody giving voice to the aching sadness in her heart.

The variations were soothing to play. All that mathematical precision, that intellectual beauty. But at the end, when she played the Aria da capo, it was like waking up again, waking up and remembering the real music. Not the dazzling fireworks but something so real she felt it deep in her body.

As the last notes resonated through the drawing room, she realised the rest of the guests had fallen silent and were all watching her. Surprised applause erupted, and Mrs. Drayton asked her to play again. Rose demurred that she'd already monopolised the instrument too long, and eventually, two other guests were prevailed upon to perform while Rose drifted back to the main part of the room.

Gil rose from his chair and walked toward her, smiling, though with a hint of uncertainty about his eyes.

"That was beautiful," he said when he reached her, his voice low and intimate. "I remember you playing that piece at Weartham, but it sounded very different tonight."

She frowned, thinking back to his arrival at Weartham two months before. "I don't recall playing that at Weartham when you were there."

"Oh, you did. When I first took you there, I mean, after our wedding. You played it straight through without any music, and I remember how impressed I was."

Rose stared at him, surprised he remembered something she'd evidently forgotten from all those years ago. Even more surprised that she'd impressed him.

"Would you like some tea?" he asked.

"I'd rather go home," she replied, her voice barely above a whisper.

Gil looked rueful. "We should stay a little longer, if you can bear it. We *are* the guests of honour."

He was right, of course, and she sighed and nodded her agreement, allowing him to lead her to a chair and fetch her a cup of tea.

She made an effort to converse with the other guests seated around them, but it was a trial. The last thing she wanted to do was to make idle chitchat. After a while, she excused herself and made her way to the ladies' withdrawing room, for no other reason than that she longed to be alone, if only for a few minutes.

She was just reaching out her hand to push the door open when the first voice spoke up, ringing with astonishment.

"He was *engaged* to Tilly Drayton? *Lord Stanhope?*"

Rose's hand dropped before it made contact with the wood.

Her breathing stilled, and her heart began to beat fast. Another voice answered.

"Shhhh..." it admonished. Then, "Not formally engaged, but everyone knew they had an understanding. It was just a case of waiting for the announcement. And then, all of a sudden, it was announced he'd married *her*, a girl not even out yet!"

"Perhaps he realised he wasn't in love with Mrs. Drayton after all," the other voice suggested in a wistful tone.

"No, it wasn't that." That assurance came promptly, smug with knowledge.

"How do you know?"

"*Well*—" The second voice grew confiding, promising a delicious revelation. "It was a very good friend of Tilly Drayton herself that told me—now, Martha, you mustn't ever tell anyone this—"

"Of course I won't!"

"I mean it, Martha. My friend was sworn to secrecy by Tilly Drayton." She paused while the other muttered assurances before she carried on, her voice more hushed now. "Well, apparently, Stanhope *had* to marry Lady Stanhope—something to do with debts—and he was *distraught* about it. Told Tilly his wife-to-be was hideous or something and how he could never love anyone but Tilly—"

"She's hardly hideous!"

"Not now, but apparently she used to look very different. And that's something I've heard from quite a *few* people..."

The sound of one of the speakers moving in the withdrawing room, skirts swishing, footsteps falling, broke Rose's frozen concentration. She stepped back, tiptoeing halfway down the corridor before turning back and walking forward again, making her approach audible this time. By the time she entered the withdrawing room, the two ladies were chatting about their children. They looked up and greeted her, one's cheeks a little pink with embarrassment. Rose forced herself to converse pleasantly with them for a few minutes until she was quite sure they believed she'd overheard nothing.

When she returned to the main drawing room, she felt oddly dazed. She accepted yet more tea and joined a conversation about bonnets, in a desultory way. She was aware of Gil on the other side of the room, talking to two older gentlemen and sending her concerned glances. Later, she noticed Tilly Drayton approaching him and, helplessly, her gaze was drawn to the two of them, again and again. They talked for a long time, and Gil smiled fondly at his old love as she twinkled charmingly up at him. They looked well-suited, everything between them easy and familiar and amiable.

Tilly Drayton. Gil's lost love. Sweet, beautiful and biddable.

No wonder he'd hated Rose. No wonder he'd resented marrying her so very, very much.

It was another full hour before they were finally able to depart, and by the time Rose climbed into the carriage, she felt utterly exhausted. As soon as the door closed, she let her head fall back against the leather upholstery and closed her eyes. Her face ached with the effort of maintaining her social smile, and a dull, insistent headache had settled behind her eyes.

It wasn't just physical tiredness, though. She felt thoroughly down.

It was unlike her to be like this. Even at her worst moments, she'd never felt quite so bleak. But tonight had been singularly awful. First her argument with Gil, then Mrs. Hornby, and finally her discovery about Mrs. Drayton. And underneath all that was a roiling, resentful anger against Gil. That he had agreed to marry her and then abandoned her; that he had made her an object of gossip and pity. Those women had known everything: that he hadn't wanted to marry her; that he'd been forced to. It seemed that *everyone* had known except Rose herself.

He'd even told Tilly how ugly Rose had been.

She should hate him. She really should. But all she felt was wounded, and the only person she hated was herself. Five years ago, she'd been weak and timid and silent. She'd had doubts, but she'd married him anyway, and then she'd let him walk away and leave her. And when she'd finally worked up the courage to face up to him? She'd lied about who she was.

Her gaze flicked to the other side of the carriage. Gil was watching her with a troubled expression.

"Are you all right?" he asked.

"I have the headache," she muttered. She could see that her words did not reassure him. But then, they were not meant to. They were only intended to stop the conversation. If he forced her to speak, she didn't think she'd be able to control herself. All of her jumbled, anguished thoughts would come spilling out of her.

They accomplished the rest of the journey back to Stanhope House in silence.

When they arrived back at Stanhope House, Gil followed Rose into her bedchamber, closing the door behind him and leaning against the paneled wood. Rose ignored him, calmly walking to the armoire to remove the pearls at her throat and ears.

Her self-possession astonished him sometimes. All through that awful scene with Mrs. Hornby, she'd looked controlled and dignified, wearing the same expression he remembered from their wedding day. Calm, collected, bland. The same expression she wore now. It worried him now, that look of hers.

"We must talk, Rose." He levered himself away from the wall and walked toward her, though he didn't try to touch her. "What happened tonight—it was embarrassing for both of us, but we must get it in perspective. Mrs. Hornby was really quite foxed. I realise it upset you, but it is not something that should happen again."

Rose gave an odd laugh, a scornful, disbelieving sound, and shook her head. She began to unpin her hair. Evidently, she did not intend to answer him.

"Rose—" He touched her arm lightly, but she jerked it away.

"Don't touch me!" she hissed, and just like that, the mask cracked. Her eyes glittered with angry tears that she dashed away impatiently.

Gil stepped away, watching with concern as she began wrenching pins out of her hair until it tumbled around her shoulders, then pulled violently at her gown, trying to reach the buttons at the back. He knew she wouldn't want his assistance, but when he heard the delicate fabric tearing, he stepped toward her again.

"Let me help you—"

"Just leave me alone," she cried and moved farther out of his reach. "I don't want you in here, Gil. Not tonight."

"But we should talk about what happened."

"There's nothing to talk about," she gritted out and began hauling at her dress again. He didn't see how she was ever going to reach the damned buttons.

"For God's sake—" He reached out to her.

"Leave me alone!" she cried, backing away from him till the wall prevented her retreating any farther, a wave of hostility coming off her that was almost physical in its force.

He dragged his hand through his hair in frustration. "Why are you so angry with me, Rose? It wasn't my fault Mrs. Hornby arrived in a drunken state."

"I don't care about Mrs. Hornby! Tonight was farce enough without her assistance. A dinner in our honour? With you fawning all over Mrs. Drayton at the top of the table?" She laughed harshly. "Although it is a fitting tribute to our marriage, I must admit."

Was she was jealous? Of Tilly? He almost smiled.

"Tilly and I are merely friends," he said soothingly. "I can assure you that she is quite devoted to Dray. She would never look at another man."

It was her sudden stillness that made him realise his attempt at reassurance had fallen flat. She stared at him until his smile faded, and he felt himself shifting uncomfortably under her steady gaze.

"I know she's the woman you wanted to marry, Gil."

His mouth felt suddenly dry. "How?"

"I overheard some ladies—they were gossiping about it."

His immediate reaction was anger. No one other than he, Tilly and their respective families had known about the almost-engagement—but Tilly must have told someone. Then he saw Rose's distraught expression, and his own resentment withered.

"I'm sorry you heard about it in that way," he said. "But it's in the past, and there's nothing I can do about it. Yes, I was going to marry Tilly. But things changed. I married you, and Tilly married Dray—"

And I'm not in love with her—I'm in love with you. But he didn't say that. *Couldn't* say it. It would have been easier to stick his hand in the fireplace.

Rose shook her head in a helpless gesture. "I know you can't do anything about your past with Tilly. But the way you behaved after we married was something you *could* have helped. You chose to break your vows and dishonour me. And you chose to do it publicly so that everyone knew."

He stared at her, bewildered. "Why drag this up now? It's in the past."

She looked right at him with those clearwater eyes of hers. "Is it?"

He was appalled at the implication. "Of course!" he exclaimed. "*All* of that is in the past. There has been no one else, not since I met you at Grayson's ball. When we met that

216

night, I was..." He braced himself, determined to try to make her understand. "God, Rose, I was *undone*, don't you realise that? Don't you know what that night did to me? Don't you know what *you* did to me?"

Gil swallowed. Just saying that much made him feel raw and exposed. And it didn't work anyway. Rose still looked angry. Completely unmoved by the words he'd forced out with such difficulty. But really, what had he expected? Gratification that she'd brought him so easily to his knees?

Well, there was nothing like that in her gaze, just weary anger and disappointment. And it was then, in that moment, that he realised, not only that he was in danger of losing her— he might have lost her already.

"You could have a mistress right now, and I wouldn't know," she said in a flat little voice.

"There is no one else!" he protested, shaken. "You must believe me, Rose! You are my wife now."

"I was your wife before," she pointed out.

He forced himself to be honest. "It didn't feel like that to me." And that was the truth of the matter. He'd gone through the wedding ceremony and consummated the marriage, but he hadn't felt like he owed her commitment or fidelity. Not then.

"So, what happened to make me suddenly *become* your wife, Gil?" she asked, voice icy.

"You know. We became lovers. You became pregnant with my child."

"I don't need to be your wife to be your lover or, indeed, to carry your child," she replied. "There is only one thing that makes me your wife, and it is not the fact that I lie beneath you when you want me or that you planted your seed in me. The only thing that makes me your *wife* is that farce of a wedding ceremony we went through five years ago. The fact that I'm carrying your child doesn't change what happened then. You can't *pretend* the last five years never happened because it suits you now. You can't expect me to forget it!" Her voice had risen by the end of her speech, and her face was flushed, the depth of her anger and resentment suddenly very clear.

Two months ago, Gil had thought himself very magnanimous, offering to forget the Eve episode and proposing that they get on with their marriage for the sake of the child. In truth, he'd taken it rather as read that his part of their shared history was forgiven. Or, perhaps, he thought with painful honesty, that it didn't need to be forgiven.

"I didn't realise you felt this way," he said, feeling desperate now. "And I wish to God there was something I could do about it. But there is not. We have to put it behind us."

"No, we don't," she retorted, "We don't have to put it behind us at all. Why should *I* forget the past? *You* won't! You won't even let my father sleep under the same roof as you because of the past."

She turned and stormed away from him and into her dressing room. At first, he just stared after her. Not her father again! How had everything got back to Miles Davenport? The very mention of the man was like a red rag to him, but he was determined not to be riled. Rose's tears over Davenport earlier had made him feel like the lowest sort of cad. He wanted time to think over her request that Davenport stay with them properly before they spoke about the man again.

By the time he followed her into the dressing room, she had managed to get the dress off somehow and was stripping away her stockings with sharp, angry movements.

"Don't bring your father into this argument," he said calmly. "My views about him are between him and me. They have nothing to do with you."

"*What!*" she cried, lifting her head to stare at him in disbelief. "They have *everything* to do with me. The reason you hate him is because you were forced to marry *me*."

"I hate him because he blackmailed me into a course of

action I did not choose," Gil corrected through clenched teeth.

"He did not blackmail you," she retorted, enunciating each word slowly and clearly as though he was an imbecile.

"He blackmailed my father. It is the same thing."

She ignored his warning tone. "For God's sake, Gil!" she cried. "When are you going to face up to the fact that it was *your* father who did this to you? Yours. *He* gambled away your family's property, no one else!"

The silence that followed was crashing. It was one thing for him to think such things of his father. It was quite another to hear the words from someone else's mouth.

"I'm sorry!" she snapped eventually, breaking the silence, though her angry tone belied her words. "But it's true, and if anyone needs to put the past behind him, it's you, not me. I've spent every day of the last few months putting the past behind me. Every day, telling myself not to mind, that it doesn't matter. Every day, that the past is the past. And then tonight—" She broke off, shaking her head. "Tonight, I realised that it does matter. That I hate what you've done to me. When I think of the—God, *years*—that I've wasted, hoping..." She broke off again, and they stared at one another across a silence that grew heavy with five years of accusations and bitterness.

He saw, at last, what he'd done to her. And he hated himself.

"I truly did not think," he said at last, "that you would hear about the—the other women. I certainly did not think you would care. You said—the night before I left you at Weartham after the wedding—you said you never wanted me to touch you again. That you wanted nothing further to do with me."

"And do you blame me?"

"No. No, I don't. I know I behaved abominably. All I can say is that I felt so very..." He paused, searching for the words that would explain his appalling behavior, and added finally, inadequately. "Cheated."

She gave another of those scornful laughs. "Well, you were not the only one. I thought I was marrying someone willing. When I learned how you really felt, I wanted to shrivel up and die."

He swallowed, sick at heart. "I'm sorry, Rose."

She turned away from him and opened a drawer of the armoire. There was something about her bowed head and slumped shoulders that made him want to pull her to him and never let her go but he knew, instinctively, that she'd shove him away. Instead, he stood, impotently waiting as she selected a nightgown from the drawer. Only then did she let the last layer of her clothing, her shift, fall in a puddle around her feet.

For a moment, she was naked, the elegant line of her back long and ivory-pale in the candlelight. The next moment, white linen spilled down her body to cover her, pure and demure and remote.

When she turned back to him, all the anger seemed to have gone out of her. She looked bone-weary.

"For what it's worth," she said dully, "I'm sorry you had to marry me. If I'd known you were unwilling—if I'd known you were all but promised to Tilly Drayton, I'd never have agreed to it. But there's nothing to be done about it now. Your love is married to someone else, and you are married to me."

Her hand went to her belly. He wanted to slide his own hand over hers. Wanted to feel his child inside her and tell her how much the baby—her and the baby both—meant to him. But when he reached out to her, she flinched back.

"Rose, please, I—"

"I wish I could release you," she continued, interrupting him. "But there is the child to think of." The sight of her small hand resting protectively against her belly made him ache.

"I don't want to be released," he whispered. "Everything's different now."

I love you.

Maybe he was a coward, but he didn't think Rose would welcome a declaration of love from him right now. Plainly, she did not return his feelings, and that discovery, though hardly a revelation, was proving to be surprisingly painful. "I never wanted to hurt you," he said instead, after a careful pause. "I was selfish and thoughtless, but I did not *intend* to cause you pain."

She sighed and looked away. "I'm tired." And he could see that she was, her eyes shadowed with weariness, her face drawn with exhaustion.

"I'll leave you to your rest," he said. "We'll talk again in the morning."

"Fine," she said tonelessly, not even looking at him.

He let himself out of the bedchamber as she was climbing into bed. Once he'd closed the door behind him, he leaned against the wall for a moment, feeling gutted and empty.

The house was unbearably quiet, the atmosphere heavy in the aftermath of their dispute. He had no wish to spend the rest of the night here, replaying their conversation in his mind.

He strode downstairs and called for the carriage.

Chapter Twenty

The first twinge woke Rose in the early hours of the morning.

She came to, blearily blinking into the blackness. And then she felt a cramping pain, low in her abdomen. After a moment or two, it was gone, but in that moment she came to full wakefulness, fear quickened her heart. She lay in the dark, her eyes wide and alert, staring at the ceiling as she waited.

Nothing.

Several minutes passed of nothing. Her panic faded, and her eyelids began to droop. And then it happened again. The same low cramping she was used to experiencing during her courses.

And she knew.

She put her hand between her thighs, and her fingers found unexpectedness wetness, a sticky, quick-drying sort of wetness. Even in the profound darkness of this ungodly hour, she could see that whatever coated her fingers had colour. And she could smell the faint coppery tang of blood.

"No," she whispered into the indifferent darkness. "No, God, no."

Shaking, she sat up.

"Gil!" she called. Then again, louder. "Gil!"

He couldn't hear her. She sat up and got out of bed. Her legs felt wobbly. She felt something trickling down her thigh in a thin line as she stumbled to the connecting door between their chambers. She could ring for Sarah, but she wanted her husband.

"Gil!" she cried again as she fumbled with the door. Another cramp seized her, more insistent than the last. Her thighs felt sticky. She threw the door open. "Gil?"

He wasn't there.

His bed was untouched, the coverlet pristine, the pillows plump and smooth.

With a choked cry, she went back to her own room and reached for the bell.

Sarah arrived minutes later, a wrapper over her nightgown, a candle in her hand. She looked concerned. Rose never rang in the night. "Milady?"

"It's the baby, Sarah," Rose said wildly.

Sarah's eyes flickered around the room. Rose saw her noticing something on the floor. She followed the direction of Sarah's gaze. Blood. A trail of fat drips from the bed to the connecting door. The maid's face went white. "I'll send Jenkins for the doctor," she said and dashed out.

She was soon back, followed by a scullery maid with an armful of linen.

"Sarah," Rose whimpered. "I'm frightened."

"You'll be all right, milady," the maid said reassuringly, but her gaze held concern, and she didn't mention the baby. Not that she needed to. Rose knew the baby wasn't going to be all right. She was not quite five months pregnant. The baby was dead. Or soon would be.

By the time the doctor arrived, the cramps had become quite painful. Rose lay on her back, and, after a brief examination, the doctor took her hand in his and looked into her eyes.

"My dear," he said. "You know you are miscarrying, don't you?"

She nodded. She had known since she saw her fingers coated in her own blood. And yet, to hear it confirmed by this stranger made it real. Tears leaked from the outer corners of her eyes and trickled through her hair to soak into the pillow beneath her head.

The doctor calmly told her that the next hour or two would be rather like having a baby, that her body was going to expel the foetus. He told her he would stay with her and examine what came out to make sure nothing was left inside. If it all came out all right, she would be fine. She would recover. In all likelihood, she would become pregnant again. All would be well. She would be a mother some other time.

She was grateful to him for his soothing words and did her best to believe him—about the being-all-right part, anyway. She knew she would never be pregnant again. Once Gil realised she was no longer having his child, he would not be so keen to have a real marriage. He had lost interest in having her in his bed weeks ago. And tonight, they had argued again. She had become a burden and a bore.

The doctor confirmed her suspicion that the baby was dead. It was better that way, he said, because it meant the baby wouldn't suffer. He held her hand when he told her that. His hand was broad and warm and dry, and he stroked his thumb over her palm soothingly. And then he let her hand go and went to his bag to get his instruments out, and Sarah lit more candles until the room blazed with light. Rose watched as the doctor laid out a thick white cloth and placed his metal instruments on it. They looked barbaric.

It took another hour. The cramps got more intense and closer together, just as they were supposed to in childbirth. And as they reached their zenith, she sat up and got on her knees, driven by an inexplicable agitation.

"Milady," Sarah said, placing a hand on her arm. "Come, you should lie down."

"Leave her," the doctor said gently. "She knows what she's doing."

She thought, What does he mean? And then, in the midst of another cramp, she began to feel a new flowering of pain.

Sudden, surprising pressure brought her hands to the mattress in front of her and a soft, keening cry to her lips. And then there was a blooming sensation between her thighs, and her dead child began to emerge from her body, forced out by the convulsing of her womb. There was a moment of crowning pain and then an instant later, it left her body, warm and slick and rounded, and she cried out, with pain and with loss.

The doctor took the dead baby away from her to examine, all bundled up in a clean white linen.

Rose felt hollow. She stared at the bloodstains on the sheet, and all she could think was that everything had gone back to the way it was before. There was no baby. No Gil. She was alone again.

Warmth settled on her shoulders. A shawl. And Sarah's hands wrapping it round her. She patted the maid's hand with cold, shaking fingers.

"What's this?" a loud male voice demanded outside the door. "What are you doing out here at this hour?"

James. There was the sound of murmuring, then his voice again, quieter this time, though still audible.

"Is she all right?"

"Sarah," Rose pleaded. "Go and tell him what's happened. Make him go away."

Sarah hurried to the door and went out, closing it softly behind her. Rose could make out scraps of their conversation, particularly James's side.

"But where is my brother?" he demanded after a minute or two. Then, after hearing Sarah's response, he cursed and said, "I'll find him."

A few moments later, the door opened and closed again, and Sarah returned to her side. And then the doctor came over to tell her that he needed to examine her now to be sure everything had been evacuated. Rose couldn't suppress a shudder when he said that word, but she lay down obediently.

The doctor's hands were warm and intimate on her body. Mortifyingly thorough.

Eventually, it was over.

"There's nothing left inside," he said. Did he realise how his words pained her? "You must rest now, your ladyship. Keep to bed. I will come and see you tomorrow, and for a few days after to make sure all is well and that you do not succumb to fever."

She nodded wanly, uncaring, and the doctor departed with one last sad-kind smile.

And then there was Sarah, guiding her to the armchair and pressing hot, sweet tea into her hands and having the bed remade with clean linen. Helping her into a clean nightgown.

"Thank you, Sarah," she whispered as she crawled between the freshly laundered sheets.

"It'll be all right, milady," her maid said in her quiet, capable voice. Unflappable and certain.

"Yes," Rose lied.

Her eyelids felt like they were made of lead. She closed them. Heard Sarah depart, taking the light with her. At last it was dark and quiet again.

She slept.

Gil was relieved to see his brother.

"James!" he bellowed, waving.

He'd retreated to a corner of Belle Orton's gaming hell with a decanter of brandy after Ferdy had left him, grumbling about married fellows who should know better. Since then, he'd been alone with his thoughts. James was a welcome distraction.

"Come an' 'ave some of this brandy with me, Jimmy!" he slurred as James approached. He lifted the decanter in invitation, only to frown at its near emptiness .

"No, thanks," James said easily.

"Oh, don't be a spoilsport!" He stood unsteadily and threw an arm around his brother's shoulders, urging him toward the chair Ferdy had vacated but James resisted, disentangling himself with disconcerting ease.

"Not like you to refuse a drinky, Jim," Gil grumbled. He sat down again heavily, his knee colliding with the table, making him frown.

"You're drunk, Gil. You need to come home."

Gil shook his head. "The night's young."

"It's five o'clock in the morning, old man."

"Christ, is it?" Could it really be that time already?

"Come on." James hauled him upright. Gil rattled the table with his knee again and steadied himself by leaning on James, who stumbled slightly under his weight.

"Where we goin'?" he asked. He suspected, distantly, that if he were less drunk, he'd be embarrassed.

"I told you. Home."

"Lor' Jim, anywhere but there!" Gil protested, but he let James lead him out of the club and down the front steps to a waiting carriage. He felt dizzy and sick as James pushed him in, slumping heavily over one of the seats. James climbed in and settled on the opposite bench, slamming the door behind them. The carriage lurched sickeningly as they set off. The swaying motion and the smell of the leather upholstery made Gil want to vomit. He moaned a protest.

"Not like you to get like this, Gil," James observed mildly. "More my sort of thing."

"Rose and I had 'n argument." Gil explained, forcing himself to sit upright. He let his head fall back against the seat as a wave of sickness washed over him and closed his eyes. "'Bout all the women I had."

There was a brief silence. "Annoyed, is she?" James asked at last.

"Y' could say that," Gil said faintly. His stomach roiled unpleasantly. "Disgusted with me is more like it. Don't blame her."

"Better get you home then, old boy. Sober you up."

Gil couldn't open his eyes. "Hmmmm," he agreed. And then he must have drifted off into a half sleep, waking up only when the carriage reached Stanhope House.

It took him a few moments to get himself together, stumble out of the carriage and follow James. Once inside, Henry the footman took their greatcoats, then lit the way upstairs with a branch of candles. Feeling groggy and increasingly queasy, Gil climbed the stairs behind Henry, James at the rear. Halfway up, he tripped, cracking his chin on one of the steps. His stupid hands hadn't moved quickly enough to save him, and he stared at them, annoyed.

"Shhhh! Quiet!" James hissed behind him. He was being awfully stern. It was most unlike him.

"You need food, coffee and a bath." James declared when they reached Gil's bedchamber. He rang the bell rope, and after a few minutes, a grumpy-looking Crawford appeared. Gil let James give his valet instructions, while he slumped in an armchair, half asleep.

It wasn't until he was drinking his third cup of coffee in the bath some time later that it occurred to him to wonder why James was trying to sober him up, rather than just letting him sleep off his intoxication. Indeed, why had James come to find him and fetch him home? He'd never done such a thing before.

"What's going on?" His voice sounded oddly loud in the too-early morning silence of the house. James was lounging in the armchair now. And drinking coffee too. Before seven in the morning when he was never up till noon usually.

James's gaze was level, considering. "I couldn't let you see Rose in the state you were in," he said at last.

"Why on earth would I want to see Rose at the crack of

dawn?" Gil asked, but even as the words left his mouth, his brandy-soused brain was beginning to work, and he lurched up, spilling water over the side of the bath and splashing hot coffee on his chest.

"Something's wrong," he said suddenly, certain of it. "What is it?"

He could see by the expression on James's face that something *was* wrong, and he stood up in the bath, water streaming off his body as he climbed out, soaking the Persian rug.

"Is it Rose?" he demanded, reaching for a towel and beginning to quickly dry himself. He was aware of his heart pounding with anxiety. James looked guilty and uncertain. "It is, isn't it?"

"It's the baby," James muttered. "I'm so sorry, Gil."

The two men stared at one another, James concerned, Gil beyond shocked.

"Has she—has she lost the baby?" Gil asked eventually. "Oh Christ, is she *all right*? Jesus, James, why didn't you tell me something had happened before now?" He yanked the shirt Crawford had laid out for him over his head and reached for the pantaloons.

"I couldn't have told you anything in the state you were in, Gil! You needed to sober up first. It wouldn't have done either of you any good for you to go stumbling into her chamber reeking of brandy." James paused, looking away. "It was over by then anyway. It was over by the time I came looking for you."

Gil's hands shook as he fumbled with his buttons. He felt sick again, but this time not from the brandy. "What happened?"

"She miscarried during the night. When I came back at four this morning, there were servants milling around outside her chamber. I told her maid I'd fetch you home."

"Did you see her?" Gil asked shakily. "How was she?"

"I didn't see her," James said gently. "But her maid said she was as well as could be expected."

Gil stared at his brother, vaguely aware that he hadn't yet felt anything except panic. He tried to calm down, but all he could think was that he needed to see Rose. He glanced in the mirror and saw that he looked dreadful, like the drunk he was. His feet were bare, and his shirt gaped open. But he was just about decent enough to see her. At least he no longer stank of brandy. Without another word, he strode to the door that connected his chamber to Rose's.

"Gil?" James's uncertain voice halted him, and he turned back to his brother, whose expression was troubled. "Perhaps you should let her sleep."

"I won't wake her," Gil promised. "But I must see her."

Chapter Twenty-One

Rose didn't so much as stir when Gil entered her chamber. Her hair spilled richly over the pillow, a dark contrast to the pinched paleness of her face. Violet shadows were smudged under her eyes like bruises. Gil carefully pulled a chair up next to the bed and sat down to watch over her.

She was so still he put his hand above her mouth and nose, hovering a quarter of an inch above, just to check that she was still breathing.

There was no trace in her bedchamber of what had passed here while he had been away. The bedsheets were smooth, and Rose's nightgown was pristine. It shamed him that all the evidence of what had happened had been cleared away by the time he got here.

It was strange, but the baby had never been more real to him than now, when it no longer was. He had seen some hints of Rose's pregnancy—small, subtle changes to her body—but it hadn't been real to him yet. He hadn't thought of the baby as a person. Just a sort of vague idea. But now that there wasn't a baby anymore, he wondered about it, if it would have been a boy or a girl. And what had happened to its little body. Had it just been discarded? He felt intensely sad at the thought. But he didn't want to ask anyone, least of all Rose.

He felt sick with guilt too. He should have been here. While he had been getting drunk, Rose had been losing their child. He ached when he thought of her going through that ordeal alone, and of the baby that would never be. His absence would have been nothing new to Rose. He had defined himself as a husband by his absences. She would probably have expected no more of him.

During the hours that he sat watching his wife sleep, his head pounding and his gut rolling, Gil forced himself to face some painful truths. He'd been brought to his knees by guilt, grief and self-loathing this dawn. And suddenly, it was obvious to him that all he'd managed to do since he'd brought Rose to London was make her miserable. She'd been reasonably contented at Weartham. Loved, by Harriet and her friends. He'd torn her away from all that, from everything and everyone she was familiar with.

He admitted to himself, finally and now, that he'd made the decision to bring Rose to London out of sheer bloody-mindedness. Making her leave Weartham where she knew everyone, and come to London, where she knew no one, had served little purpose for all his talk of being seen to be reconciled. But it had been a way of making her dance to his tune; of showing her he was in charge and that her deception would not go unpunished.

He'd brought Rose to London to exercise his authority over her, but he had wanted to reach an accommodation with her too; he had wanted their marriage to stand. He might not have been imagining a perfect marriage of the sort he'd once dreamed about, but he'd imagined one perfect in its way. One that let him both have Rose and hold on to all his affronted pride and resentment too. A marriage in which he was the perpetually aggrieved party.

He'd been arrogant and selfish and full of stupid pride. And he was sorry for it. He hadn't known what it meant to be sorry—really sorry—until this moment. The regret that ate at him now was a physical pain in his chest.

At last, he saw that Rose had every right to feel as aggrieved as him. More, in fact. At last, he saw that if anyone in this room needed to seek forgiveness, it was him.

He wanted their marriage to be real—not because he wanted to bed Rose, or to keep any children she bore him under his watchful eye—but because he loved her. But now he saw that the baby had been the only glue holding them together. Without that, Rose had no reason to stay with him. Except for propriety's sake, perhaps.

Through all this self-flagellation, Rose slept. She lay profoundly still, her skin looking waxy to Gil. At one point, he grew so worried he leaned forward to check yet again that she was breathing, holding his cupped hand over her face. Even the warm huff of her breath against his palm didn't completely reassure him. She could have died last night, without him being here. The thought of being without her was bad enough; the thought of her existing nowhere in this world wasn't to be borne.

Was there even the slightest chance she would want to stay with him after this? It seemed hopeless. But one thing was sure. No matter the cost to him, Rose's future would be her choice, not his.

He must have fallen asleep in the chair eventually. He woke feeling cold, his neck stiff and sore. The fire had died away in the grate hours ago, and the ⁕room was chilly. Gil stretched, groaning, and glanced at the bed, starting when he realised Rose was awake. She half sat, half reclined on a pile of pillows, and her eyes held a bleak expression that hurt him.

"Rose," he said and, leaning forward, took her hand. Her fingers were icy and unresisting as she turned her head to look at him.

"I take it you've heard," she said, her voice remote.

"I'm so sorry," he whispered brokenly. "I don't know what to say. I should have been here with you."

She stared at their loosely linked hands for a few moments before gently withdrawing hers. It was absurd to feel rejected by the small gesture, but he did.

"Can you bear to tell me what happened?"

She stared at the wall, her gaze fixed on a spot over his

right shoulder. "I started bleeding," she said listlessly. "The doctor came. He told me I was miscarrying. After that, it was an hour, maybe two." She fell silent again.

"James came to find me." Gil said after a pause, when it became clear she had no more to say. "He was concerned about you."

"Was he?" Her disinterested tone made him wince. "I think I can guess where he found you," she added, letting her gaze wander over him, and suddenly, he was very aware of his unkempt appearance. He sat up straighter, running a hand through his hair, which he could feel was standing on end in odd peaks. A heavy growth of stubble shadowed his cheeks and chin. He suspected his eyes would be bloodshot. They felt hot, and a headache pounded behind them.

"I'm so sorry," he muttered, aware more than ever of how badly he had let her down.

"It doesn't matter," she said automatically. As though his apology was of no interest to her.

"It *does* matter. I should have been here with you." He swallowed, forced himself to say it. "You lost our baby while I was out drinking myself into a stupor."

She said nothing, but he saw her swallow, and he knew she was hurting. He wanted to do something to comfort her, but how could he when his touch was probably the very last thing she wanted?

After a while, she said tonelessly, "The doctor said I should stay in bed for a few days. But as soon as I'm able, I'm leaving. There's no reason for me to stay now."

Even though he'd expected this, he still felt the shock of her announcement, like he'd been punched in the gut and left winded. He sat back in his chair and searched his mind for a suitable reply, but none came to mind. He wanted to beg her to stay. Or order her. But he would issue no more commands to her.

So when he finally spoke, he merely said in a voice so calm it astonished him, "Is that really what you want?"

Her expression didn't alter by so much as a flicker. It was as though she was buried under layers, somewhere he couldn't reach. She'd always had that tendency to hide her distress behind her bland mask, but this was different. She seemed fathoms away, totally unreachable. "Yes," she whispered at last, "I want to go."

That unhesitating confirmation mangled what was left of Gil's heart. He wanted to crawl into a hole somewhere and howl. Instead, he forced himself to be practical.

"Where do you want to go? To Weartham again? Or Bath? I have a small townhouse there."

"You do not need to house me," she said. "My father is returning to England. I can go to him."

"No. Even if we never lay eyes on one another again, I will always provide for you. You must know that. We are still married."

"But we need not remain married."

Gil ran a shaky hand through his rumpled hair. "You cannot be thinking of divorce?"

She looked away. "I don't know. I need to consider it carefully. It is not an easy thing, a divorce. You would have to make the complaint, and it would be very scandalous."

"And I have nothing to complain about. You have not been with any other man."

"These things can always be arranged when you are rich. It would be no difficult thing to find someone to say it happened. You could—we could both be free."

He fought to contain his instinctive outrage at what was she was so calmly suggesting. With effort, he adopted a reasonable tone of voice. "Nothing of what you propose is easy. The simplest thing to do, if you wish to be free of me, would be to remain married and live separate lives. Plenty of couples do

235

that. It is unexceptionable. If you leave me, however, you will have publicly deserted me. You will not enjoy the same respectability that you do now. And if you divorce me, it will be far, far worse."

And suddenly, that remote mask of hers fell away. She turned anguished grey eyes on him and whispered, "You don't understand. I can't bear to live like this anymore."

His heart wrenched at her hopeless words and her distraught expression—and at what this *meant*. Staring down at his hands, he bit down on the soft flesh inside his cheek till he drew blood to distract himself from the lump in his throat and the hot, unfamiliar press of tears in his eyes.

When he had himself under control he said, "If you truly wish to leave me, I won't stand in your way. But I want you to return to Weartham for now, and I'm not agreeing to a divorce. Not yet." After a moment, he added more softly, "Don't ask such a thing of me yet."

She stared at him with those wide grey eyes and slowly nodded her agreement.

They sat together in the cold room in silence for a few more minutes. The air was freezing, and Gil felt like a block of ice, sitting in his open shirt and bare feet.

At last, he stood up, aching in every bone, weary to his very marrow. "I'll send a maid to make a fire up for you," he said and quietly left.

Part Five

How like a winter hath my absence been from thee...
William Shakespeare
Sonnet 97

Chapter Twenty-Two

December 1814

Three weeks after Rose arrived back at Weartham, a packet arrived from Mr. Andrews, Gil's secretary. It was waiting for her at the breakfast table with the rest of her post. She had taken to dressing and going down to breakfast, because her father was visiting and it had always been their time together when she was a girl.

She sat down and opened the packet while the footman poured her coffee. It contained a letter and legal documents. After two paragraphs of enquiries after her health and expressions of regret that he had not had the pleasure of making her acquaintance during her brief visit to London, Mr. Andrews informed her that his lordship had seen fit to have Weartham made over entirely to her. Although Gil owned all her property as her husband, Mr. Andrews assured her that henceforward, Weartham was Rose's to do with as she wished, including making provision for its disposal to whomsoever she chose on her death. The documents Mr. Andrews had enclosed dealt with these matters and should, he advised, be kept safe.

Rose put the letter down and untied the documents. They were written in impenetrable legal language, and she felt too agitated to try to make sense of them, so she tied them up again with shaking fingers and re-read the letter twice more.

"Why the frown, Rosebud?"

She looked up. "I wish you wouldn't call me that, Papa," she said for the hundredth time.

"You'll always be my Rosebud," he replied as he spooned devilled kidneys onto his plate. "What have you got there?"

Rose gestured for the footman to leave the room and waited until the door closed behind him until she answered. "It's a letter from Gil. He's giving me Weartham. Outright."

Miles paused and looked at her, the spoon hovering over his plate. "Really? How—unexpected."

"Yes, there's no real need. He's already assured me I may remain here all my life if I wish. Perhaps—perhaps it is to settle matters between us once and for all?"

Miles sat down at the table and poured himself coffee. "Well, what does he say in the letter?"

"The letter's from his secretary—there isn't even a note from Gil."

Miles seemed to consider as he chewed his breakfast. He swallowed and took a swig of coffee. "It is generous settlement, though of course the estate still technically belongs to him."

"His secretary acknowledges that but says Gil has stated it is to be mine in all ways." And Gil would hold to his word, she knew that. Weartham was truly hers now. If Gil predeceased her, no one could remove her. The running of the estate would be at her say-so. Improvements she had previously felt to be beyond her discretion as the estate's chatelaine were now within her gift.

The enormity of it hit her then: Gil may not be able to love her, but he had given her this estate. And by gifting it to her entirely, he had put her beyond ever needing anyone's grace or favour again. For the first time in her life, she was independent.

"Well," Miles said. "It's no less than you deserve after the way he's behaved."

Rose sighed. "We've already spoken about this, Papa. Please don't start again."

Miles scowled. He was still angry at Gil. It was no wonder, really. No sooner had he arrived back on English soil than he'd had his daughter knocking on the door and telling her marriage was over for good. The very daughter he'd been so anxious to get off his hands five years before.

Rose had told him why she'd left and, although she'd spared him some of details, she'd let him know how unhappy she was about his part in securing Gil as her husband in the first place. Annoyingly, he'd been unapologetic. He'd wanted to go and have words with Gil then and there, but she hadn't let him. Instead, she'd asked him to accompany her to Weartham, and, amazingly, he'd agreed, escorting her on the long journey north and staying on for several weeks. He was going back to London tomorrow, though, and she could tell he was itching to be away. He hadn't mentioned the reason for his eagerness to be gone, but she knew Lottie had returned to England last week. And perhaps, for Lottie, Miles would finally settle down. Rose hoped so.

After breakfast, Miles announced he was going to supervise his packing—a sure sign of his excitement to be going back to Town. Rose decided to seek out Will. She'd had little contact with him since her return, but she wanted to share this news with someone who would understand what it meant to her.

She put on her warmest cloak and hat and walked down to the home farm. The day was cold and dank, the sky a heavy, low grey. The chill from the ground seeped through the leather soles of her boots as she walked.

She found Will in the courtyard, talking with Josiah, the head farmhand. When Rose arrived, they both looked up, and Josiah doffed his cap while Will looked surprised for a moment, then made a small bow.

"Good morning, milady," he said

"Good morning, Mr. Anderson," she replied, always careful to give him his proper title in front of the hands. "And Josiah. How is your wife? And the children?"

"Very good, milady," the hand said, smiling. "The twins is ten now, would you believe. And my Mary almost seventeen!"

"Time goes so fast, doesn't it?" Rose replied. "And Mary is

doing well up at the house, Mrs. Hart tells me."

"Aye, she's a good lass, that one." He beamed.

"And what were you two gentlemen talking about, if I may ask?" Rose turned her gaze to Will.

"Josiah was just telling me your neighbour Mr. Benson has found some footrot in his sheep."

Rose frowned. "Have they been anywhere near ours?"

Will shook his head. "No, thankfully. I'll go and see Mr. Benson shortly and examine the animals myself. We can't have it spreading."

She nodded. "When you've finished, could you come up to the house? I have some matters I would like to discuss with you."

"Of course, milady. Would one o'clock be all right?"

"That would be ideal. Thank you." She smiled then, at both of them. "Well, I will take my leave of you, gentlemen. Good day."

Josiah beamed again and tugged his forelock as she left, and Will gave his usual formal bow, though he still had that curious look in his eye.

She knew that Will would be hungry by one o'clock, so as well as tea and cake, she asked Mrs. Hart to send meat pie and a flagon of ale up to the library. Being a very proper sort, Will took some persuading to partake of the food, but eventually, when Rose helped herself to a small slice of the pie he relented, polishing the rest of it off and eating three slices of seed cake besides.

"You were hungry," she observed when he finished.

"I was up early—breakfast was a long time ago," he admitted, finishing his tea and placing the empty cup back in the saucer.

She refilled his cup without asking if he wanted more. She knew he did, and he'd only say no. "You've been working hard," she said, nodding at the ledgers, which she'd looked over this morning and found completely up-to-date.

Will shrugged, not denying it, and Rose felt a stab of guilt. He must've been working all the hours God sent to get everything done. She'd been thinking about hiring an assistant earlier in the year but had left for London with Gil without doing anything about it. And without her own contribution, Will must've been hard-pressed.

"It's time we hired someone to help you, Will. Can you think of anyone suitable offhand?"

For a moment, Will looked taken aback, but he recovered quickly. "The vicar's youngest son Christopher is a quick lad, and he's interested in farming. He's done well at school, and the vicar can't afford to send another to university. I think he'd be keen."

"If you think he's suitable, I'm happy for you to hire him," Rose said. She trusted Will's judgment. He was a shrewd judge of character and popular with the hands.

Will smiled, but his expression was slightly troubled.

"Is something wrong?" she asked.

He shook his head. "No, it's just that—are you suggesting I hire an assistant because you do not intend to be involved in running the estate any longer? You don't have to answer me, of course..." He trailed off, his face flushed.

"That's not the reason, no. I was thinking of hiring someone before I left for London, as it happens. And it was quite unfair of me not to do so before I went. I'm sure you've been running yourself ragged. The fact is..." She lifted her tea cup and took a sip of tea, thinking about how to put it. "The fact is, I've returned to Weartham for good. Stanhope has given it to me outright, you see. And I want to make some bigger changes this next year. So we're going to be very busy. We'll need the extra help."

"I thought you and his lordship—" He broke off. "I beg your

pardon. It is not my business."

There was a brief, strained silence; then Rose said, changing the subject, "Perhaps you could tell me what you've been doing since I left?"

Within a few minutes, the awkwardness had passed. Will told her about his decision to plant the north field with clover for grazing. They'd be moving the cattle up there in the spring. He was still unsure what to plant in the old grazing pastures, though, and they had a lengthy debate over the respective virtues of barley and wheat. Before long, it was as though Rose had never been away. They talked about the things that had to be done before the end of winter, and of other things that might be possible if the weather was kind and a few other imponderables came good. They talked about the more drastic changes Rose had in mind for the future. And all the while, Rose made notes while Will scribbled sums on the blotter.

By the time Will took his leave, Rose had a list of tasks half as long as her arm. It was a relief to have so much to do. The last few weeks had been difficult. Losing the baby had left her in a deep mire of sadness. She wasn't sure whether to call it grief. It wasn't the same as the pain she'd felt when she'd lost her mother. Rather, an awful, empty regret. A profound disappointment. It sounded such a mild, inoffensive thing, *disappointment.* But now she knew what that word meant. Now she knew that disappointment could feel like a wave crashing down on you, crushing you and leaving you empty and wanting.

She missed Gil too. When she thought of him, she felt a yawning ache in her chest. She'd been missing him before she even left London. Before the night they'd argued about her father and she found out the woman he loved was Tilly Drayton. Before she lost the baby. She'd been missing him since he left her bed, weeks and weeks before she left him. Back when she'd still had a bit of hope left in her.

Hope was a terrible thing. It filled the empty spaces inside in you for a while, and then, when you realised your hope was misplaced, it felt worse than before. She wasn't going to allow hope to fill the empty spaces again. Hope made you think that things that were irretrievably broken could be salvaged, when the truth was that some things could never be fixed and some actions could never be forgiven.

And so here she was, back at Weartham. Discovering that life went inexorably on, no matter what happened. It was much easier when finally you accepted that truth and stopped trying to stand against the current that wanted to push you forward. Today's letter had made her see that. And her meeting with Will. And the list of things to be done she had written down during that meeting. Each task finite and achievable.

Rose looked down at the list and saw that the first task was to write to one of her neighbours about the crumbling drywall on the boundary between their lands. She opened the desk drawer and pulled out a fresh sheet of paper. Then she picked up her pen and began to write.

That night was Miles's last night at Weartham. Harriet and Will joined them for dinner, and afterwards, Rose played the pianoforte while Harriet embroidered and the men played chess. It was companionable and pleasant, even though Rose could sense her father's eagerness to leave. As the day of his departure had grown closer, his barely suppressed excitement became more and more apparent.

At ten o'clock, Will and Harriet departed. Will, ever the perfect gentleman, would escort Harriet back to Honeysuckle Cottage before returning to his own house at the edge of the estate. After waving them off, Rose returned to her father in the drawing room. He sat at a small table, playing Patience and sipping Port. When he saw her standing in the doorway, he put his cards down and leaned back in his chair.

"Well, now, Rosebud—" Then he stopped and looked at her reflectively. "You're right. I really must stop calling you that.

You're a rosebud no longer. A full-blown flower is what you are."

She walked to the fresh tea tray that had been brought in her absence. After pouring herself another cup of tea, she sat down opposite him. "Let's hope I keep my petals for a while." She smiled.

"Rose, there is...something I've been meaning to say—" He stopped and sighed heavily, then started again. "Before I go back to London, I wanted to tell you that I, well—I know I've been a rotten father. I brokered a bad marriage for you and left the country before I even knew you would be all right."

Rose said nothing. In truth, she was surprised.

"All I can say is that I'd assumed you would be fine." There was a long pause; then he added peevishly, "Why didn't you write and tell me you weren't?"

Rose suppressed her irritation at that final question—as though he'd have come back to England if she'd written! "There was nothing to be done, Papa. No use crying over spilt milk. We were married."

She saw him flinch and couldn't quite be sorry, though she added, "It wasn't as if Gil beat me. He merely ignored me."

Miles sighed. "Is there no chance you might try again?"

Rose stared unseeingly at the half-played card game on the table. "No. The way this marriage came about, Gil will always feel trapped. And I don't want to be his gaoler anymore. I think that's why he's given me Weartham, you know. To release me from my dependence on him. And him from his obligation to me."

And maybe that was why she felt all right about accepting Weartham? Because it wiped away the debts of the past—on both sides.

Miles frowned. "Is that what you really think? That you trapped him? That *I* trapped him? That's rot!"

"It's not rot," Rose replied angrily. "Gil had no choice but to agree to marry me—what else was he to do? Impoverish his whole family?"

"He had a choice," Miles retorted mulishly. "It may not have been much of choice, but it *was* a choice. The way old Stanhope was playing, he was going to lose everything, one way or another. He was lucky he lost to someone looking for a husband for his daughter. There are plenty of men who'd have kept the properties Stanhope wagered, and they'd have been entirely ruined."

"He was in love with someone else, Papa!" Rose cried, clattering her cup down on the saucer. "Did you even think to ask if his affections were engaged? Did you imagine I would've wanted to marry a man *who did not want me*?"

"Rose—"

"But you didn't care about that, did you?" she cried, furious now. "You just wanted to be gone. You just wanted to be *rid* of me. The opportunity came along to marry me off, and you couldn't leave England fast enough! I've never once come first with you, have I? *Have I?*" She only stopped shouting when she ran out of air.

The silence that followed seemed unnaturally quiet, the ticking of the clock on the mantel oddly loud.

Miles looked appalled. "Rose...I'm sorry. I don't know what to say. You're right—I was incredibly selfish—but it wasn't that I didn't *love* you."

"No?" She laughed bitterly.

"No! I wanted you to be secure. And yes, this was an opportunity. A chance to marry this well wasn't going to come up for you again. It seemed like—like a safe bet!"

Rose made a disbelieving sound "That's just it, Papa. You *wagered* on my future. With as little thought as you'd have given to a game of cards. But I can't treat this like a game of cards. I can't shrug my shoulders over the fact that Gil lost the game and had to give up someone he loved. That he did not *consent*."

"He did consent. He had a choice—"

"Hobson's Choice is not choice, Papa! Not when it comes to marriage. When you're in love with someone, you want them to love you back. You don't want to force them to wed you."

"But Rosebud, you weren't in love with Stanhope. It was—"

"Yes, I was!" she cried. "I fell in love with him at that very first meeting. He was charming and handsome, and he looked like a pirate. He was kind to me without knowing why I was there, and I thought he was wonderful!"

Her father stared at her, and she realised her cheeks were wet.

"He wasn't awfully wonderful after that," Miles pointed out, his tone almost curious.

No, he wasn't. And she'd quickly suppressed that incipient adoration and told herself she hated him, but the truth was, those feelings had never fully gone away. And five years later, on Nev's moonlit terrace, without even realising it, she'd fallen again. And all the anger and resentment and recriminations that had come later hadn't stopped her continuing to fall over the weeks and months that followed. Falling, falling. All the way, this time.

"Why don't you try again, then, if you love him?" Miles asked gently.

"You still don't understand, Papa, do you?" Rose said, shaking her head. "I'd never have forgiven myself if I hadn't set him free when I had the chance."

Chapter Twenty-Three

When he couldn't sleep at night, Gil would go into Rose's bedchamber. She hadn't taken quite everything away with her when she left. She'd bought new things in London—clothes, cosmetics, trimmings for bonnets she hadn't got round to doing anything with—and in her haste to be gone, she'd left some of them behind, suggesting in a note that Antonia help herself to whatever she wanted and dispose of the rest.

Gil had thrown the note away. He instructed the servants to leave the room exactly as it was, and as a consequence, it looked as though she'd just stepped out and might return any minute. Several gowns still hung in the wardrobes. One of the smallest drawers in her armoire seemed to have been overlooked entirely—it was brimming with silk stockings in pink and white and black. A few jars of cosmetics and ribbons decorated the top of the armoire.

Sometimes, he handled her things. Sometimes, he just sat for a while. Or lay on the bed. It didn't make him feel any better, but still he came, most nights.

Tonight, he'd been at his club with James, and he felt as though he'd spent the entire evening fielding questions about Rose. When he'd admitted she'd returned to his estate in Northumbria, there had been a lot of good-natured teasing about not leaving his lovely young wife alone for too long, and certainly not over Christmas when nights were long and beds were cold. He'd made a poor job of laughing along and, in the end, he'd come home early, leaving his brother swilling Port and talking about horses and women with Ferdy.

Once Crawford had Gil's coat off, he dismissed the valet,

and no sooner had the door shut behind the man than Gil entered Rose's chamber. He left his candle on the armoire and picked up an ivory comb lying there. Staring at the intricate design, he smoothed his thumbs over the fine carving, remembering Rose wearing it, the unblemished whiteness against her simply dressed dark hair. Putting the comb down, he opened the drawer of stockings and pulled a handful of the fine, silky garments out, letting them drift through his fingers. At length, he wandered away from the armoire and sat on the end of the bed.

He smoothed his hand over the coverlet and thought of the first couple of weeks he'd had with her here. Making love to her in this bed each night before returning to his own. Why had it seemed so vital never to stay the night and sleep beside her? He regretted that now. He regretted many things, of course.

Though not his latest decision: to give Weartham to Rose. He'd told James tonight, and his brother had stared at him as though he'd sprouted a second head, though, to his credit, he'd made no protest.

It had seemed obviously right to Gil as soon as he'd conceived the idea. He'd already been thinking about speaking with James, to ask him to agree that if Gil died, Rose should be allowed to remain at Weartham. And then it occurred to him that if he and James both died, it would be Cousin Horace who would inherit Weartham. Horace would have no compunction about evicting Gil's widow.

It was a short step to get from there to gifting Weartham to Rose entirely. Knowing she was provided for, for the rest of her life, gave him some small comfort.

Gil sat on the bed, stroking the coverlet till the clock chimed the hour. Midnight. Sighing, he levered himself up off the end of the bed and lifted his candle from the armoire. He returned to his own chamber, closing the connecting door behind him with a soft click.

The next day, Gil received a note that surprised him. It was from Rose's father, and it asked Gil to meet him at Brooks that afternoon.

As he made his way to the club, Gil wondered what the purpose of the meeting was. Was he finally to be called to account for his dereliction of husbandly duty? Or did Davenport merely wish to have a discussion about some sort of settlement? Did he know about Weartham?

Gil was the first to arrive. He sat down in a private corner with a newspaper and awaited Davenport. At first, he stared at the pages unseeingly, waiting for the other man's arrival, but after a while, he got drawn into an article.

"Good afternoon, Stanhope."

He raised his head, startled and annoyed that he hadn't noticed the older man's approach.

Davenport looked different, his face darkened by the Mediterranean sun. His eyes glinted silver, and his teeth flashed white in a brief smile. He still looked too youthful to be the father of a grown woman.

Gil stood and held out his hand stiffly. "Davenport."

"Sorry to be late," the other man murmured, shaking Gil's proffered hand briefly and taking the opposite chair.

A waiter brought wine and glasses, and Davenport dismissed him with a wave of his hand, pouring the wine himself before settling back in his chair, glass in hand. He seemed in no hurry to speak, and it was Gil who eventually broke the silence. "Why did you want to speak with me?"

Davenport smiled. "Why do you think? I wish to talk about my daughter."

"Oh yes?" Christ, but he'd known he would feel like this when he met Rose's father. Angry and awkward and wrong-footed.

Davenport regarded him over the rim of his wineglass with

eyes that were disturbingly like Rose's.

"When I left England after your marriage," he said, speaking softly but succinctly, "Rose was still recovering from a very grave illness." He paused briefly. "I must say I find her much altered." The man's tone was conversational, his expression bland.

"Indeed?"

"Yes. She is a full-grown woman now. She has lost the gaucheness of youth." He smiled tightly. "And much of its optimism."

Gil did not look away from Davenport, but he felt his face heat. For all their mildness, the other man's words were a stinging accusation.

After a brief silence, he leaned forward and fixed Gil with a steely gaze. His voice was still quite deceptively gentle. "You abandoned her in Northumbria as soon as the ink was dry on the wedding contract, Stanhope. It was not well done."

"No," Gil admitted, unflinching. "It was not. At the time, the best thing seemed to me to be to leave her there. But I do not make excuses for my behaviour. I behaved badly, and I am sorry for it."

Davenport watched him with his shrewd gambler's gaze. "Rose told me you were in love with someone else when you married her," he said.

It was the last thing Gil had expected to hear, and he gazed at the other man in surprise for long moments, heat creeping up his neck, before he replied.

"I believed myself to be in love with someone else at the time, that is true. But I made my wedding vows, and I ought to have kept them. I intended to, when I made them. But things went...awry."

"So it's true what Rose says," Davenport said. "You were unwilling."

Gil shook his head. "I had a choice. It might not have been

a choice I liked, but I could have said no."

"So why did you agree?"

"My father—" Gil began, then he broke off again. His neckcloth suddenly felt too tight, and he raised a hand to tug at it. "My father lost everything to you."

"Not Stanhope Abbey," Davenport pointed out.

"Stanhope Abbey wasn't able to support itself—not then, anyway. We needed the unentailed properties to shore it up. When my father lost those properties to you, he ruined himself."

Davenport's face was unreadable. "I see."

"So I agreed to marry Rose."

"And the girl—the one you loved?"

Gil frowned. Had he really *loved* Tilly? He supposed he must have, though the memory of that boyish admiration felt very different from the way he felt about Rose.

He shrugged. "I couldn't have married her without the means to support her. Her father would have turned me away." Strange to realise that thought brought him no pain or even the smallest stab of regret now.

Davenport sighed. "I assumed you were happy with the match. I would not—I *hope* I would not—have allowed the marriage to proceed had I known." But he looked doubtful, that oddly familiar gaze of his troubled.

"What did my father tell you?"

"Merely that you were agreeable. I did not ask for more than that. I should have done so, of course. I was careless with Rose's future, carried away with arranging such an illustrious match for her and eager to be off on my travels." He passed a hand over his mouth, rubbing at his cheek with long fingers. "I'd wanted to travel since I was a boy and the thought of handing Rose over to a husband to look after was...heady." He sighed heavily again, then looked at Gil, his gaze flat and grey, like flint. "I do not say this to absolve you of blame, you understand."

"I don't ask to be absolved. I deeply regret the way I have behaved toward Rose. It has been the besetting sin of my life."

"Then what will you do to put it right?"

Gil stared into his glass of wine for a long time. "I would do anything in my power to put it right," he said in a low voice. "But I cannot. I cannot give her what she deserves."

"And what is that?"

"To go back and choose a better life than the one she got with me. To choose a husband who would treat her as she deserves to be treated."

"But why can *you* not treat as she deserves?" This in an impatient tone.

Gil looked up from his wine. Davenport was leaning forward in his chair, waiting for Gil's answer. He wore an expression of mingled confusion and irritation.

"I'm not going to impose myself on Rose again," Gil replied. "She has suffered enough of my company these last months. The best I can do for her now is to leave her alone."

Davenport stared at him for a long time, his expression unreadable, and Gil steadily gazed back. At last the older man shook his head. "I cannot believe what I am hearing," he said. "Do you really believe that?"

"I *know* it," Gil replied. "She made it very plain to me that she wished to leave me, and I will not ignore her wishes in this. The least I can do—"

"Has anyone ever told you that you are a fool, Stanhope?" Davenport interrupted.

"I beg your pardon?"

"A fool," Davenport repeated succinctly.

Gil stiffened. "I do not believe I understand you."

"Tell me this, and no more of this pokered-up attitude. Do you love my daughter?"

Gil stared at his father-in-law. At the man—or rather one of them—who had brought his disastrous marriage about. The man he had hated and resented for five years. The feelings he'd been bottling up for months seemed to swell inside him, forcing a confession to his lips he'd never uttered before.

"Of course I do," he said hoarsely. "More than anything."

There was an infinitesimal softening of Davenport's expression. "Then go to her. Tell her. Ask to start again."

"She does not want me to—"

"Just *ask* her. Have you asked her?"

"No—she told me she couldn't bear to live with me again. How could I ask her to stay?" He still felt a shaft of pain when he recalled her anguished expression when she'd said that.

"Trust me, my boy. If she knows you love her, she'll be able to bear it." Davenport smiled, seeming almost amused, though his eyes looked sad.

"You don't understand. I don't want her to have to tolerate me. She deserves more than that."

Davenport looked at him oddly. Then he sat back in his chair and lifted his wine again, taking a slow sip while Gil squirmed in his chair, wishing he hadn't given in to the lure of confession. This was an odd form of torture. The pain of talking about Rose and his one-sided feelings, not quite balanced by the pleasure and relief of being able to speak her name aloud.

"Let me tell you something about my daughter." Davenport made a performance of putting his wineglass down and sitting back again. "When she was a young girl, there were times when I left her with friends. She always smiled and said she was sure she'd have a lovely time and would see me when I returned for her. And it was much easier to believe her than to question her when I wanted to go." He stopped and took a deep breath, averting his eyes from Gil's as though ashamed. "Recently, an old friend took me aside and told me how it really was. Rose had told her how terribly upset she was whenever I left her, how she cried herself to sleep until I came back for her. And sometimes I left her for weeks at time." The man looked stricken, remembering. "I never knew. I never *noticed*."

"She is good at hiding her feelings," Gil murmured, thinking of that mask she wore so often. "Even at the worst of times."

"Yes, she is. And it's because she doesn't expect much of anyone. So please do not imagine that *she* knows you love her. I wonder if she's ever felt truly loved by anyone."

Gil felt an aching sadness at those words, right in his chest. He remembered how she'd looked on their wedding day— thin and plain and hopeful. And then he thought of her on Grayson's terrace six months ago, beautiful and vivid, but sad when she spoke of her marriage. And the morning after she lost the baby. God, he never wanted to see her like that again.

"She deserves to know she is loved," Davenport said, "and I'm going to try to convince her that, despite my shortcomings as a father, I do love her."

He stood then and motioned to a footman that he wanted his coat. Automatically, Gil rose too, waiting while the coat was brought and Davenport shrugged it on. He thought their conversation was over, but when Davenport offered his hand, and Gil took it, the older man looked him in the eye and said, "And what about you, Gilbert? What are you going to do?"

Chapter Twenty-Four

24 December 1814

Rose couldn't concentrate on her book. Couldn't settle to anything, in fact.

She glanced at Harriet, sewing contentedly by the fire, and sighed. It was Christmas Eve, and everything was ready for tomorrow. She should be feeling happy and relaxed. She usually loved Christmas.

She loved decorating the house with greenery and singing carols and entertaining her neighbours. She loved the preparations and the festivity of it all. The busy hours and the quiet, contemplative ones. The lull of Christmastime between the difficult end of autumn and the hard beginning of January.

This year, though, she couldn't shake her melancholy. She had managed to busy herself with a thousand and one tasks, and still her sadness would not go. It sat heavily in her soul, a persistent presence, always there. Or perhaps an absence. A constant absence.

She put her book aside with a sigh and stood, causing Harriet to glance up from her sewing, a questioning expression on her face.

"I'm going out for a walk," she announced. Harriet looked surprised. It was very near the shortest day of the year—it would be dark in an hour or less—and while the weather had been mild for the last fortnight, they'd both remarked earlier on the heavy grey clouds and blustery wind.

"Are you sure, dear?" Harriet asked mildly. "It looks awfully cold."

"I'll wrap up," Rose replied. "I just need some air."

The sun was low in the sky when she left the house, wrapped in a heavy wool cloak, thick mittens covering her hands. She headed for the gardens. The kitchen garden was bare-looking, the dark loam of the empty raised beds touched with frost. Rose carried on, into the orchard, past the barren fruit trees and down to the wild garden. She walked all the way to the little temple of Persephone before she stopped.

The wind was getting quite strong now, and she stepped inside the temple for shelter, sitting down and wincing at the chill from the stone seat. The cold quickly permeated her skirts, but she ignored it, just pulled her cloak closer around herself and stared at the fresco, squinting to make out the details in the fading light. She used to think Persephone looked hungry as she contemplated her pomegranate. Now she thought the goddess looked sad.

Preoccupied as she was, she didn't even hear him approach.

He was only a few feet away from her when she caught the wild flutter of his coat in her peripheral vision and turned her head.

"Gil..." She breathed his name, and her heart felt as though it was stuttering into life again for the first time in weeks, beating a ragged and unfamiliar tattoo to see him standing not ten feet away, so solid and real.

Why is he here?

She schooled herself to present a calm expression as she rose, despite her inner turmoil. Time seemed to slow, and she felt as though she was walking through water as she stepped forward to greet him. "Gil—this is a surprise."

His gaze travelled over her face, lingering till her smile began to feel taut and tense.

"Hello, Rose," he said at last, lifting his hand to take off his hat. The wind immediately ripped through his dark hair, making it wild and unruly. It was whipping about his face, and his coat was fluttering, and the ends of his neckcloth were flying about too, but Gil, at the centre of all that movement, was as still as a rock. His hazel eyes fixed on her with an odd, wary look she'd not seen on his face before.

"Suddenly, I find I don't know what to say," he said with a humorless laugh. "After coming three hundred miles to see you."

She stared at him, not knowing what to say either. She couldn't imagine why he was here. After a moment, he closed the distance that separated them. It took him two long strides. She had to tip her head to look into his face then, and when she did, it was to see that he appeared deeply troubled.

"What's wrong?" she asked.

"You didn't invite me for Christmas," he said at last, and she wondered if she'd misheard him. His words were so unexpected, so at odds with his unhappy expression. "Every year, you invite me for Christmas," he added. "Except this one."

She attempted a smile, but it was a poor thing, wavery and uncertain. "I rather assumed you would not wish to come."

"Your assumption was wrong," he retorted, and she felt an odd little flutter in her chest. She quashed the feeling quickly, sternly reminding herself that hope was a terrible thing. That she'd given it up.

"I don't understand," she replied, watching him carefully.

He gave another of those self-mocking laughs, his jaw tense and set. "God, I'm awful at this." And then he took a deep breath. "The thing is, Rose—I miss you."

"You *miss* me?" Her heart began beating wildly, and she struggled to maintain her calm façade.

"Yes, I miss you. I didn't want you to leave London."

"No?" For the life of her, she couldn't utter another word. It was an effort just to get that single syllable out on a whispered breath.

"In fact, the truth is, I very much wanted you to stay. With me, I mean."

She frowned at that, her initial reaction one of disbelief.

"But after you lost the baby, I thought I should let you go," he continued. "I thought that it would be wrong to ask you to stay."

Her heart wrenched. "Did you?" she said. "I wish you'd told me."

"I wanted you to decide for yourself what you wanted, and you seemed desperate to leave." He raised a gloveless hand to her face and stroked her cheek with his thumb. "And who could blame you? I've been the worst of husbands. I wasn't even with you when you lost our baby. And I'm so *sorry*, Rose. I'm so, so sorry for all the times I failed you."

His gaze was bleak, without hope, and she stared into his eyes, torn between the urge to comfort him and fascinated wonder as to what he might say next.

"Would it have made a difference, if you'd known?" he asked, his voice husky, his hazel eyes pleading.

And in that instant, something quickened deep inside her, a seed of hope germinating when she'd thought she was done with hope forever. "Yes," she whispered, gazing into his eyes. "It would have made all the difference in the world."

Gil let out a shuddery breath—she didn't know if it was from relief or fear. A smile trembled at the edges of his mouth, but he looked sick with nerves too. "There's something I must say," he began. The wind buffeted them, and he closed his eyes. She saw him steel himself for what he was about to say next.

"Rose." He paused. And then he opened his eyes and looked straight at her. "I love you."

"Do you?" she whispered. A lump in her throat made saying more than that impossible.

"With all my heart. And I realise that you do not feel as I do, but perhaps, in time..."

He trailed off, his gaze going from earnest to puzzled, and

she supposed it must be the sight of the smile that had broken out over her face that made him stop talking. It was a laughing-and-crying sort of a smile, watery and wobbly but possibly dazzling too—it certainly felt as though she was smiling just as widely as she could.

She put her mittened hands—absurd mittens!—on his chest and said, "No, I do! That is, I love you too, Gil." And it was such a relief to say those words aloud. Words that had been rattling around in her sore heart for so long.

He took hold of her shoulders, his hands a little too tight. "Do you?" he asked hoarsely. "Despite everything?"

"Yes. Yes, despite it all." She wanted to explain it to him, but that would mean she'd have to stop smiling and clutching his waistcoat and drowning in the expression of stunned disbelief arresting his dear face. She gave a joyful little laugh.

"God, Rose—" He pulled her closer, dipping his head to capture her lips with his own in a hard, desperate kiss, and she returned his embrace feverishly, crushing her mouth to his and welcoming the invasion of his tongue, the rasp of his bristles on her jaw.

When he finally pulled back, he cupped her face in his hands and stared down at her for the longest time. Then he dropped to his knees, heedless of the frosty ground, and took possession of her hands.

"What are you doing?" she squeaked.

He looked up at her, serious and determined. "Rose Davenport," he said. "Will you do me the honour of becoming my wife in truth? A wife I will love and cherish and honour every day of my life?"

She returned his gaze with the same gravity, clutching his ice-cold fingers with her own mittened ones. "I want to," she said, after a heartfelt pause. "I do love you, Gil. But you must understand that I can't go back to the way things were before."

He shook his head. "Nor can I. I want a real marriage this

time. If you're prepared to give me one last chance, I swear that I will spend the rest of my life trying to earn your forgiveness."

She met his intent gaze, seeing her own hope and fear mirrored there. Her own love.

"You don't have to earn my forgiveness," she whispered. "You have it already."

He paused, staring at her, then closed his eyes. "I don't deserve that."

"Well, that's the point of forgiveness, I think. What use would it be if it was given conditionally?"

He laughed ruefully. "I never realised how wise you are till now. I need you to come back so you can keep me on the right path."

She smiled and tugged at his hands till he gave in and got to his feet.

A single white snowflake drifted between them.

"Let's go inside," she said, "and get warm."

Gil had been greeted by Harriet when he first arrived at Weartham, but by the time he got back to the house with Rose, she had returned to her cottage. Making herself tactfully scarce, Gil realised gratefully as Rose pulled him toward the stairs.

He felt twenty again, his heart light as a bird. He felt as though he had pure happiness running through his veins. When they reached the earl's chambers, Rose leaned against the door, looking at him through half-closed eyes, inviting and challenging. He couldn't stop grinning. He loved her. She loved him. It was a miracle.

Bracing one hand against the wall, he lowered his head. Her eyes gleamed, breathing quickening. When his lips finally, finally reached hers, descending slowly to meet and press and meld, it felt like breathing for the first time in forever.

He poured everything into that kiss—lust, need, love—and Rose sent to him all her own yearning and joy. He didn't even know how long he kissed her before he was hefting her into his arms, kicking the door open and striding into the bedchamber.

Once inside, they made their way to the bed in an inelegant tangle of arms and legs, undressing as they went. A path of discarded clothing mapped their route.

And God, but holding her in his arms was heaven itself. He'd never felt this perfect mingling of lust and love before; a coincidence of body and soul that elevated his lust to a spiritual thing and made of his love something even more profound. Perhaps the difference, he thought hazily, was knowing that he was loved in return.

Rose loved him. She *loved* him.

Soon, all thought was gone. There was only feeling. Gil moved without thinking, senses reeling. Her skin was satiny against his lips, her familiar scent surrounded him and she sighed in his ear, breathing his name like a prayer.

He surged into her, fusing his mouth with hers, groaning as he kissed her. Her legs wrapped around him, her thighs clutching him as he drove into her again and again. He could feel her rippling around his flesh in waves as they climaxed together.

Afterwards, he lifted his head and opened his eyes, wanting to see her. She was beautiful, eyes half closed, face flushed and smiling at him, happy and loving and brimming over with pleasure.

And his.

By half past four it was fully dark, and Rose was tucked cosily into the shelter of Gil's big body.

"Are you awake?" he rumbled into her ear.

She squirmed and laughed, the low reverberations of his

voice ticklish.

"I'll take that as a yes." He turned her in his arms and kissed her, a long, slow, unhurried kiss, and she kissed him back happily.

When they broke apart, he said, "Where shall we live?"

"I love it here," she murmured, tucking herself against him again, her head on his shoulder. "But do you realise I've never been to Stanhope Abbey? I should go there at least once, I think. It's terrible form to be the countess of somewhere one's never been."

He chuckled softly. "Stanhope Abbey after Christmas, then?"

She smiled against his shoulder. "Yes."

"You'll love it," he said dreamily. "It's beautiful. Not wild like Northumbria. But lovely. Great rolling green downs, and the best farmland anywhere."

She snorted. "We'll see," she said, reserving judgment.

Gil kissed the top of her head.

"May I ask you something?" she whispered after a while.

He stroked her hair. "Of course."

"Do you still love Tilly?" She added hurriedly, "I shan't mention it again, but—well, I'd like to know."

Again, his hand smoothed over her head. "No, I don't. And even when I did, it wasn't the way I love you. I loved her as a boy loves."

"What do you mean?"

"Silly, worshipful stuff. She was like a goddess to me, I suppose."

"And I'm not?" Rose demanded, lifting her chin to look up at him, only half-jokingly.

He shifted his position to meet her gaze, but his expression was shrouded by the darkness, and she couldn't read him. "You are better than any goddess. You are the very real woman that I love, and what I feel for you is deeper, more profound, and much more wonderful than anything I could feel for a mere goddess."

The seed of hope inside her, the one that had sprouted in Persephone's temple, had been slowly growing ever since. And now, suddenly, dramatically, it flowered. A thousand blooms opened their petals in her heart. She felt her eyes flood and turned her face back into Gil's shoulder, pressing a few kisses there between the tears.

"Sorry," she mumbled on a half laugh, half sob. "But if you will say lovely things like that to me, you must expect me to leak all over you."

"Leak away," he said, and she heard the smile in his voice. "I mean every word. Oh, Tilly seemed perfect to me when I was twenty: she was sweet and domestic, the epitome of womanhood, I thought, back then. I suppose even recently she was still a sort of ideal at the back of my mind—but then Eve Adams came along, and she was so passionate and exciting. I thought no one could eclipse her." He kissed her nose and chuckled softly. "But *then,* there was Rose. And when I got to know Rose, I saw that she had it all. The passion and excitement and the sweetness too. And more besides. Rose was kind and quick and bright and surprising. She made me laugh like no one else does. And there's not a woman in the world— Tilly Drayton included—who can hold a candle to her."

Rose gave another hiccoughy sort of laugh-sob and kissed his shoulder again.

"I love you," she murmured when she could manage words, and the phrase whispered over his skin like a blessing. A benediction.

And then they were drifting, drifting, in the December dark. Until finally, and at long, long last, they fell asleep in each other's arms.

About the Author

Joanna Chambers always wanted to write love stories but she studied law, became a practising lawyer, married and had two children before she finally got beyond staring at empty notebooks. She thanks the arrival of her children for the discovery of her muse and/or destruction of her social life.

Joanna is a passionate believer in the transformative power of love. She lives in the UK with her family. When not working, looking after children or writing, she can be found with her nose buried in an ebook.

She loves to hear from readers and can be reached at:

Twitter ID: @ChambersJoanna

Website: http://joannachambers.com

Facebook: https://facebook.com/joanna.chambers.58

A ghost whisperer. A devilish captain.
A killer thirsting to destroy their passion...

Silken Shadows
© *2012 Jennifer St. Giles*
Killdaren, Book 3

On the day of her sister's wedding ship, Gemini Andrews's spirit heard the siren call of the sea. Over the past year it has become a friend that whispers to her heart, promising a full, blessed future.

That future is threatened by a string of gruesome murders that are too similar to those of a killer who vowed to destroy her sisters to be coincidence. She knows her psychic gifts can stop this evil, but her sisters think her too delicate. The enigmatic Captain Deverell Jenson, who stole her heart with one Christmas kiss, thinks her too young—for anything.

Determined to prove them all wrong, Gemini steals aboard Deverell's Northrope-bound *Black Dragon*. Never realizing she is about to sail into a storm of passion as deep as the ocean...and a battle that will threaten not only their lives, but their eternal souls.

Only Deverell, a man too haunted by his past to believe in a future, has any hope of discovering the truth before the evil destroys them both.

Warning: Contains a devilish captain, scorching nights, and an evil that will chill you to the bone.

Available now in ebook and print from Samhain Publishing.

Enjoy the following excerpt...

"Are you reaching for the moon or the stars?" came Captain Jansen's deep voice from behind me.

Lowering my arms, I swung around, shivering from the timbre of his voice. He stood in the shadows, leaning against the castle's stones, smoking a cheroot. That he didn't immediately extinguish the smoke, as propriety demanded, quickened my pulse. I didn't want propriety. I stepped a little closer to see him better.

"Both the moon and the stars," I said as my breath caught, hitching on the devilish shadows darkening his face. They revealed a dangerous edge about him, one that I realized I'd overlooked. For in the night, in the shadows, alone, without the comforts of home and family surrounding us, I could well see this man not only leading his ship through the fiercest of storms, but also slaying any foe...with deadly competence.

"Wanting what can't be had leads a man to his downfall." His gaze raked down my form with the same heat that had sizzled across the parlor. Suddenly the moon and the stars weren't in the heavens, but were on the balcony in the shape of a man just a few steps away.

Drawn to him, I moved even closer. Much closer than was proper. He dropped and ground out his cheroot with the heel of his boot before bringing his gaze up to meet mine.

"That goes for young ladies as well," he added, letting me know that he was well aware of my interest in him and telling me it was an impossible want.

A bristle of irritation scrubbed at me. He made it sound as if the reason was because I was a mere schoolgirl even though he didn't look at me that way. My petite size might lead many to think I was younger, but eighteen was past the schoolroom door. I lifted a challenging brow and instinctively acted on the fire in his eyes by leaving less than an inch between us. "You not only make me wonder if you speak from experience, Captain Jansen, but also have me curious as to who determines what is acceptable to have."

The heat radiating from his body seeped into mine. All I had to do was draw a deep breath and my bosom would likely brush the open edges of his coat. He'd dressed for dinner, wearing a black coat over a silver vest and crisp white shirt, but no matter how stylish his suit, the length of his unruly hair and the rugged cut of his features would always place him on the bow of a ship at sea rather than a formal parlor. I wondered where his hovering ghosts were. It was the first I'd seen him without them.

"Reason," he replied. "And fact."

"Whose reason and what facts?"

After studying my face a moment, he swore under his breath. "Do you even have a clue as to what you've been asking from me all night?"

I dampened my suddenly dry lips, feeling compelled to swallow. Wanting him to kiss me was one thing. Having to boldly state that desire aloud was another.

"Of course. I'm not ignorant of such things." It wasn't as if I hadn't been kissed before. Both Lord Percy and Lord Ashton had brushed my lips with theirs. And I knew there was more to it. I'd inadvertently seen Sean kissing Cassie a few times and had to back away from them before being discovered.

"Such things?" His words came on a snort of amusement.

Before I could respond, he caught my shoulders, pulling my body flush to his in a dizzying rush. Pleasure, like a line of fire, ran from my breasts to my toes, weakening my knees. I leaned into him, clasping my hands into the material of his coat and silken vest.

His lips claimed mine, hot and demanding. This was no Lord Percy/Lord Ashton ghost of a kiss. This was real and my pulse raced as my heart pumped with dizzying force. A sigh of pure pleasure escaped me and I pressed my breasts harder against him, wanting more of the burning sensations, wanting to feel him with every part of me.

He cursed under his breath and thrust his tongue between my lips, caressing inside my lower lip before delving deeper and tangling with my tongue. The intrusion surprised me, but not enough to pull away. The kiss was suddenly so much more than I imagined it could be, so demanding and intimate and exciting. I opened to him, tasting him, wanting to know more, eagerly responding to his exploration by matching the stroke and swirl of his tongue with mine.

He stiffened and set his hands on my shoulders, as if he were going to ease back from me. I pulled him tighter to me, unwilling to end the excitement that was making me feel more alive than ever before.

He growled—there was no other word for the primal sound—deep in his throat and thrust his leg between mine. He ran his hands down my back to clutch my bottom and lift me to the demand of his mouth. I wrapped my arms around his neck, threading my fingers into his silken hair. He swung around, pressing my back to the cold stone as his thick thigh made contact with my feminine flesh so thoroughly that my feet didn't even touch the ground.

He kissed me harder then, his tongue relentlessly thrusting against mine, sliding out just enough to make me want more before he invaded again. Between my legs, his thigh jerked slightly in tiny repetitive contractions that sent hot pulses of pleasure through my most intimate places, matching the rhythm of his tongue. Tension curled inside of me, a wild, heated need that made me want to shout and weep at the same time. My breathing became ragged. I moaned deeply when his hand cupped my breast. Then, as his fingers caught the tip of my breast and squeezed, I jerked and cried out sharply from the pleasure that had me so crazy I could do nothing but demand he give me more. My legs opened wider, needing him closer. I slid my knee up and encountered the hard ridge of what I knew had to be his male sex. I'd examined the nude statues at Killdaren's Castle rather closely and I'd read everything I could, even medical journals from the library, so I knew what I was feeling, but I didn't expect for it to be so alive and on fire against me. I pressed again.

"Bloody hell," he said, lifting his head from mine, forcing me to release him. His chest heaved and his hands shook. A gust of chilly, salty wind blew in from the sea, cooling the air between us and rifling through his hair and mine. His ghosts were back. They were staring at me over his shoulder, their eyes bulging as wide as their jaws hung open. I ignored them. I had to, or I would have shouted at them.

The captain sucked in air and that is when I realized I wasn't breathing. That I was getting faint from the lack of oxygen. I drew in a bracing breath, only to drown in the exotic flavor of his scent. It was nearly as potent as his touch. My legs, still clasped about his thigh, contracted.

He caught me up under my arms and lifted me from him, almost with the air of lifting an errant kitten out of harm's way. Then he set me on feet that I wasn't entirely sure I could stand on.

"Miss Andrews," he gasped. "I suggest you refrain from 'such things' until you're older and you know just what end you're headed to. I may be a murdering devil to a lot of men, but I don't despoil virgin schoolgirls, no matter how desperately they ask."

Murdering devil?

What was that supposed to mean? Surely I'd misunderstood him. "Luring devil" was more like it.

My head was still spinning and my senses were still burning, but I wasn't so far lost in the storm of his passion that I didn't realize he'd not only insulted me, but he'd adeptly absolved and denied his whole part in the passionate encounter. I knew enough to realize that. And, much to my chagrin, I couldn't think of a single thing to say before he'd quickly turned on his heel and hurriedly left, going down the steps that led to the sea-swept shore.

It's all about the story...

Romance

HORROR

www.samhainpublishing.com

CPSIA information can be obtained at www.ICGtesting.com
Printed in the USA
LVOW12s0552221213

366391LV00002B/30/P